# When I Trust You

# Dedication

For Mariah
Thanks for reading, sweetie
You bless my heart

*Trust in the LORD with all your heart...*

*Proverbs 3:5*

# Chapter One

Amber felt unsettled. She had been feeling this way all week. Getting up from her desk, she decided to go for a walk around campus. It was a beautiful March day, and she couldn't concentrate anyway. She had wanted to stay out in the sunshine and fresh air earlier when she parted from Seth. He had two more classes this afternoon, and she needed to study for her midterms. But she couldn't keep her focus on any of it.

"I'm going for a walk," she told Kerri. Her roommate, and future sister-in-law, only had one afternoon class today, and it was at three.

"Okay," Kerri said. "I'll probably be gone by the time you get back."

"See you at dinner then," she said. "Or are you going into town tonight?"

"No. Kevin's coming here."

She went out the door and took the stairs to the bottom floor. Stepping outside, she breathed in the warm sunshine and followed the path toward the center of campus. She didn't have any particular route in mind, she just needed to get out. She needed to think.

Her wedding was coming up at the end of May, and she was excited. This Saturday she and Seth were driving up to Oregon to spend the week with their families during Spring Break, and also take care of wedding details. Her mom had been doing what she could, but there were things she needed to make decisions about. She didn't think her restlessness had anything to do with that, or with her relationship with Seth. They were as solid and steady as ever, and there wasn't a doubt in her mind she wanted to marry him on the date they had set.

But their plans following the wedding were up in the air. They hadn't decided what they were going to do with their summer. They basically had three choices. They could move into their apartment in the married-student housing complex in June if either of them took summer classes. Another option was to remain in Oregon, rent an apartment, and return to school in late August. That would require them to find jobs up there and an apartment while living here until mid May. They could stay with family if they had trouble finding something, but she wanted them to have their own space if possible. And she wanted to go home with definite plans, not try and wing-it once they got there. She believed God would provide for them, but she didn't think that meant they couldn't decide anything until the last minute.

The third option was to not take any summer classes but return here in June, live in town, work at Tony's, and be involved in the summer ministries going on at the church they attended. That had been their original thought, and the one Amber felt most comfortable with. She didn't want to take summer classes, and Seth didn't either. Finding an apartment here in the summer was easy because many of them were vacated during the summer months. There was even the possibility they could stay at Kevin's apartment because his sister was getting married in early June and Kevin was going to Alaska for six weeks. He was trying to convince Kerri to go too, but if she decided not to, Kevin wasn't going either.

If she didn't go on the trip, Kerri was staying here to take summer classes. She had decided she had a calling to teach children with special needs, and she wanted to finish school as soon as possible. Seth had no doubt she could graduate in three years instead of four. She could be very ambitious and goal-oriented once she set her mind to something.

Walking all the way to the tennis courts and back up the path past the gym, through the courtyard, across the street, and down the path that circled the small lake in the student housing area, Amber knew what had her feeling restless. She really wanted to go to camp this summer. Not at the expense of delaying the wedding, but she would miss being there, and she knew it.

*I'm trying to believe You have something else for us that will be as rewarding as spending the summer at camp, but I can't imagine doing anything else. It's like my second home, Jesus. Even more than here. You always meet me there in a unique way. Help me with my unsettled thoughts and emotions and heart that feels displaced somehow. I know you will lead us exactly where we need to be. Help me to believe that. Restore my joy and give me peace.*

*** 

Amanda Smith entered the house and could hear her grandmother rattling around in the kitchen. Going to see what she was up to that was making so much noise, she stepped through the door and saw her mom there too. They were cleaning out the refrigerator, and her mom had dropped one of the racks after taking it out.

"Hi, honey," her mom said. "You're home early today."

"Matt has a meeting with Pastor John this afternoon, so he had to go," she said, setting her backpack in the chair and laying the mail on the table. Sorting through it, she saw there were two things for her, and she opened one of them.

"I got accepted to Lifegate—again," she said. "Big surprise."

"Congratulations," her grandmother said. "I guess Jesus is ignoring my prayers about you and Matthew staying here with us."

She stepped over and gave her a hug. "Sorry, Grandma. We'll miss you too."

"I have your dress ready for you to try on," she said. "If I had known you were going to be here this soon, I would have put this task off until tomorrow."

"That's all right," she said. "I'll be here for the rest of the day. Whenever you're ready, let me know."

Mandy resisted the urge to go into her grandmother's bedroom and look at the half-completed wedding dress. She would let Grandma show her all she had gotten done since her last fitting. Her wedding wasn't until August, but her grandmother

12

needed to get it done before June because she was going on a trip with a group of senior citizens to Italy, Switzerland, Austria, and Germany.

Going to her own room, Mandy opened the other envelope she had gotten and read the letter from Amber. Her cousin sounded unsettled about school, her own upcoming wedding, and the summer, so she took a few moments to pray for her and then decided to call and see if she was in her room. No one answered, and she made a mental note to try later this evening. Normally she spent Tuesday evenings with Matt, but he had a Performance Review with Pastor John this afternoon, so she felt a little lost about what to do for the rest of the day. She had term finals to study for, but she was mostly prepared and didn't feel like doing that right now, so she called Matt instead. His meeting wasn't until three o'clock, and it was only two-forty.

"Hi, it's me," she said.

"Hi, me. Did you make it home all right?"

"Yeah, I'm here. Where are you?"

"Almost Downtown—about two minutes away," he said. "You're praying for me, right?"

"I said I would. But I think it's going to be fine."

"I don't know. He sounded weird when he mentioned it on Sunday. I think something is up."

"Like what? He's going to fire his most hard-working, dedicated, and energetic intern?"

"No, but he might ask me to reconsider staying after August."

"I told you I'm okay with that if you decide you want to stay here."

"I know, but I don't know what I'm supposed to be doing. I really want us to go to Lifegate."

"I got my letter today."

"Okay, that's it. We're going."

She laughed. "Go to your meeting, Matthew, and don't stress. Call me later if you have anything significant to tell me."

"Can I call you even if I don't?"

"Yes. I miss you already."

"I miss you too, sweetheart. And I love you. Very much. You haven't forgotten that, have you?"

"It's kind of hard when you tell me every day."

"I have to, Amanda. I can't keep it to myself."

"And what am I going to do when you're gone for ten days?"

"I have a surprise for you."

"What? You're not going to Mexico?"

"No, you'll see on Thursday."

"I'd say 'I can't wait', but I can. I'm really going to miss you."

"You'll have Amber there."

"Not the same, Matthew. I'm glad she's coming, but I'd rather have you here too."

"Just don't break up with me while I'm gone like Amber tried to do with Seth last year."

She laughed. "I won't. I'll be counting the days until you're back."

"I'll miss you too," he said. "I would get out of it if I could."

"I know you would, but I don't want you to. This is what you do, and I'm proud of you."

"Thanks, baby. I'll call you later."
"Okay. Bye."

\*\*\*

Chad decided to stop by the Chapel after his Western Civ midterm. He was glad that one was out of the way, but without his toughest exam on his mind, his thoughts had returned to the decision he had to make by the end of the week.

He knew what he wanted to do, and he felt at peace about not going to camp this summer and having time with his family instead, but he wasn't sure how to tell Jessica about it. He would miss her.

He couldn't believe he was nearing the end of his first year of college. His mom was proud of him, but she missed him too. A couple of weeks ago, she had asked if he would go to Florida with them in June. Going on vacation with his family would be possible if he didn't go to camp this summer, and he was okay with that. Last summer he had needed to get away, be on his own, and show his family he was serious about going to college and doing what he felt God calling him to do. But he didn't believe God wanted him to leave his family behind while he pursued his goals. He had plenty of seeds of truth to plant, and love to show, right in his own family.

He had Jessica in his life now too, and he didn't want her to think she was any less important to him than she had been at Christmas, because she wasn't. He loved her, and he didn't see that changing. She had every right to expect him to spend the summer with her at camp, but he couldn't ignore the leading in his heart.  He needed to tell her what he was thinking. Putting it off any longer would be dishonest.

He knew he could pray anytime, anywhere, but being inside the Chapel walls made him be more complete in his prayers.  In addition to praying about his summer plans, he also prayed for his relationship with Jessica, her family, his family, his dreams, her dreams, Seth and Amber, Kevin and Kerri, his sister whose cat had died yesterday—any burden on his heart; he laid it before Jesus, and he felt the weight of everything being lifted.

Going to his room to get some studying done before he needed to leave for work, he could hear Seth tapping keys on his computer before he called out to him.

"Is that you, Chad?"

"It's me," he said, setting his backpack on his bed.

"Come here when you have a minute."

He stepped to the other side of the suite and saw an astonished expression on his roommate's face. "What's up?"

"Look at this," Seth said, pointing to the computer screen.  "Remember what I asked you to pray about?"

Looking over Seth's shoulder at the email message, he read the whole thing and smiled.  "All right, brother.  You've got good news for your girl."

## Chapter Two

Seth wanted to reach for the phone and tell Amber the news, but he decided to plan a special time to tell her. Maybe Saturday at the lake. They were going home for Spring Break, so it was an ideal opportunity, but it seemed like a long time to keep something this exciting from her.

He had been feeling stressed about their summer plans. In his heart he knew God was going to take care of them, but he was a planner. He liked to have a course marked out—a course led by God, but still some kind of concrete plans for any major life-change, like what to do when Spring Semester ended and how to support himself and his wife after the wedding—two things that happened to go together this time.

God had laid something on his anxious heart last week, and he had decided to pray about it. He almost called Dave at camp to see if they had any positions open this summer he and Amber could fill. Normally the staff was made up of single people because they didn't have the housing arrangements to take on married couples. Since setting the date for their wedding, they had been looking to remain in California this summer, but as the weeks had gone by, he felt that familiar tug to return to camp.

He hadn't called Dave and instead decided to pray for two weeks and then contact him if he felt God leading him to. He'd asked Chad to pray too but was amazed at Dave's words.

Going to meet Amber for dinner, he didn't know if he could keep it from her, but he decided to try. If she could tell something was up and asked what the goofy grin on his face was for, he would tell her. But waiting for a special moment at a special place appealed to his romantic tendencies, and it had been a few months since he'd had a good surprise for her.

"Hey, sweetheart," he said, meeting her outside the dining hall with a kiss on the cheek. "How was your afternoon?"

"Fine," she said. "How was yours?"

"Good. I think I did all right on my exam."

"I'm glad," she said.

They went inside and got in line for dinner, but Seth wondered if she was all right. She seemed a little subdued, and he watched her carefully for the next ten minutes as they got their food and found a table with friends who were already here. She talked and smiled at the right moments, but she wasn't herself. When he caught her staring into space while Adam was telling a funny story, he slipped his arm around her back, stroking it gently and getting her attention. She turned and smiled at him, and he said simple words he never got tired of saying.

"I love you, Amber."

"I know," she said, leaning her head on his shoulder.

"Are you spending this evening with me?"

"If you want me to."

"I want you to," he said. "Do you want to spend it with me?"

She lifted her head and smiled at him. "Of course I do."

"Okay, just checking."

They sat there talking with their friends like usual and then left the cafeteria. Normally they parted for a few minutes to get the books and notes for the classes they needed to study for, but tonight he kept his arm around her and let her know in a direct way he had noticed her pained expressions and fake laughs during the last thirty minutes.

"Let's go for a walk," he said, pulling her toward the path leading to the lake. "You look like you need some good kisses."

She went with him but didn't say anything. By the time they reached the lake, he could tell she was on the verge of tears. He pulled her close and kissed her gently.

"What is it, sweetheart? Stop pretending to be fine when you're not."

She clung to him and let the tears fall. He thought back to when he had last seen her. He didn't think he'd said or done anything to make her upset, but there were other people in her life and anything could happen on any given day. He felt responsible for her happiness even if this had nothing to do with him.

"I'm scared, Seth," she said. "I know I shouldn't be, but I am."

He released her enough to look into her eyes. "Scared of what?"

"Life. This summer. Getting married."

He knew what she meant. "It's coming up fast, huh?"

She nodded.

"Do you still want to marry me?"

"Yes."

"In May?"

"Yes," she said, giving him a smile. "I can't wait."

He knew she meant that, and he felt the same way. He gave her a kiss and allowed himself to envision their honeymoon. He couldn't wait to be with her. Kissing and holding her only got better with time, and his desire was stronger when she needed an extra dose of love and comfort from him.

"What scares you?" he asked. "Specifically."

"Where we're going to live. What we're going to be doing this summer. If we're ready for this."

He smiled because Amber was usually the more steady and optimistic one. Whenever he voiced similar concerns, she always said, 'Don't worry about it. God's got it all taken care of. You'll see.' And he knew she was right, especially today, but it was nice to see she had her weak moments too.

"I know, I know," she said, before he could voice his own thoughts. "God's got it all worked out, but what are we doing, Seth?"

He laughed at her whiny tone. This really was not like her, and he knew if he hadn't heard from Dave today, he would be feeling the same way and really panicking about now. His own faith wavered often, but if Amber's did too, he was in big trouble. He wanted to tease her because he didn't often have this opportunity, but he knew she was genuinely upset, so he took the chance to do something else—being the one to remind *her* of the faithful God they had.

"We're doing what we've done all along, Amber. We're waiting on God to show us the right paths to take. We're trusting Him with all of our heart. Has He ever failed us when we've done that?"

"No."

He kissed her again, and he loved her all the more. He would be nowhere near where he was today in his relationship with God and walking the path He had for him if it wasn't for her. How many times had he been the faithless one and she had gotten him to face the next day?

He had something to tell her he knew would melt her anxiety away and bring her an overflow of joy, but he decided to pray for her, and them, and their future together first. Amber didn't just need to hear some good news to lift her out of this, she needed to allow her own heart to cling to what she knew was true— that she could have faith in her incredibly loving and powerful God even when she couldn't see what was around the corner. To hope and have peace when she had no tangible reason to have it. Because next time around, God may very well leave them in the dark until the last possible moment.

\*\*\*

Kerri sat on the steps leading to the parking area, waiting for Kevin to arrive. When she saw his red car come around the corner, she stood up and watched to see which open parking space he chose and then went to meet him.

They both worked on Monday evenings, so she hadn't seen him since Sunday night. His wide smile emerged as soon as he spotted her coming toward him, and she smiled in return. After five months of dating Kevin, she still got goose bumps every time she saw him and longed for his gentle touch and sweet words. He might have seen her two days ago, but he acted like it had been weeks.

"Hi," she said, cherishing his warm embrace.

"Hi, Kerri," he said.

She lifted her face, and their lips met easily. She let Kevin kiss her for as long as he wanted to, instantly transporting her into another dimension of reality. Kevin's reality where love was love and there was no reason to doubt or question it. His love for her didn't fluctuate, and she felt the same way about him. It was just there: strong and real and exactly what she needed.

"I missed you," he said.

"I missed you too." She smiled at him, and he smiled back. "You brought your books."

Sometimes he did, and sometimes he didn't. If he didn't, she usually didn't study until after he left unless there was something he could help her with, but if he came prepared to study, then she did too, and tonight she needed to for the same reason as him.

"I have a test tomorrow," he said. "Genetics. It's tough. I get mixed up."

"Maybe I can help," she said, leading the way to The Oasis. She already had her books with her. She was taking a biology class this year, and they had studied genetics a few weeks ago. She liked science. It usually made sense to her, especially anything related to real life, like how two parents with brown eyes ended up with a child with blue eyes.

Kevin didn't argue with her. Sometimes he did if he knew she would have no clue about what he was studying, but she had helped him with this class before. He had been planning to graduate this spring, but after looking at the remaining classes he had to take, his counselor had advised him to save two of the classes for next fall rather than trying to tackle them both along with genetics. He wasn't anxious to graduate and had been fine with it. He loved to learn and he was happy.

But he wasn't so happy an hour later when she had been helping him with his work and he wasn't getting it. She didn't completely understand the material herself, so it was hard to explain to him, but he was getting some of it—enough of the study-guide to pass tomorrow.

"I hate this," he said, pushing the paper away from him in a way that was characteristic of his autism. "I'm not smart. I'm too tired to think."

"It's tough, Kevin, really. It's not just you."

When Kevin said he was tired, he didn't mean physically like he needed to go to bed, he meant his brain was tired of thinking because it didn't make sense to him, and that made him feel angry. Angry at his stupid teachers and the stupid subject, and mad at himself because he felt stupid. Jenna had explained that to her several weeks ago when he had first started taking this class and they had been at the apartment together. Kevin had been studying and then he suddenly closed the book, got up from the table, and went to his room. Jenna said it wasn't the first time since the semester had started, and she was worried he wouldn't understand enough to pass. That was always hard on him when he had to drop a class. He liked to learn, and he didn't like it when he couldn't.

Kerri knew what Kevin understood, he got, and what he didn't, he wasn't going to get by tomorrow, so she closed the book and put it away and then reached for his tense hands folded together on the table. She knew he was using every ounce of strength he had to not get up and leave. He'd done that once here, and when she caught up with him, she asked him not to do that because it made her feel like she was the problem instead of the work.

"Look at me, Kevin," she said, gently stroking his hands.

He did. His eyes were watery and lost-looking.

"You're smart, Kevin. You're very, very smart."

"I don't get it," he said.

"So? I don't get calculus most of the time. Does that mean I'm not smart?"

"How can you get this and not calculus? Calculus is easy compared to this."

"For you, but not for me. My mind doesn't work that way. I get this, but not complicated math. You get math, but not this. It doesn't mean you're not smart. It means you get some things and not others, just like everyone. You can't be good at everything."

"I should study more," he said, reaching for the paper. "Where's my book?"

She took the paper from him and stuck it in his backpack. "You don't need to study anymore," she said. "You need to have some fun with me. Come on."

She got up before he could argue, and he came with her. "Where are we going?" he asked once they were outside. "I should study more."

"Nope. No more studying tonight." She was in the mood for a good game of pool, and the rec center was just around the corner. Kevin was a master at it, and she loved to watch him play and to play with him.

As soon as they stepped inside, Kevin looked like a puppy who had finally found his way home after a long night in the streets. He could never say no to a game of pool and followed her without argument to an empty table.

"I am going to beat you tonight," she said. "No more being Mr. Nice Guy. You will see how I can really play."

He looked at her like he wasn't sure if she was serious or not. The first time they had played, she thought she had a decent chance of winning. They had a pool table in the basement at home, and she'd played with her dad a lot. He was good, and he had taught her well. She hadn't wanted to beat Kevin the first time they played, however, so she played like she sort of knew what she was doing, but not really. But when he kept beating her no matter how hard she tried, she realized how good he actually was.

She smiled at him, knowing she had already been successful at getting his mind off of his studying. But she had one more diversion tactic at her disposal, and she used it even though she didn't need to at this point. Taking two sticks from the wall and handing him one, she didn't let go when he grabbed it, pulling him close to her instead.

"I think I need a kiss first," she said.

He had to shift to a different gear to go there, but he willingly did so. "I love you, Kerri," he said, seeming to realize she had pulled him a million miles away from his frustration.

"I love you, Kevin," she said, kissing him softly one more time. "And I am going to beat you."

"Nah-uh."

"Uh-huh."

"No, you're not."

"Yes, I am!" She tickled him, and he laughed, moving away from her and going to the other side of the table.

She asked him to break. She found that always gave her a slight advantage because by the time he missed, he had cleared a lot of the balls out of the way for her to have some clear shots of her own.

She gave a serious effort, but he beat her anyway. She talked him into one more game, but during the second one he seemed less interested in pool and more interested in her. At first she thought she might have a chance because he missed several easy shots, but he was as much of a distraction to her with all of his sweet touches and soft-spoken words in her ear when she was trying to set up for a shot.

It was a longer game than usual, but he still beat her. He walked her back to the dorm after that, and he was very quiet. She thought maybe his mind had shifted back to his frustration with his studies, and she was going to suggest he not go home and try to cram any more in there tonight, but he stopped on the path leading to the front door of her dorm. Normally he walked her all the way up and said good night to her there.

She turned to face him, knowing he must have something to say, but he remained silent. She could hear crickets chirping in the cool night air, and no one else was around.

"You're being quiet," she said, wrapping her arms around his waist and leaning into him. "What are you thinking about?"

"You."

She smiled. "What about me?"

He didn't answer immediately, and she waited. If they hadn't been having such a fun time, she would have been alarmed, but she didn't think this could be anything bad, especially when he began kissing her. His kisses were always the same: passionate, controlled, and amazing.

"Can we get married now, Kerri?" he asked. "I want us to be married now."

She smiled at his phrasing. One thing she could never accuse Kevin of was not being honest with her. But she wasn't sure what to say. Yes, she wanted to marry him. She wouldn't be doing this otherwise. But now? She wasn't sure about that.

"When do you want to get married?" she asked.

"Now."

"Tomorrow, next week, next month?"

"In June," he said. "Jenna and Caleb are getting married then. I want us to get married too."

She decided not to say anything and gave him a hug instead. He held her close with so much love, she felt both scared to death and at total peace she was actually thinking of saying yes.

When she released him, she took his hand and led him the rest of the way to her dorm. Turning to face him before she said good-night, she could tell he was waiting for an answer.

"I want to marry you, Kevin, but I'm not sure if I'm ready yet. I'll think about it, okay?"

"Okay."

"Are you okay?"

"Yes."

"Are you sure? You're not going to go home and stare at the refrigerator, are you?"

He laughed. "No."

"And you're not going to study anymore tonight? You're going to do fine, I promise."

"No, I won't study anymore."

"Will you think about me?"

"Yes."

"I'll be thinking about you too," she said, giving him a tender kiss. "I love you, Kevin."

"I love you, Kerri."

"Good night."

"Good night. I'll see you Thursday?"

"Yes. I'll be there."

She squeezed his hand and turned away to go inside. She waved before she rounded the corner and walked to the elevator. Once she was inside the cubicle all by herself, she leaned against the back wall, closed her eyes, and sighed.

"Okay, Jesus. What am I supposed to do now?"

## Chapter Three

Emma Jones peered over the top of her textbook to stare at the couple on the other side of the lounge. She had seen them here together before and knew the girl lived in this dorm, but she had never spoken to her. Emma didn't have any classes with the brown-haired girl, but she had seen her at Chapel and in the dining room many times. She knew her name was Amber because she'd heard someone call out her name once and Amber had turned to look at her friend as she approached her, but beyond that she was a complete stranger.

She also knew the guy's name was Seth because he was in her history class this semester. He hadn't been last fall, and in January it had taken her a few days to figure out where she knew him from when she saw him sitting in the lecture hall. Once she figured it out, she wondered if he was still with his girlfriend, because if he wasn't, she wanted to try and get to know him herself, but then she had seen them together the next day.

Emma had never had a boyfriend, and she wanted one so badly. She had come here alone from Monterey along the central coast of California. She had been homeschooled all her life, gotten a nearly perfect score on the SAT, and received a full-ride scholarship to come here. Last semester had gone okay. She had gotten A's in all of her classes with relative ease, she liked one of her roommates, and she had been on the cross-country team.

This semester she had more spare time on her hands without cross-country, and she felt lonely. The roommate who had shared her side of the dorm suite and she liked the most hadn't returned, and her new roommate was kind of a snob. Tiffany had a boyfriend and was with him most of the time, and she had caught them alone in the room together a few times. They'd only been lying on the bed and kissing, but that wasn't allowed here, and it made her feel like she was interrupting something.

Last semester she only studied here occasionally and had seen Amber and Seth together a few times, but this semester she had been down here a lot more and had figured out they were usually here on Tuesdays and Thursdays and sometimes Saturdays. They had other friends who were sometimes with them, but more often it was just the two of them, and whenever they were here she couldn't ignore them. There was something about them she found very watchable. Sometimes it made her mad because she wanted something like that for herself, but other times they made her smile, especially tonight.

She could see they were trying to say good-night to each other but were having a difficult time doing so. Sometimes Seth would walk Amber up to her room, but he always came back down within a few minutes and left the girls' dorm. But if it was past ten o'clock, like tonight, then he couldn't go upstairs so he would say good-night to her here.

Standing up from the couch they had been sharing, Seth slung his backpack over his shoulder and Amber rose to give him one last hug. He held on and then did something Emma had never seen him do before. He took Amber's left hand and kissed it, saying something about the ring on her finger that made Amber smile. Emma suddenly realized they must be engaged. She'd never noticed Amber's ring before.

Emma sighed. Her hopes of them breaking up and being able to get Seth's attention, by some miracle, officially died at that point. They could still break up, she supposed, but she scolded herself for having such thoughts about two people who were obviously very much in love. She didn't hate them, she just wanted what they had for herself.

She studied for awhile longer without anything to distract her. There were other students scattered around the room, but no one caught her eye for any particular reason. She was a people watcher. She wasn't trying to spy on anyone or meddle in other people's business, she was just fascinated. She had always been that way. Some people could walk into a room and not notice anyone, being caught up in their own little world, but not her. Whenever she entered a room, she noticed everyone and everything, and her eyes were always drawn to particular people for whatever reason. Amber and Seth were like that.

There were a few guys here besides Seth who had attracted her attention. She was certain none of them knew she existed, but still, she watched them with hope in her heart. Maybe one of these days one of them would notice her too.

*** 

Chad left Tony's at ten. He had hoped to get off work sooner so he would have more time to talk to Jessie, but it had been a busy night and he hadn't wanted to leave Blake to do all the deliveries on his own. Their other driver had called in sick tonight.

He had seen her this morning at breakfast but not since then. That was normal for a Tuesday. They both had classes all day, their lunch break at different times, and he worked at Tony's from five to at least nine, sometimes later. He would usually go to the library when he got back, study with her until eleven, and then walk her back to her dorm before going to his room to study longer.

He liked everything about being here at college, except for the limited amount of time he had with Jessie. She seemed fine with it and told him she knew he was doing the best he could. But he wasn't fine with it. He needed more time with her. More and more as the weeks went by, it seemed, and yet he simply didn't have it. He wasn't taking any more classes than he needed. He had to work or he couldn't be here. And Jessica had other friends besides him, so sometimes when he was free, she wasn't.

Arriving at the library and finding her in their usual spot, he sat down beside her on the small couch and gave her a brief kiss when she looked at him. "Sorry it's so late. Tate was sick tonight."

"That's all right," she said. "I'm sorry for you. You look tired."

"I stayed up late last night studying for my exam."

"How did you do?"

"All right, I think. I never know how much to study for that class. There's too much for the professor to cover everything, but you never know which stuff he's going to choose."

She gave him a sympathetic smile. It was his toughest course, and he mentioned that often. "Just remember you got an A last semester. I'm sure you can do it again."

He kissed her more seriously then. He knew it was more than midterms that had him stressed, and he couldn't carry the burden any longer. He needed to tell her what he had to say, even if it was late.

He hated this part of being in a relationship. He hated the feeling of letting Jessica down in any way, whether it was something he could control or not. Most of the time it was good because it kept him from being selfish and only acting in his own interests, but he knew this might feel that way to her.

"I need to tell you something," he said.

"Did something happen? Did you get bad news?"

"No," he said. "I've just been thinking about something."

She waited for him to go on, and he told her about his mom asking if he'd like to go to Disney World with them this summer. Keisha and Darius had never been there, or on any big family vacation like that, and he hadn't been during his growing-up years either.

"At first I was thinking I could talk to Dave about being gone from camp for a couple of weeks, but the more I thought about it, the more I knew God was leading me to be home this summer."

"Then you probably should, don't you think?" she said.

"Yes, but are you okay with that?  With me not being at camp with you?"

She smiled at him in a way he couldn't read.  "I love that you follow God, Chad.  I need that from you more than anything you do to please me or make me happy."

"It will be tough for me to be away from you.  I want you to know that.  I will miss you very much."

She was still smiling at him, and he started to feel uneasy.  He was trying to pour his heart out, and she didn't care one way or the other.  The doubts began to surface about whether or not she wanted to be in this relationship, if he meant as much to her as she meant to him, and...

"Ask me what I'm doing this summer," she said, interrupting his private thoughts.

"Why?"

"Ask me."

"What are you doing this summer?"

"The same thing," she whispered.

He wasn't sure what she meant.  "The same thing as last summer?"

"No," she laughed.  "The same thing as you. Spending it with my family instead of going to camp."

"When did you decide that?"

"Just now.  I've been praying about it, and I've been waiting for God to show me if that's the right choice or not."

He had more studying to do, but he couldn't think about anything besides Jessica and the One who had brought them together. In spite of his past. In spite of their differences. In spite of his own lack of initiative in the beginning. In spite of everything, here they were falling in love with each other and with their God—more and more every day.

Jessica brushed his tears away with her fingertips and kissed him. He kissed her gently and passionately in return, longer than he usually allowed himself. He couldn't kiss her like this when they were completely alone, and he didn't feel comfortable in an exposed setting, but tonight he didn't care. He needed her to convince him this is what she wanted. She wanted him. She wanted this relationship. And he believed God wanted it for them.

"I love you, sweetheart," he whispered. He had told himself to wait a year to say that, but he was never going to make it until August.

"I love you, Chad."

Pulling her close and holding her securely against his chest, he said something else he'd been thinking about lately.

"I need you, Jessica. I need you to walk this path with me. I feel scared to death most of the time about what I'm doing here, where God is leading me, and if I can really be the man He wants me to be; but you give me strength when I feel weak, you always say the right thing, and you make me believe I can be used by God in a special way."

"That's because I see what's there, Chad. I see your heart, and I know it's the kind of heart God is looking for. I know He has to get the biggest smile on His face whenever He thinks of you."

*Just like that, baby,* he thought but didn't say. Jessica was as good at receiving compliments as he was, so he let it go this time and allowed her support and encouragement to sink deep into his soul.

An exciting thought entered his mind: He had heard God speaking to him. God had been the One leading him this way, but he kept saying, 'What about Jessica?' And God kept saying, 'You let Me take care of Jessica. You listen and follow Me, Chad. Trust Me. I'm trying to bless you and lead you into the summer I have for you, just let Me do that.'

## Chapter Four

"Good night, Tony," Blake said. "See you on Thursday."

"Good night," he replied to both him and Colleen. "Sorry it was a bit late tonight."

"No problem," he said, hearing the door open behind him. He turned and saw Kevin coming into the restaurant that only had a few late-night customers remaining. "Hey, Kev."

"Hi, Blake. Hi, Colleen," he said, and then in the same breath added, "Hi, Dad. Can I talk to you?"

"Sure, Kev."

Blake wondered what that was about. It was late and Kevin seemed very urgent about something, but he stepped away with Colleen and left the pizza place, heading for the car and looking forward to having a few minutes alone with his girl at the end of this very long day. They worked here together on Tuesday and Thursday evenings, but he was making deliveries most of the time so he didn't get to see her much unless it was a slow night, and this had definitely not been one of them.

Before he opened the car door, he gave her a kiss and asked something he'd asked her before, but he wanted to make sure she was happy.

"Are you still glad you're down here with me, even on nights like this?"

She smiled. "Of course I am."

"Why? You never see me."

"I see you a lot more than I did when I lived eight hours away."

"And that's enough?"

"I'd love more, but it's enough, Blake. I promise."

"I'm looking forward to next week."

She smiled. "Me too."

"I have another interview in Portland."

"You do? Besides the two you already told me about?"

"Yes. I called on that other one this afternoon."

"I can't believe you're looking up there."

"Why?"

"You're only doing that because of me."

"*Only* because of you?" He laughed. "Colleen, if I can't find something around here so you can keep going to school with your friends and be near me at the same time, I want you to at least be close to your family. I've told you that."

"I know, I just can't believe you're considering me so much. Girls go to college away from their family and friends all the time, and if I go wherever you go, I'll already have at least one friend there."

He shook his head, not understanding how she could be thinking of herself so little and knowing he needed to make her understand he was committed to her well-being as much as the path God had for him. As far as he was concerned, it was all one and the same: her best, his best, and the best God had for them.

"I love you, Colleen.  Do you believe that?  Do you know what that means?"

"That you like kissing me?"

He smiled.  "It means I want the best for you—always.  In everything we do.  This isn't just about me, it's about us.  It's about our life together.  Are you interested in that?"

"Yes."

"Do you believe I am?"

"Yes."

"Do you doubt my love for you?  Even a little?"

"Sometimes," she admitted. "Not because you don't show it, Blake.  It's just me.  Sometimes I ask myself, 'What do I possibly have to offer this guy?  Why me?  How long can he keep pretending?'"

"I'm not pretending, Colleen."

"Me neither," she replied.

"Then let me take care of you, okay?  I need you to let me do that."

"Okay," she said.

***

"What's up, Kev?  Everything all right?"

"Y-Yes. Yes, Dad.  E-Every—Everything is g-good."

"So why are you stuttering, and why are you here?"

Kevin leaned across the counter and softened his voice.  "I-I want to marry Kerri.  C-Can I d-do that—n-n-now?"

His dad smiled and came around the counter to meet him.  He led him to one of the booths in the roped-off area they didn't use unless it got really busy. They sat down, and Kevin waited for his dad to speak.

"Did you ask her?"

"Yes."

"What did she say?"

"She said she would think about it."

"How soon do you want to get married?"

"In J-June. When Jenna does."

"Did you tell Kerri that?"

"Yes."

"And she said she'd think about it?"

"Yes."

"Are you going to be okay if she says she doesn't want to do that yet?"

He didn't answer.

His dad reached across the table and took one of his hands, speaking in a tone Kevin recognized as one he needed to really listen to. "You have to let Kerri decide what she wants, Kev. There's no reason why you can't marry her in June if that's what she wants too, but you have to let her decide for herself. Understand?"

He nodded.

"This isn't like talking her into going to New York and Alaska with you. This isn't just a trip. This is the rest of her life. If you push her into this, and she's not ready, you'll end up pushing her away and possibly losing her. Understand?"

"Yes."

His dad lightened up then, sitting back and asking him something else. "Why do you want to get married in June?"

"Because I want to."

"But why?"

He hated that question. *Why?* He had to think to answer that. He told Kerri he wanted them to be married now because he just did. His heart wanted it. He wanted to marry her. But why? He closed his eyes and thought really hard: about the last five months and all the time he'd spent with her, about their time in New York at Christmas, about meeting her family in Portland and spending a week there with her, about tonight and how she'd made him feel—there had been something about tonight. What was it?

"Did you want to stay there with her tonight instead of leaving?" his dad asked.

That was it. "Yes. I want her and me to live together. In the same place."

"Anything else?"

"I was frustrated. I was so frustrated, and she got me out of it—way out of it. I completely forgot. I—She—I—We fit together. Her and me together. I want that all the time."

\*\*\*

Kerri lay in her bed and closed her eyes. She hadn't said anything to anyone about Kevin telling her he wanted them to get married in June, and she had managed to do the rest of her studying without letting it be too heavy on her mind. But lying in the darkness of the quiet room, she let her mind replay her evening with Kevin, from the moment he first arrived, to their time at The Oasis and rec room together, and their walk back across campus.

*I want us to be married now.* She smiled at the memory, and she wondered what made him say it in that moment. She didn't think it could have been something he had been waiting to say. He didn't function that way. He said what he wanted to say when he wanted to say it. He didn't plan moments like that. He didn't have that capacity. It had been spontaneous, honest, and completely genuine. Straight from his heart.

His tender heart made her eyes fill with tears. There was something about Kevin's love that was intangible and yet completely real at the same time. He couldn't always express it, but he didn't hold back either.

He hadn't said, 'Will you marry me, Kerri?' or 'Do you want to marry me?' He already knew the answer to that. Of course she wanted to marry him. That was a given.

He'd said, 'Can we get married now?'

She had to admit she wasn't opposed to that. She had a strong sense of wanting to take care of Kevin and his unique needs by simply loving him. She knew she had the ability to reach a place in his heart very few could, and she had no desire to hold Kevin at a distance. He touched her heart in unique ways. He met needs she didn't know she had until she was in the middle of receiving them.

More than once she'd been having a difficult week, tried to hide it from him and be her usual happy self, but he dropped whatever he was doing to get her talking, letting her blow off steam and then saying something adorable like, 'When I'm frustrated and you kiss me, I always feel better. Maybe if I kiss you, that will help.'

*Oh, Jesus. Please tell me what to do. I can think of a hundred reasons to say no right now and a hundred reasons to say yes, but what is right? For me? For Kevin? For our life together? Is there any harm in waiting? Is there any harm in not waiting? The last thing I want is to hurt Kevin in any way. Please don't let me do that. Prepare his heart for what I feel I need to tell him, whatever that is. I ask for wisdom, Holy Father, as only you can give it to me, because only You know what's right for both of us.*

She fell asleep with relative ease and realized she had done so in the morning. She had a completely grace-filled day. One where everything went smoothly and she had peace in her heart about the decision she had before her. She went to Chapel at noon, and she allowed it to be an uplifting time of joy and peace. Throughout the day she found herself thinking about the joy Kevin brought to her life, and she didn't see this as a bombshell he'd laid on her she felt completely overwhelmed by. She felt blessed to know him and to be so freely asked.

She didn't usually see him on Wednesdays because he worked and she needed the study-time, but she wanted to see him and make pizza by his side. She also wanted to make sure he was okay. She hadn't heard from Jenna and assumed he must be fine, but it was good to see that for herself when she snuck into the kitchen to surprise him and he welcomed her easily.

"What are you doing here?" he said, finishing the pizza he was working on as she held him around the waist.

"I wanted to see you."

He turned and held her as soon as he was finished, and neither of them said anything. She had the feeling he was thinking about it, but he didn't say so.

"Can I work with you tonight?" she asked, stepping away to grab an apron and wash her hands.

"Sure," he said. "You can have this easy one, and I'll do the Special."

After she had washed her hands, she returned to his side and went to work with the "easy" one-topping pizza. Laying the exact number of pepperoni slices without having to rearrange them to make them all fit, she enjoyed the simplicity of having this time with Kevin in the same way their relationship began.

While she was working on the simple pizza and Kevin did ten times the work on a Tony's Special, she thought about how Kevin and her relationship with him was like making a pizza. It had started out very basic and they'd added new things along the way until it had become as complex as a Tony's Special, and yet it wasn't a mess. It was perfect, exactly as it should be. A work of art that could only be put together properly by a master pizza maker—Someone who knew exactly what He was doing.

She stayed until it was time for Kevin to take his dinner break, and she ate with him. After they had both finished, she leaned against him in the booth where they were sitting side by side, and she felt the need to say something to let him know she was thinking about it.

"I'm praying about what you asked me last night."

He didn't respond.

"Do you still want that?"

"Yes," he said. "But my dad said I have to let you decide."

She looked up at him. "You told your dad?"

"Yes."

"Did you tell anyone else?"

"No. Just my dad."

She smiled. She could picture how that conversation had gone, and since Tony had greeted her in his usual way tonight and hadn't pulled her aside at some point to say, 'Don't let Kevin talk you into this. He's not ready', she knew it would be perfectly okay with him and the rest of Kevin's family.

Laying her hand on Kevin's cheek, she asked him to kiss her. He did, and she imagined being alone with Kevin where he would be free to touch her in every way and the amazing amount of love that would pass between them. He was so gentle—always. So caring. So protective. She wanted to be wrapped in that love for the rest of her life.

"I think I want to say yes," she whispered.

"I want you to say yes," he was quick to add.

She smiled. "Tell me you love me."

"I love you, Kerri."

"Ask me again."

He didn't hesitate. "Can we get married now?"

"Yes, Kevin. I'd really, really like that."

He smiled. "Does that mean you'll go to Alaska with me too?"

She laughed. "Yes, I'll go with you. I'll go anywhere with you, Kevin. For the rest of my life. Anywhere you want to take me."

## Chapter Five

"Okay, what's your big news you've made me wait all day to hear?" Mandy asked Matt on Wednesday afternoon.   After talking to him on the phone last night, she had no idea what to expect.   Apparently Pastor John had told him something significant at their meeting yesterday, but he hadn't wanted to tell her over the phone, or today until they had sufficient time to sit and talk.

Matt took her hand.   She had driven him to the MAX station to catch a train back to Portland for the midweek youth gathering at the church, but he didn't have to leave for another hour.   By the look on his face, she couldn't tell if this was good or not good, or somewhere in between. He had seemed a little spaced-out most of the day like he wasn't sure himself.

"Okay, here's the deal.   The church has three full-time youth pastors.   Pastor John has been there for ten years and he's over everything, and then they have Pastor Mike, and he's in charge of the high schoolers, and Pastor Jeremy who's over the middle school students.   Each of them have an assistant who are part-time and Bible college students in their third or fourth year. Once they graduate, they move on and find full-time positions at other churches."

"And the interns are under them?"

"Mostly yes, except for me and Travis. We're directly under John and cross over between junior high and high school."

"And he doesn't want to lose you?" That was her best guess.

"Yes, but he doesn't want me to be an intern next fall. He wants me to be Pastor Mike's assistant."

"How is that different from being an intern?"

"More time, more pay, and a lot more responsibility."

"And you would have to go to Bible college at the same time?"

"No. This is the crazy part. Pastor John thinks the position would be great for me, but he's afraid of me working at the church, trying to go to school at the same time, getting burned-out on all of it, and quitting all together. He knows I'm not a classroom-type learner. He thinks I can learn more from him and being in youth ministry than from plugging my way through school. Being a Bible college student has been one of his requirements in the past, but he's willing to let me do it if I agree to stay here."

"And you want to?"

"I don't know," he said. "I know it's a great opportunity, but I don't know if I'm ready for it. I think Pastor John has too much faith in me, but he has a point with the school-burnout thing. If you really want us to go to Lifegate, it's fine, Amanda. Honestly. But I told him we would pray about it for at least a week, and we have more time to decide than that.

Mike's current assistant isn't leaving until the first of June."

***

Seth replied to Dave's email on Wednesday afternoon, letting him know he was interested in his offer but had decided to wait until Saturday to tell Amber, so he would get back to him by early next week. He also read Matt's message and thought that was very exciting. He'd been looking forward to having him down here next year, but he knew Pastor John was likely right about Matt learning better from on-the-job training, especially under their beloved mentor.

On Thursday afternoon he had another message from Dave waiting for him, but this time Dave's news depressed him a little from the happy-high he'd been on for the last two days. Trying not to dwell on it too much until he had a chance to discuss it with Amber, he did some reading and greeted Josiah when he came into the room. He was getting ready to leave to spend Spring Break with Rachael and was in a great mood.

Josiah went to get the door when someone knocked, and Seth thought it might be Amber, but it was Kerri. She chatted with Josiah for a minute and then came back to say 'hi', and Seth asked what she was doing here.

"I need to talk to you. Privately, please."

She didn't seem upset, so he wasn't worried this was anything bad. Josiah was the only one here and graciously excused himself, saying he would catch an early dinner. Seth and Kerri thanked him as Kerri sat on his bed, and Seth remained in his chair but turned around to face her fully. "What's up?"

She smiled broadly, and he waited. She seemed giddy, and he hadn't seen her since Tuesday night at dinner. He knew she had seen Kevin that night, and he wondered if she had decided to go on the trip with him to Alaska this summer.

"Well," she began, "on Tuesday night Kevin was here, and before he left he asked me something, and I prayed about it, and I decided to tell him yes last night."

"About the trip?"

"No, not that, but I am going with him. I decided that last night too."

"What else did he ask you?"

She sighed. "He asked me to marry him."

Seth stared at his sister, feeling speechless. "Wow. And you said yes?"

"Yes. I know it's what I want, Seth. Kevin didn't talk me into it. He didn't have to."

"Are you getting married sometime soon, or is this like 'someday'?"

"Soon."

"When?"

"June. We're not sure what day yet. I have to talk to Mom and Dad and to you about when will be good for you and Amber."

"Do Mom and Dad know?"

"I want to tell them on Saturday. Only Kevin's family knows right now, and you. You're the first person I've told."

Seth didn't feel like he could say, 'You're too young to get married.' They were the same age, and Kevin was twenty-four. He knew this wasn't the same as if he and Amber had decided to get married after only six months when they were sixteen. But still, it seemed crazy.

"Are you sure, Kerri?" he said. "Amber and I prayed about getting engaged for two months. You shouldn't feel like you need to decide in one day."

"I'm sure, Seth. It's just right. I can feel it. Like I knew it was right when I let Dylan go. Like I knew it was right to let something happen with Kevin on the night of his recital. Like I knew I was supposed to go to New York with him. It's all the same Voice. It's the same warm feeling in my heart that makes me want to be with him and wouldn't let me wait more than a day to tell him yes."

Seth knew he couldn't argue with that, and he moved over to the bed to give her a hug and say what he knew she needed to hear. "That's great, Kerri. I love you. I'm very happy for you."

"Thanks. I love you too, Seth."

They held each other for a minute and then Kerri sat back with tears on her cheeks and said, "Jesus gave me everything I asked for, Seth. Everything. It came in a different package than I was expecting, but it's all there."

***

Rachael checked her phone before going to bed, and she had a message waiting from Josiah. In addition to little texts throughout the day, he always wrote her something lengthy at some point too. She missed him very much, but she knew this time away from each other and his daily words of love and encouragement had been good for her continued healing process.

He was her best friend and had become so easily. The ten days they had together before Christmas, along with the two weeks after New Year's hadn't been a lot of time to fall in love with each other, but they had. And Rachael was certain it wasn't a rebound relationship. Her relationship with Steven had been that, but this was the real thing. What she wanted. What she had prayed for all during her teen years. What God had waiting in the wings for her when she needed it the most. And Josiah didn't have to be here physically to give her what she needed.

**Hi, Beautiful. How was your day? I had two midterms, but all I could think about was seeing you tomorrow night. I hope you're prepared for some major loving-on, because I've been dreaming about it all week.**

**I read these verses this morning from Matthew 16. The disciples are worried because they forgot to bring bread on the boat with them, and Jesus says, "Won't you ever understand? Don't you remember the five-thousand I fed with five loaves and the baskets of food that were left over?"**

**Sometimes I worry this thing between us will go away, and I was thinking that this afternoon because I worry about seeing you tomorrow and having it not be the same as it was two months ago, but today Jesus said to me, "Don't you remember the way I brought you two**

together?   That wasn't you going after some girl.   That was Me bringing you together at the right time.   You never thought it would happen, Josiah, but I did it!   Don't forget that."

Rachael smiled because she had been having the same worried thoughts, and she needed to be reminded God had done this.   Having Josiah in her life was a miracle, but too often she tried to analyze their relationship instead of just letting it be.   Her relationship with Steven had been so wrong, and she'd known that from the beginning.   Her relationship with Gabe had been more on the right track, but looking back she could see areas they'd had trouble in too.

But her relationship with Josiah—there was no downside.   Even being away from him was a good thing.   She needed him more emotionally and spiritually right now than physically, and yet when they were together, that aspect was great too.

Personalizing the verse for herself, she replied to Josiah's message:

"Won't you ever understand? Don't you remember the day I brought Josiah into your life, and everything changed?   I gave you everything you needed and more!"

That's the truth, Josiah, and I can't wait to see you either.   Yes, I am prepared for some major loving-on.   To feel you holding me again will be like heaven.

Emma didn't usually go to The Oasis in the evenings. She sometimes went for her afternoon study-break on Tuesdays and Thursdays when it wasn't crowded, but otherwise she chose the library or the dorm lounge over the more social-type of hangouts on campus. It wasn't much fun to go to those places alone.

But when her roommates decided to go on Friday night and they invited her to go with them, she said yes. They hardly ever invited her anywhere. With midterms over, she didn't need to study, and there wasn't much else to do. She had decided to wait until tomorrow to drive home. She could have gone this afternoon, but she would have been driving late, and she preferred to not do that.

On the walk down to the lobby and across campus, her roommates talked and laughed with each other, but she was quiet. She didn't have anything to say relating to their topics of conversation that jumped from one to another without any break in between. Even when she did think of something, by the time there was a lull in the conversation, they were onto another topic entirely.

All three of them currently had boyfriends. Elissa had been dating the same guy for about four months, since before Winter Break. Tiffany, her newest roommate, had been dating her boyfriend since high school. He had come here in the fall, but she'd gone to Biola in southern California before deciding to transfer here for Spring Semester. They were pretty hot and heavy whenever she saw them together, and she always made sure she went to the room right after dinner if she wanted to study there because if she didn't, then she would undoubtedly find them together, and she always felt like they wanted her to leave and she would have to spend the rest of the evening in the library or the lounge. She had already decided to request a new roommate for next year, and she wished she knew someone who was looking for a roommate so she could choose someone she liked rather than having random girls chosen for her.

Her other roommate was currently dating someone she had only been with for a few weeks. There had been five or six others before that. Abby was her least favorite. Elissa and Tiffany were sometimes nice to her, especially if she was alone in the room with one or the other, but Abby was rude, condescending, and looked down her nose at her all the time—when she bothered looking, which wasn't often. Most of the time she completely ignored her, and Emma was certain Abby was the main reason Caitrin, who had been her roommate before Tiffany, had decided not to return for Spring Semester.

Caitrin had said she was homesick and didn't feel ready to be away at college, but Abby had said mean things to her several times. Emma almost hadn't come back herself for the same reason, but she really did want to be away from home and going to college, so she had decided to stick it out another semester and then pray for new and better roommates next year. She knew they were here. Most of the girls in her classes were really nice, but not the three she had been stuck with.

They all got something to drink at the counter and decided to share fries and nachos. Abby's newest boyfriend had left this afternoon. Elissa's boyfriend was working tonight, and Tiffany's had gone with his friends to the rock-climbing gym and said he would meet her later.

Emma found herself just sitting there while the other girls continued to talk, and she wasn't sure why she had decided to come. She watched other people like usual, and she felt embarrassed when she had been staring at one guy and he caught her doing so.

She looked away and didn't look back. It wasn't anyone she knew or could recall seeing before. He was sitting with two other guys, one who was in her economics class and the other she had seen before, but she wasn't sure where.

"We're going to the rec room to see if Robbie is there," Tiffany said after they had been there for thirty minutes. "Do you want to come?"

"No, I think I'll go back. I'm tired. I'll probably read and then go to bed."

"Okay," Tiffany said. "Bye."

Emma sat there at the table for another minute until she saw other girls leaving. It was late and she didn't like walking across campus by herself after dark. Following the other girls out but remaining a few paces behind, she was glad when she saw them take the path heading toward the dorms rather than to the rec room, and she kept pace with them for a minute before one of them turned around and noticed her.

"Hi, do you want to walk with us?" she asked.

"Sure, thanks," she said, jogging a bit to catch up.

"You're Emma, right?"

"Yes," she said, wondering how the girl knew that. She looked older, and Emma was certain she didn't know any of them. The whole group was likely juniors or seniors.

"I saw you run in cross-country," she explained. "You were good."

"Thanks," she said. "Do you have a friend on the team?"

"My brother. Tate Morgan. Do you know him?"

"Yes," she said. "I mean, I don't really know him, but I know who he is."

"He's a sophomore. I'm Danae, by the way. Are you a freshman?"

"Yes."

"Where did you go to high school?"

"I was homeschooled. I'm from Monterey."

"Oh yeah? We're in Santa Cruz. Me and Tate, I mean. Evangeline is from Monterey, aren't you, Evangeline?"

One of the other girls turned around. "Yes, I am. Born and raised."

"So is Emma."

"Hi, Emma. Oh, you're that fast girl from cross-country. The one Tate went on and on about, right Danae?"

"Yep. This is her. We're walking with a star tonight, ladies."

Emma appreciated the praise. She certainly didn't get this kind of attention every day. Most of the student body didn't follow cross-country too closely. You had to either be on the team or be close to someone who was.

Danae and her friends were in the girls' dorm that was mostly upperclassmen, and they parted at the fork that split in front of Priscilla Hall where she lived. "It was nice meeting you, Emma. Are you driving home tomorrow?"

"Yes."

"All by yourself, or with a friend?"

"By myself."

"Would you like to ride with us? Me and Tate are driving down, and Evangeline is driving Pam and Katy to San Mateo, and she could take you all the way to Monterey. We have plenty of room if you don't like traveling alone."

"Sure," she said. "When are you coming back?"

"Next Sunday."

"Okay. When are you leaving?"

"About nine. I'll come by. What's your room number?"

"205."

"Okay. I'll see you then."

"Thanks," she said. "Good night."

"Good night," Danae said as if they'd been friends for years.

Emma walked the remaining steps to the building and jogged up the stairs to the second floor. The reality of what had happened didn't hit her fully until she entered the room and began to finish her packing. Other than when she had placed first in several meets last fall, this was the highlight of her year.

## Chapter Six

Mandy enjoyed the feeling of Matt's arms around her and listened to the steady rhythm of his heartbeat through his soft t-shirt, wishing she didn't have to let go. She had known about this day for several months, but that didn't make it any easier.

"I love you, Amanda," he said gently. "I'll be thinking about you every day."

She didn't respond. His words were sincere, and she knew he meant them. She wanted him to go on this trip, and she had never considered asking him to stay. It was just hard to imagine the next ten days without him.

"Will you be thinking about me?" he asked.

"Yes."

"Do you still love me?"

She looked up at him to respond. "Yes."

He kissed her, and she felt loved, like always. "Will you meet me here next Sunday, or will I have to wait until Monday to see you?"

"I'll be here," she said. "Anxiously waiting for more of those."

He smiled. "There was a day not long ago I never imagined you saying something like that. You used to be so reserved with me. I'm glad you're not anymore."

She was still a quiet and reserved person with a lot of people, but she wasn't that way with Matt, and she wanted to tell him exactly what she was thinking.

"I like who I am with you, Matthew. I'll miss that this week."

"I like who you are, Amanda. And I like who I am with you too."

Matt kissed her one more time and then turned away to get in line with the others who were flying out of here in an hour. Matt was one of three interns who were going on the mission trip to Mexico along with thirty high school students from the church, some parent sponsors, and the lead youth pastor. She was so proud of him. A year ago he had barely made the cut of students Pastor John was willing to take along on the intensive mission trip, and now he was one of the leaders.

She waited in her place until she could no longer see him, and then she turned away to walk back to the parking garage alone. On the drive home, she prayed for him and the rest of the team, and she also prayed for Amber and Seth who were driving up tomorrow. She wondered if they knew about Matthew's job offer, and she supposed Matt had told Seth.

She had been feeling excited about going to California in the fall, but now that she knew it might not be happening, she didn't feel disappointed. Being anywhere with Matt was better than being anywhere without him.

Driving the last stretch of highway between Eugene and Corvallis as the clock neared eleven p.m., Josiah felt tired, but he didn't regret making the long drive this evening rather than waiting until tomorrow. He had been doing all right with not seeing Rachael for several weeks, until the last two. They had seemed to drag on forever.

He could hear Seth's words of warning spinning around in his mind. 'My most vulnerable times of weakness with Amber are when I've been missing her and only have a limited amount of time before we'll be separated again.' He was facing the same now and had been praying like crazy, but he already felt weak.

Their time together during Winter Break had been easy for him to control because it was all new, and he always had a definite sense of what was too much for Rachael before he hit that point himself. He knew she was vulnerable because she had equated physical affection from Gabe and Steven with their love for her, something she had come to realize wasn't the same thing, but it was difficult for her to separate the two.

The last couple of days he'd been having thoughts about her he knew he shouldn't be having. Whenever he imagined kissing her, his mind took the next step, and he wasn't even with her yet! He told Seth about it last night, and Seth's advice had been to not kiss her whenever they were completely alone.

"If you're at her house and her parents are there and they're awake, then go ahead and take the opportunity to enjoy kissing her the way you want to, but if they're not there or it's late and they're already in bed, don't even think about it."

Josiah knew Seth's words needed to be taken seriously, but he didn't know if he could follow them. He had desires for things he wanted to experience with Rachael—like he needed it. He kept praying until he arrived at her house but wondered if he shouldn't have come tonight.

*Okay, Jesus. Here I am. If I've already been ignoring you and shouldn't be here right now, I know my chances of listening at this point aren't great. But I have to see her. I can't wait another day. So please help. My strength is gone.*

Getting out of the car, he walked to the front door and began to knock softly, but the door opened and there she was, standing right in front of him like he had been anticipating all day.

"Hi," she said, reaching for his waist and wrapping her arms around him.

He pulled her close and held her in return, and she felt good. But it was a different good than he was expecting. He kept holding her and didn't want to let go, not even to kiss her. She smelled good. She felt good. And she needed this, so he didn't let go. He needed it too.

"Oh, Rachael. I've missed you," he said.

"I've missed you," she echoed.

He kept holding her securely in his arms and experienced something he had never felt with another person. He had an overwhelming desire to take care of her. He knew she felt safe and loved in his arms, and he liked that feeling. His vivid imagination of selfish acts of pleasure seemed dim in comparison. He wanted this all week, not something they would regret, and an idea came to him he hadn't considered until now.

"I need to tell you something," he said before he talked himself out of it.

"What?"

"I can't kiss you this week.  I can hold you like this, but I can't kiss you.  So please don't let me, and please don't ask."

She didn't say anything, but he didn't care if she liked it or not.  He loved her, and this is what he needed to do for them right now.  He knew it, and he knew he could do that.  He couldn't stop himself from coming here tonight, and he might have a difficult time stopping with kissing, but he could do this.  He could hold her like this forever.

She stepped back and looked into his eyes, and she smiled.  That was a good sign.  He shared his thoughts with her.

"I love you, Rachael.  I've been looking forward to this so much, and you feel so good to me."

She lifted her arms and slipped them around his neck.  He pulled her closer, stroking her back and saying the words once again.

"I love you."

"I love you too," she whispered.

***

"Blake, I need your advice."

"What's up?" he asked, putting on his shoes and looking at his roommate.

"Do you remember that girl I told you about last fall? The one on my cross-country team who ran past everyone most of the season?"

"The one you liked?"

"Yes. Emma. Her name is Emma."

"What about her?"

"Danae saw her last night and found out she's from Monterey, and she invited her to ride with us."

Blake smiled. "Does Danae know you like her?"

"No. Or maybe she does. I never told her that, but sisters—they always know everything."

"What's the problem?"

"What's the problem! What am I supposed to do?"

"I don't know. Talk to her? You have at least one thing in common, and she knows you. That's half the battle right there."

Tate put his elbows on his knees and his head in his hands.

Blake laughed. "You're almost twenty, Tate. You're going to have to start talking to girls one of these days."

"I talk to girls, just not her."

"What's she like?"

"Smart and beautiful."

"How do you know she's smart?"

"One of my friends told me she got a perfect score on the SAT."

"So? What do you think she's going to do, give you a math test before she'll let you take her out?"

"That's easy for you to say, you're good at math."

"You're a sorry sight, Tate. It's a car ride. What could possibly happen—especially if you don't let her know you like her?"

Tate didn't respond, and Blake almost let it go, but as he took his bag from the bed and headed for the door, he couldn't resist adding a little advice about his own experience of taking a chance on a girl and ending up with way more than he ever dared to dream.

"Of course if you actually asked her out for sometime next week while you're home, Tate, now that would be interesting. That would be something to be all bent out of shape over, but since you're not going to do that—no worries. Just play it cool and she'll never know the difference."

***

Amber saw Kerri and Kevin together on Saturday morning. Kevin was riding up with them for Spring Break, and having him along on the trip was one of the highlights of her year. She loved Kevin. She thought he was the neatest guy she had ever met, besides Seth, of course. And seeing him in this unstructured and relaxed setting was especially fun. He was really funny. He didn't try to be, except sometimes when he was teasing Kerri, but he had a natural humor in the way he said things and saw the world.

Amber felt incredibly happy for Kerri. She knew Seth was concerned this was happening too fast, but she saw it the same way Kerri did. She had been praying and waiting for two years. Why shouldn't they expect Kevin to be perfect for her?

Amber was looking forward to seeing her family and friends. As they drove the final stretch along the mountain highway after stopping to drop off Kerri and Kevin in Portland, Seth asked if she would like to go to the lake first. She said that was fine. She was feeling better after talking to Seth this week about waiting on God to lead them, and with Kerri and Kevin going to Alaska this summer, that left their apartment open for them to use. Spending the summer in California seemed to be the way God was pointing them, and she had made up her mind to be happy about it.

Seth drove to the lake, and they got out of the car to go for a walk. She knew there would be other times this week they could come here, but having a few quiet moments with Seth tonight after the long drive was nice. She needed it.

When they stopped to share sweet kisses, Seth said he had something to tell her. "I have good news and bad news," he said. "And I have to tell you the good news first, or the bad news won't make sense."

"Okay," she said. "I like good news."

He smiled cautiously. "A couple of weeks ago, I asked God for some clear direction for this summer, and I felt like He was telling me to call Dave and talk to him about the possibility of us working at camp."

Amber tried not to get her hopes up, but that was very difficult to do.

"I decided to keep praying to make sure I was hearing right, but before I got around to calling him, he sent me an email."

She smiled and laughed. She couldn't help it. "About what?"

"Having us there as senior counselors for the crew team. He asked Adam and Lauren about it, but they both want to be counselors again."

"Would we be able to stay together, or would you be sleeping with the guys and I'd be with the girls?"

He laughed. "That doesn't appeal to you?"

"No. If we're going to do that, we may as well wait until the end of the summer to get married."

"I know, and Dave knows that too. He said we could have the new room above the staff lounge. Remember the one they were starting to build at the end of the summer? It's small, but it does have its own bathroom."

"I can live with that. Can you?"

"Yes. I'd love for us to go. I think it's where God wants us."

She hated to ask. "What's the bad news?"

Seth had a look she knew well. He didn't want to say it, but he did. "Elle applied to be on staff. Dave is willing to let her come, but not at our expense. If we're fine with having her there, then she will be, but if we're not, he'll turn her away."

Amber didn't want her there. Elle had hurt her deeply last summer with her lies and false accusations. It had taken the rest of the summer for her to heal from the pain, and the scars still twinged if she spent any amount of time dwelling on it.

"What do you think?" she asked Seth, hoping he felt the same way she did.

He didn't answer immediately, and her heart dropped. "If Dave is willing to give her another chance, I think we should consider it."

She couldn't believe he said that. How could he? "How long do we have to think about it?"

"Dave would like to know as soon as possible if we want to come so he can look elsewhere if we don't.

We can take longer deciding about Elle. The letters to the general staff don't go out until next month."

She didn't know what to say.

"How do you feel about it?" he asked gently, giving her a hug and keeping her from bursting into tears.

"I want to go," she said, knowing that for a fact. She had felt that tug to be at camp too strongly to deny it.

"But you're not sure about Elle?"

*I'm sure I don't want her there!*

"I need to pray about that," she whispered instead.

"It's okay for us to say no, Amber. She hurt us, both of us, a lot, and forgiving her doesn't mean acting like it never happened."

## Chapter Seven

Kerri always enjoyed coming home after she had been away, but she was certain she had never felt more excited about it. Kevin seemed happy to be arriving with her. She was amazed by the way he fit in with her family. It usually took Kevin longer to warm up to new people. It had taken him several weeks to let her into his world completely, but with her family—especially her mom and dad, it was just there. She had noticed that with Seth too. If she was close to someone, Kevin could sense that, and it made him see them the way she did.

"We have something to tell you," she said to her parents after Seth and Amber had left and it was just the four of them. Taking Kevin's hand and pulling him close to her, she said it. "Kevin asked me to marry him this week, and I said yes."

Her parents didn't seem surprised. She hadn't expected them to object, but she thought they might be shocked by the sudden news.

"Did Seth tell you?"

"No," her dad said. "Kevin did."

"Kevin?" she laughed. "When?"

"I think it was Thursday you called us, wasn't it, Kevin?"

"Yes. Thursday," he agreed.

Now she was the one who was shocked. "Why didn't you tell me?"

"You didn't ask," Kevin said.

They all laughed. "I told you I wanted to tell them tonight."

"I know. And you did. But I told them on Thursday. My dad said I should."

She wasn't surprised now that she thought about it. Tony had been involved in this whole process and uninvolved at the same time. He had a way of letting Kevin make his own decisions and guiding him every step of the way.

"He told me I should buy you a ring too, but to wait until we got here to give it to you. Do you want it now?"

She laughed. "You silly. Of course I want it now!"

"Okay," he said. "I'll be right back."

He left the main family room to get the ring out of his bag they had left by the stairs, she assumed.

"Thanks for saying it was okay, Daddy. Were you too shocked?"

"A little. We hadn't heard you talk about wanting to get married anytime soon."

"I know. I was not expecting this for—I don't know how long—but when he asked, I knew I wanted to say yes."

Kevin returned in a simple manner and came to her side. She half-expected him to hand her the ring and say, 'Here you go,' as if had bought her a candy bar, but his dad had coached him better than that.

Getting down on one knee in front of her with her parents looking on, he handed her the closed ring box.

"That's for you, Kerri," he said. "I want you to wear it. It's from me."

"Thank you," she said, taking the case and opening it. She stared at the ring for several seconds and allowed the tears to come.

"Do you like it?" he asked. "I picked that one."

"Yes," she said, laughing softly with her tears. "It's beautiful, Kevin. Thank you. Will you put it on me?"

She handed the ring to him, and he slipped it onto her finger. Her emotions overwhelmed her. All week she'd had a feeling of, 'I'm getting married. Kevin asked me, and I said yes,' but it was a little unreal. This made it real for her, and she knew she couldn't be any more blessed.

"I love you so much, Kevin. Don't worry. These are happy tears."

"I know," he said, giving her a sweet kiss. "I make you happy."

***

Emma couldn't remember when she'd had such a fun day. Danae and her friends were happy and fun, and they included her as if they'd known her for years. Every time they stopped along the highway, she felt like a part of the gang, like she'd seen in other groups of girls having fun together on campus. But it wasn't like spending time with her roommates where they talked about things she couldn't relate to. Danae and her friends talked about good things. They laughed a lot but not at the expense of others. They laughed at themselves. They teased each other, but in good ways. And not once all day did any of them say anything to make her uncomfortable or tear her down. They asked her a lot of questions about herself, and they accepted her for who she was.

She talked to Danae the most because she rode in the front seat with her. Her brother Tate was in the back, and he was mostly quiet. Evangeline and two other girls she dropped off in San Mateo were in the other car. Danae and Evangeline had been roommates since sophomore year when they were randomly placed together. The other girls lived on the same floor as Danae and Evangeline, and they all attended the same college group at one of the churches in town.

Emma had been attending a smaller church close to the campus. She had tried some of the larger churches a lot of the students went to, but they were too big. She'd grown up in a small church, and she and Caitrin had discovered Redwood Chapel back in November. They only had one service on Sunday mornings, and it was small—about a hundred people, but they liked it. The people were mostly locals who lived there year-round, and they were all nice and welcoming. The church didn't have a college group, but that was okay with Emma. She usually felt intimidated and socially backwards in group settings.

Danae said she had been in smaller churches growing up, and she missed that sometimes, although during her college years she had needed a lot of people around her to help her stay on-track spiritually. She had gotten into an unhealthy relationship with someone during her senior year of high school that took her some time to heal from. Emma was surprised by how open Danae was about it, but she didn't feel uncomfortable, like it was more than she wanted to hear. It made her thoughtful on the drive to Monterey with Evangeline.

"Danae probably talked your ear off today, huh?" she said.

"She likes to talk," she laughed. "But that's okay. It was fun. It must be nice to have a roommate who's also such a close friend."

"You don't?" she asked, sounding sympathetic.

"No, not really. I got to know my roommate from last semester pretty well, but she didn't return after Winter Break, and the three roommates I have now are very different from me."

"Bingo, girl! The same thing happened to me my freshman year, and I almost didn't come back, but then I ended up with Danae, and wow! What a difference a year makes. She was more quiet then and still working through some things, but she was such a sweetheart, and in three years I have never once been mad at her. Now that's the kind of roommate you pray for."

"I've been praying, so we'll see."

"I did hear of someone the other day who is looking for a roommate for next year, who was that? Oh, it was Blake's sister, Lauren. Her current roommate is great, but she's getting married this summer."

"Is she nice?"

"Yes, very nice, and quiet like you. Blake is one of Danae's best friends. He got her through some rough days that first year, and he's also Tate's roommate. Do you want us to ask him about it after we get back?"

"Sure."

"Okay, don't let me forget."

***

Rachael felt so happy she could hardly stand it. From the moment she had stepped onto the front porch and into Josiah's arms last night, she had been on happy-overload. Last night had been perfect, just sitting there in the living room talking with him until one-thirty in the morning, enjoying a face-to-face conversation with him instead of a long-distance one.

She had been concerned all week about doing something to tempt him beyond his limits, or Josiah becoming more affectionate with her and not wanting to stop him, but Jesus had definitely answered those prayers in a way she never would have expected, and Josiah's solution had been perfect. She knew she would love to feel him kissing her, but his other less-risky displays of affection were enough—especially when he held her in his arms, as he was currently doing.

They'd had dinner with her family tonight after a day of sleeping-in, going into town for lunch, taking a drive up to Marys Peak, and returning to go for a walk around the neighborhood. She loved having time with Josiah all to herself, but she loved having him here with her family too. It felt easy and right.

She could remember when Gabe had spent time with her family. She always felt the need to prove to her parents he was worthy of her, and to prove to Gabe she was independent and mature. But with Josiah she didn't feel that way. Josiah's words and

74

actions spoke for themselves. She knew she wasn't strong and independent from her parents yet, and Josiah was fine with that. He never said things both Gabe and Steven used to say: 'You're a big girl, Rachael. You don't have to listen to your parents. You can make your own choices.'

He also didn't tell her parents they were going to do one thing and then take her someplace else or keep her out later than he said. When they left this morning he told them where they were going and said they would be back for dinner, and he'd stuck with that plan.

And now, sitting on the couch together with her parents and older brother in the room, she knew they had nothing to hide. There was no shame in being with Josiah, and she had no fear of him changing that. He said he loved her, and she believed he knew what that meant.

Josiah wanted to call his parents this evening, and he went to do that after sitting there and talking with her family. Today they had talked about possibly going up to Bellingham on Monday, staying with his family for a few days, and returning here on Thursday. She wanted to meet his parents, and that was important to Josiah at this point in their relationship. He had asked her mom and dad if it would be all right to take her there, and they said it was fine.

While he was in the other room talking with his parents and letting them know their plans, her mom asked if she told him about receiving her acceptance letter to Lifegate, and she said yes. She told him this afternoon while they were at Marys Peak, taking a walk in the picturesque setting and enjoying the view of the valley below.  She had wanted to tell him in person about her acceptance into the school and the final decision she had made this week about attending there in the fall.

They were planning to work at Camp Laughing Water this summer, along with some of his friends from school, but neither of them had received their acceptance letters yet.  Josiah's roommate didn't seem to think they would have any trouble getting accepted because they were always looking for college students to be counselors.  She was really excited about doing that, mainly because of the ministry environment they would be a part of.  She knew she really needed that at this point in her healing process.

When Josiah returned, he appeared disturbed about something.  He said his parents were fine with them coming up and spending a few days there.  They were anxious to meet her, Josiah said, and that gave her a good feeling, but she knew something was bothering him.  Her dad asked how long of a drive it would be, when they were planning to leave and return exactly, and Josiah had all of that already figured out.

Josiah had been holding her in his arms before he left the room to call his family, but now he kept his distance and she could feel the tension coming from his body language.  She knew her family noticed it too.  Taking his hand, she asked him what was wrong.  He shared the news he had received.  It was something they had been expecting, but the reality of it was a bit sobering.

"Sienna had her baby yesterday.  My mom just told me."

"What did she have?"

"A girl. She named her Brittany."

"Did everything go okay?"

"Yeah. She's fine; the baby's fine."

"And Gabe?"

"My mom didn't say. She thought I might want to try and get together with him while we're up there."

"Have you talked to him since Christmas?"

"I called him twice, but he wasn't very talkative."

Rachael didn't understand why Gabe had gone the way he had. She didn't understand how a guy she had once admired could abandon a girl he'd gotten pregnant. And she knew Josiah still carried a lot of the burden on himself.

She didn't say anything else, and neither did he. Her brother changed the subject, asking them if they wanted to see the new video project he had finished. That's what Casey wanted to do with his life, and he was a senior at OSU this year, so he'd been doing some advanced work. It was a good diversion, and Rachael knew Josiah was genuinely interested in what Casey showed and taught him, but after they returned to the living room and had time alone, she knew Gabe was still heavy on his heart.

"If you'd rather go up by yourself next week so you can have more time with Gabe, I understand," she said, throwing that option out there.

His face softened, and he apologized. "Rachael, I don't want that. I'm sorry I'm spoiling our evening together."

"You're not spoiling it. I'm concerned for you. How can I help? What can I say?"

He put his arm around her and pulled her close to him. "You don't have to say anything. And you help by just being here. What I'm thinking is I don't want to talk to Gabe while we're there. I've tried. Nothing I say makes a difference. Maybe I need to let it be. If he wants to come to me at some point and say, 'I messed up. How can I fix this?' then I'll be there for him. But you can't help someone who doesn't want to be helped."

"I know you've tried, Josiah. Don't take this all on yourself."

"I'm think I'm just grieving for him," he said.

She knew the feeling. They sat there in silence, both lost in their own thoughts. She decided to remind him of the difference he'd made in her life. The last three months had been like night and day compared to where she had been.

"There was time I thought I could never get over the pain of losing Gabe and the guilt of what I let happen with Steven, but you've gotten me there, Josiah. You and Jesus. And I am so happy. I'm happier than I've ever been in my life."

"Even if I'm not kissing you this week?"

She snuggled into him more and felt complete contentment. "I love your kisses, Josiah. But I don't need them right now to be happy. I just need you."

## Chapter Eight

Kerri led Kevin up the stairs and down the hall to Seth's room.  Since Seth and Amber were going to be staying with Amber's family for a few days, Seth had told Kevin he could have his room while he was here. Seth was going to be here for a few days without Amber next week, but he wanted Kevin to have his own space.  They all knew that was important to Kevin.  He did better in new environments if he had things he could count on remaining the same, like sleeping in the same bed every night and having a place he could retreat to when he needed that.

Stepping into her brother's room, Kerri wanted time with Kevin.  They'd been together all day, but not just the two of them.  She stepped into his arms as soon as he set down his bag, and he seemed to need it as much as she did.  He had been okay all evening with the endless talking and activity once more of her family arrived, but she knew he needed to "depressurize" after being in that kind of environment. Often after working for several hours at the restaurant, they would go out together and find a place to walk or sit—mostly in silence, and she always loved those moments.

"Your family makes me tired," he said.

She laughed. "I know. I'm sorry. It's okay if you need to get up and leave the room sometimes."

"I'd rather stay with you," he said.

"You let my family in. Why is that?"

"They're a part of you."

"They love you," she assured him. "Do you know that?"

"Yes."

"I love you."

"I know."

She smiled. Sitting down on the floor and leaning against Seth's bed, she waited for him to sit beside her. He did and held her quietly in his arms for several minutes, and it was nice. The best part of her day.

"When you asked me if we could get married, you said, 'I want us to be married now.' Why did you say that?"

"Because I do."

"I know, but why did you say it like that? Why do you want us to be married now?"

"Because people who love each other get married, and we love each other."

"Do you think we will ever stop loving each other?"

He appeared confused. "I don't stop love. It just keeps going."

She smiled. "Do you know when we get married we can sleep in the same room together? That I could stay in here with you all night?"

Kevin didn't often look embarrassed. Most of the time he was oblivious to the way others viewed him or had any form of self-consciousness, but he seemed shy about this topic.

"Yes," he said.

"How do you feel about that?"

"I don't know."

She rephrased the question. Abstract feelings about things he had no frame of reference for were difficult for him to express.

"Do you think you will like sharing a bed with me?"

"Yes."

"Why?"

"Because I won't have to say good night to you. You'll just stay."

"Do I ever make you feel tired—like you need to be away from me for awhile?"

"No."

Kerri realized something. This was the most alone she had ever been with Kevin. He had never been in her dorm room. They had never been at his apartment without Jenna there too. The only time they were completely alone was in the car, but he never kissed her in the car. They had moments where they spent time by themselves at the park or on campus, but there were always others around. Kevin often kissed her in public, and he never held back, but she often felt herself holding back because she was aware of the way others might be watching them.

Kerri didn't feel like she needed to put Kevin to the test and see how he would treat her if he kissed her in this private setting, and she didn't think he would kiss her any differently than anywhere else—but she would kiss him differently, and she wanted to.

She kissed him, and he kissed her easily in return. At first it was the same as always, but as her desire increased, she became more forward about it than she normally did. She knew the moment when she crossed the line for him because Kevin pulled back suddenly and seemed to realize the situation they were in.

"I shouldn't be—you shouldn't be—I'm not—"

She laid her hand on his tense jaw and spoke softly. "It's all right, Kevin."

He didn't respond, but she could tell he didn't agree.

"I'm sorry. I won't kiss you like that. It was me, not you."

When he didn't relax and go back to kissing her, she asked him if he was okay. Had she made him feel like when Jeff tried to take advantage of her? The thought made her sick to her stomach. When he didn't move or speak, she moved from his side and sat facing him instead, taking his hand and asking him again.

"Are you okay, love? I'm sorry. I shouldn't have done that."

He was just staring at her, and she tried one more time.

"How did I make you feel?"

He dropped his eyes and swallowed hard. "I-I wanted t-to touch you," he said. "I really, really wanted to touch you."

"I'm sorry," she whispered, sitting forward and hugging him gently. "That's my fault. I won't kiss you like that until after we get married."

He held her but seemed detached. "I can't m-marry you, K-Kerri. I can't—I shouldn't." He gently pushed himself away from her. "I need to—t-to go home now."

He stood up and turned toward the door. She felt awful, and confused. She hadn't done anything besides kiss him.

"Kevin, wait," she said, standing up and grabbing his hand. He didn't turn back to look at her, but he stopped. She stepped in front of him. "Please talk to me. You can't go home right now. We're in Portland. You don't have your car here."

He didn't say anything. She prayed from the depths of her soul for the right words. He had put up a wall. He didn't put up walls with her. How could she fix this? She thought about telling him to go to sleep now, but she didn't think leaving him alone would be the best thing. She didn't know what he was thinking. Why did he think he couldn't marry her now?

"Look at me, Kevin."

He lifted his eyes and appeared to "see" her, but he was ready to bolt at any second. She took his hands and asked him something that hadn't occurred to her until now.

"Do you know that you can touch me after we get married?"

He stared at her.

"Do you?"

"A-Anywhere?"

She smiled. He was looking at her in disbelief, but he was back. "Yes. It will be okay then. When we get married, we won't have rules anymore. You can kiss me in the car. You can be in my room because it will be your room too. You can hold me until you fall asleep. You can touch me anywhere you want, as much as you want, as long as it's just you and me alone together."

She stepped closer, speaking calm words of truth to him. "That's what married people do. It's part of being married. We're not married right now, so you can't do those things, but when we are, you can."

He kept staring at her but spoke cautious words. "I-I didn't know that. I thought I could n-never—I was never going to—but—"

"I know, love," she said. "I made you want to, and you thought you couldn't, and you didn't know how to not feel that way."

"Yes. I didn't. I don't. I—I—I'm still thinking about it."

"That's okay. You can think about it. You just have to wait until we get married, okay?"

"Okay."

"Can you do that?"

"Yes."

"As long as I don't kiss you like that?"

"Yes. You can't do that."

"I'm sorry. I want to kiss you like that, just like you want to touch me. But I won't anymore, okay?"

"Okay."

"And I won't kiss you in a bedroom again until it's our bedroom, okay?"

"Okay."

"Come here and sit with me," she said. "We were doing fine, and I spoiled it. You can just hold me now. No more kissing tonight."

They returned to the floor, and she leaned into his side. Neither of them said anything for several minutes, and she was back to enjoying the quietness and Kevin's presence when he spoke.

"Are you sure, Kerri?  My dad never told me I can touch you after we're married.  He tells me things.  He tells me what I need to know."

"I'm sure, Kevin.  Maybe he didn't tell you that so you wouldn't decide to marry a girl for that reason."

"That isn't a good reason?"

She smiled.  "Not if it's the only reason.  You should marry me because you love me, and then touching me is a way you show me your love."

"I think I love you a lot."

She didn't dare laugh, but she smiled.  "I know you do.  And I love you too, Kevin.  I love you very, very much."

## Chapter Nine

"What are you going to do with these books, Jewel?"

Amber looked up from her laptop, and she shrugged. "I don't know, Dad. I've done some research on getting them published, and Seth has too, but it's not looking too promising. Most publishers won't take submissions unless you have an agent, and the two agents I contacted said they can't take on any more writers right now."

"Has anyone read them beside your mom and Seth?"

"Mandy and my roommate Lauren did, and they liked them. Stacey read the first one, but I haven't sent the second yet."

"I think we should figure out a way to print them ourselves," Seth interrupted. "But we haven't had time to look into it yet."

Amber appreciated Seth's support and optimism, but she had begun to wonder if she was meant to write more than a couple of stories or have anyone besides close friends read them. She loved doing it, and she knew she had a good message to share, but so did a lot of writers. Bookstore shelves were already filled with books, and publishers weren't desperate for new material. Perhaps this was a dream that would be better left on the shelf of her idealistic heart, not brought into reality.

"I'm sure a lot of the girls at church would love to read them, sweetie," her mom chimed in. "I wonder if your grandmother knows someone in town who could help with figuring out how to do it."

"It sounds like a lot of work," she said.

"You've already done the hardest part," Seth said. "You keep writing, and I'll figure out a way to get them into readers' hands."

She smiled at him. There was something about the way Seth said things that made her believe anything was possible.

"We should probably get going," she said, noticing the time and closing her computer. "Where are Ben and Hope?"

"Upstairs, I think," Seth replied.

"I'll go see if they're ready."

She got up from the couch where they had been sitting for the past hour. After attending church this morning and having lunch at her grandma's house with the rest of her family, they had returned home to relax for the afternoon. Ben and Hope didn't have Spring Break until next week, but they had come for the weekend to see them. The four of them had made arrangements to meet Mandy, Colleen, and Blake in town before Ben and Hope had to head back to school for classes tomorrow.

Everyone's summer plans were the topic of conversation over pizza. Mandy shared about their decision-making process with Matt being offered the position at the church. At this point they didn't know what they were doing, but everyone seemed to agree it was a great opportunity for Matt.

"He can always go back to school later if it doesn't work out," Seth said. "But I think it will. I've never seen him fail at anything when his head and heart have been in the right place."

"You need to tell him that," Mandy said. "He doesn't listen to me."

"Oh, I think he does," Seth said. "All I ever hear whenever I talk to him is: Mandy says this, and Mandy says that. And I tell him to listen, and he says he does."

Colleen and Blake's decisions about this summer and beyond had a lot to do with what would be happening this week and if Blake was officially offered any positions. He hoped to be going back next weekend with clear direction about where he was supposed to go after graduation, but he also knew that might not happen.

Seth and Amber shared their news also, and the decision they had to make about Elle. Everyone said they wouldn't blame them if they told Dave they didn't want her there, but when she and Seth talked about it on the drive back to the house, Amber was feeling different about it than she had yesterday. She wanted to write-off Elle as someone she had every right to distance herself from, but she knew better than anyone that people did change and damaged relationships could be healed.

"I think my problem with believing that about Elle is I never got to know her to the point of caring about her. I didn't like her for other reasons that week, and then when she told a horrible lie about me, I actually hated her, and I've never felt that way about anyone."

During the last six months, she hadn't thought about Elle much, but she had caught herself being more guarded around new people, especially any girls who showed any kind of attention to Seth beyond normal friendliness. One of them had been in their Old Testament class last fall. Her name was Michaela, and she had also been in Seth's youth group in Portland. She was constantly flirting with Seth, and he had a lot of fun with her in return. She knew Seth saw her like a sister, and he treated her a lot like Kerri, but it had prevented her from wanting to be friends with her.

"You have a heart of gold, Amber," Seth said. "That's why this is so hard for you. A lot of girls would justify their hateful feelings and not give it another thought. But you can't do that because you usually love people so easily."

"What am I supposed to do, not love this time, or pretend it doesn't hurt?"

"Neither. You can love and admit that it hurts at the same time."

"Do you think we should allow her to be there with us?"

"I didn't say that. Loving her doesn't mean giving her the opportunity to hurt you again. It means you leave her in God's hands, and you do whatever you feel God leading you to do. If that's to have her there, then you trust Him to take care of you. If it's to not have her there, then you trust God to reach her in another way besides being at camp this summer. That might not be what's best for her. It's what she wants, but that doesn't mean it's what God wants."

*** 

Hope wondered what time it was, and she rolled onto her side to check. She couldn't sleep because she'd had that nap in the car on the way back this evening, and her thoughts were unsettled too. She was happier than she had ever been, and these last three months of being married to Ben and sharing an apartment with him had been fun and given her a settled feeling. She didn't have any reason to feel anxious about her own life right now, and she hadn't realized how content and happy she felt until she had seen Amber this weekend.

In the two and a half years she had known her, Amber had always been the peaceful one. Carefree and happy were words she used to describe her. Hope's goal in her recovery process had been to be like that. To find complete healing for her past, overcome her feelings of self-scrutiny and doubt, and get to the point where she felt carefree and happy.

She knew there would be difficult times to face and life couldn't always be blissful. There was too much anti-Godism in the world to remain completely unaffected by the trouble and cares of life all the time, but she wanted to do that as much as possible, especially when she didn't have any immediate problems in her own life to deal with. In the past there had been times when everything around her was fine, but in her mind and heart things weren't, clouding the happiness and joy she should have been experiencing.

But this weekend Amber wasn't carefree and happy. She was majorly stressed. Hope knew she tried to hide it, but Amber couldn't hide it. If she wasn't herself, anyone who knew her well could see it. The pain from Elle's lies went deep. That had been obvious this evening when Amber had talked about it.

Getting out of bed, she opened the door to the small balcony and breathed in the cool night air. She didn't pray for Amber with words, but she opened her weary spirit for her and asked Jesus to help Amber sort through this and find further healing through the process.

"You okay?" Ben asked when she went back to bed and he woke up momentarily. She snuggled into his arms and told him what she had been doing.

"She didn't look good," he agreed. "I wanted to say something, but I wasn't sure what."

Hope agreed. They were going home on Thursday evening after Ben's last final, and she knew they would have a few more days with Amber and Seth before they left on Sunday morning. Maybe something would occur to her to say when she saw her then.

\*\*\*

On Monday morning Josiah felt ready for the drive up to Bellingham. He was looking forward to having Rachael there with him. He'd been keeping his parents posted on how their relationship was going and often asked them to pray for Rachael in various ways.

Rachael seemed a little stressed during breakfast, and once they were in the car, he took the time to reassure her today was going to be fine. Giving her a brief kiss and a soft smile, he said what he believed to be true.

"They love you already, Rachael. All you have to do is be yourself and let me take care of you."

She nodded and appeared to believe him. He wanted to kiss her again, but he decided he'd better not. He was still committed to not kissing her in a sensual way this week and had only kissed her now as a way of making her feel loved and safe.

He asked her to pick music for them to listen to, and once they were on the road, they talked easily with one another. He hadn't told her that much about his family other than major details: his parents had been married for twenty-five years, his dad was a pastor, he had three sisters and one brother. Catherine was a senior at Seattle Pacific this year, and his two younger sisters, Emily and Kristin, were in high school. His younger brother, Alex, was fourteen.

He told her more details about his mom and dad and siblings and the church he had grown up attending. When he was little his dad had been the youth pastor there, and when the senior pastor retired fifteen years ago, his dad stepped up to the open position.

He and Rachael had similar childhoods: they had both lived in the same city their whole lives, attended the same church, had parents who were actively involved in ministry, and had been raised to believe the same things about God. But their high school years were vastly different: Josiah had been studious and limited his extracurricular activities to basketball, youth group, and music lessons; Rachael was also a good student but had been involved in everything under the sun: student government, sports, dance team, cheerleading, theater, choir, band, youth group, and children's ministry.

She began her freshman year at OSU as an active participant in the college group at church and various things on campus, taking on a leadership position within the youth group, teaching a children's Sunday school class, and helping her parents with the children's choir.  She had taken a serious step back from the busyness ever since her relationship with Steven had been exposed.  At first it had been her parents and her youth pastor advising her to take a break, figure out who she was and where she wanted to go from there, and then slowly get back into things—not taking on more than she could handle or only staying busy to avoid the emptiness and pain.

She decided to take a break from everything except the children's choir and being a part of the college group until the end of the year and then see where she was at.  It was during that time he became a part of her life, and after Christmas they had a lot of conversations about what her life was supposed to be about, and if she had been doing what God really had for her.

On the one hand being involved in a lot of things gave her more energy.  She thrived on being around people and doing things she was good at and enjoyed.  But on the other hand she could see how most of the relationships she had with others were superficial and she hadn't gone any deeper in her faith through all the church-involvement. She was so busy trying to lead others to God, she was missing Him herself.

During the last two months she had maintained her more relaxed schedule, focusing her energy on three things: her relationship with God, her relationship with him, and school. College group and her involvement in ministry were secondary, and it was working for her. She had shared that with him during the last two months, but today she talked about it more extensively, seeming to need to use him as a sounding-board for her current thoughts. He mostly listened, smiling several times when she said something he had been specifically praying for her to realize.

"You're smiling again," she said when they were an hour away from Bellingham. "You could have told me that two months ago, right?"

"Yes, but I love seeing you discover it for yourself. And I haven't thought about it in those terms. You teach me a lot, Rachael. You put into words things I already know but can't express. Several times this semester I've told Seth something, and he's said, 'That's a really cool way to think about it,' and I had to say, 'Rachael told me that.'

"You're not getting tired of me?" she asked. "All of my babbling and slow-to-learn tendencies and hopeless flaws?"

They were approaching a rest stop, and he took the exit off the freeway. He needed to take a break from driving and he wanted to hold her and assure her of something. Once he found a parking space and shut off the car, he went around to open her door and gave her a long hug right there in the parking lot with the noise of the freeway in the background.

"I love you, Rachael," he said, not knowing how else to express it. "I'm not getting tired of you by any stretch of the imagination. The more time I have with you, the more I want. Are you getting tired of me?"

She stepped back and smiled at him. "Of you? How does anyone get tired of someone like you? My friends ask me what you're like, and I can't put it into words. I feel like pulling my heart out and giving it to them for a few minutes and saying, 'That's what he's like.'"

He wanted to kiss her, and he asked if he could. She smiled and put her arms around his neck, but she gave him a hug and put her lips out of his sight.

"Hold me, Josiah."

He did, and he felt bad for asking, but her words set him at ease. They were sincere and appreciative and let him know he was doing something right in all of this.

"I've needed you to not kiss me this week. I never would have known that if you hadn't made the decision and stuck to it, but I need this more than kisses right now. I need to know you love me and care about me. I need to know you're after my heart more than my body. I need to know I can feel this way about you and hold you in my heart so tight without having to give you anything."

"You give me more than you know, Rachael. You give me you, and that's enough."

# Chapter Ten

"I think we should decide what day we want to get married while we're here this week," Kerri said. She and Kevin had gone for a walk and were currently along the perimeter of the neighborhood park where she had grown up playing.

"I think so too," Kevin said.

"We also need to decide where. Do you want to get married up here or in California?"

"Jenna and Caleb are getting married at the church."

"I know, and if you want us to all get married on the same day, we'll definitely do that too. But is that what we're doing?"

"I don't know," he said. "What do you want?"

When she had first accepted Kevin's proposal last week, Kerri felt like she didn't care. But after being home this week and having time to think about it, she had decided she would prefer to get married up here, but she didn't want to upset Kevin's mindset if he felt like it had already been decided.

"I'd like to get married here," she said. "Is that okay?"

"That's fine," he said. "I just want to get married. I don't care where."

"You don't?" She laughed. "Who are you, and what have you done with Kevin?"

"I'm Kevin," he said, not catching the joke.

"I know you are," she said. "I'm just teasing. Ever since I met you, you've always been very particular about the way you want things to be. Why not this?"

"I've never gotten married before. I don't know how to do it."

"So, it's okay if I take care of details like where and when and whether we have white flowers or pink ones?"

"Yes."

"And if we got married up here at my church on the third Saturday in June, that would be okay? That's two weeks after Jenna and Caleb are getting married and a week before we're leaving for Alaska. I was thinking we could go to the beach up here after the wedding and then travel down the coast all week to San Francisco for our flight up to Vancouver."

"That sounds good."

"Are you sure? Just like that, you're letting me decide?"

"I want you to be happy, Kerri. Whatever makes you happy."

She almost argued with him. He'd been so insistent about her going to New York and Alaska with him and wanting to see her on particular days during the week, but she realized all of those things were a part of Kevin's desire for her to be happy. He often knew what she needed before she did.

"That would make me happy," she said, stepping into his arms and giving him a gentle hug. He held her equally in return, and they stood there for a minute, feeling the mild breeze around them and listening to children play in the background.

"Do you want to have children?" she asked him.

"Yes."

"Me too."

"Where do you want to live?" he asked.

She stepped back and looked at him. "In your apartment?"

"I mean after that. After we're not in school anymore."

"I don't know. I haven't thought about it. Have you?"

"I was thinking about it."

"When?"

"This morning."

"What were you thinking?"

"My dad has always told me I can work at the pizza place however long I want, even after I'm married and have a family of my own."

"Is that what you want to do?"

"No. I don't think so."

"Where do you want to go?" she asked. With her current plans to become a special education teacher, she knew she could do that anywhere, and if she was with Kevin, she would be happy anywhere he was happy.

"I want us to live here. Near your family."

"Why?"

"Because you're happier here."

"Am I?"

"Yes. You smile more."

She smiled. He was right. She had missed her family. It felt good to be home this week.

"What would you do up here? What kind of job would you like to do?"

He hesitated before he answered. "M-Maybe a t-teacher, li-like you."

"You could do that."

"What if I'm not good at it?"

"Then you try something else."

"Would you be disappointed in me?" he asked softly, appearing as though he might cry.

Her heart nearly broke in two. "No, Kevin. I wouldn't. I will love you no matter what you do or don't do. I want you to be happy too. If you try teaching, and you don't like it, then you try something else. If you decide you don't like trying new things and want to go back to making pizza, then that's what you do."

"I need you, Kerri," he said, pulling her back to him and holding her close. "I need you t-to believe in me. T-To help me be brave. I-I was getting so scared about gr-graduating and n-not knowing what I-I was g-going t-to do. I w-want t-to do o-other things, b-but I-I'm scared."

"That's okay, Kevin. We all get scared."

He remained silent. Kevin had only expressed his fear to her one other time. The night she had gone to his recital and he told her he didn't want Jenna to get married. She quoted a verse she knew he would know. She had memorized it when she felt scared about graduating and going to college.

"*I sought the LORD and he answered me; he delivered me from all my fears.*"

He remained silent, but she knew he was listening.

"Do you know I was scared of going to your recital—the first one I went to?"

He released her and looked into her eyes. "You were? That's silly."

She smiled. "I know, but I was so scared. Not when you first asked me, but after I found out from Lauren you didn't usually ask people you'd just met. I knew it was a big step for you, and that scared me. But I asked God to help me be brave and go and see what happened, and it was one of the happiest nights of my life."

"I was scared that night too. I thought you might not like it. I was nervous about playing for you."

"But you did beautifully. Just because something scares us doesn't mean we shouldn't do it or it's going to turn out bad."

Kerri thought about her words in relation to the decision she had made last week when she had agreed to marry Kevin. Fear had kept her from saying yes right away, but after she thought about it, she knew she didn't have anything to be afraid of. It felt scary, but she didn't have any real reason to say no.

"Are you scared of getting married?" she asked.

"No. I was scared to ask you, but I'm not scared now."

"Why were you scared to ask me?"

"I thought you might say no. I-I thought you might say you never wanted to get married a-and that I could never have you like that."

By "like that" Kerri knew Kevin wasn't talking about having her sexually because he hadn't known about that until after they were engaged. He meant he could have her forever. She sometimes wondered if Kevin might eventually get tired of her. Like one of the pinball machines at Tony's they had replaced recently because Kevin said he was tired of it and wanted a new one, even though it had been his favorite for a long time.

"Do you know what divorce is, Kevin?"

"No."

"It's when two people who are married decide they don't want to be anymore, and so they get a divorce. They stop being married and live in different places again."

"Why?" he asked.

"Sometimes because they don't get along and fight too much, or sometimes because they stop loving each other and want to be alone again or marry someone else."

"Is that like being separated? My aunt and uncle say they're separated, but they still come together for Christmas and stuff."

Kerri didn't know if his aunt and uncle were only separated or actually divorced, so she said, "Yes, it's like that. People who are separated usually get divorced, but not always. Sometimes they just stay separated for awhile and then get back together later."

"My mom and dad haven't ever done that. Have yours?"

"No, they haven't. They love each other very much, and I know your mom and dad do too. And that's what I want for us. I want us to always be married to each other and to never get separated or divorced. Is that what you want too?"

"Yes."

"Are you sure? You don't think you'll get tired of me—like you got tired of *Galaxy Racers*?"

He laughed. "That's just a game, Kerri. Not a person."

"But you really liked that game for a long time, and then you wanted a new one."

"You're silly," he said. "I can't get a new Kerri. Just you."

"I know," she laughed. "I just want to make sure you understand when we get married—that lasts forever. We will be together for the rest of our lives. You can't wake up one day and say, 'I don't want to be married anymore,' and then leave and never come back. I mean, you could, but that would hurt me very much. It would hurt our children very much. Getting married is a big deal. It's a big commitment. I want to make sure you understand."

"I understand, Kerri."

She smiled, and she believed him.

"You can't go away either," he said. "I-I c-couldn't—"

"Shh," she said, putting her fingers on his lips. "I won't, Kevin. I won't ever leave. I promise. You won't have to get a new Kerri. You can always have this one."

## Chapter Eleven

Danae woke up suddenly, realizing it had only been a dream. Lying there in the darkness, she could feel her heart racing. She hated having that dream and had wondered if she would make it through the week without having it.

It wasn't actually a dream. It was worse. It was a memory of something that had happened four years ago, and all of the feelings of shame and regret came flooding back as if it had been yesterday.

She'd been through counseling and had good friends she had been able to talk to about it. She shared openly with other girls she mentored at school and led in Bible study in an attempt to keep them from making the same poor choice. She knew she was forgiven. She had moved on with a new relationship. She felt hopeful about the future God had for her. But still, the dream had returned, and she hated it.

Glancing at the clock, she saw it wasn't that late. She'd had an early morning and had gone to bed at ten. It was only twelve-thirty now, and she didn't want to go back to sleep. Reaching for her phone, she selected John's number and waited for him to pick up. He had worked late tonight so she hadn't talked to him since yesterday, and she knew he probably wasn't asleep yet.

"Hey, you're up late," he said, greeting her with a familiar softness.

"I was sleeping," she said. "I woke up."

"Bad dream?" he asked with a knowing tone. She had always been honest with him about her past and her continued struggle to overcome it at times.

"It's not a dream. It's a memory."

"It's over, Danae. It's not real. Not now."

"I know, but it feels real."

"Do you want me to come down tomorrow? It's my day off."

"No, you should rest. It's too long of a drive for just one day."

"Love does crazy things like that. I'll come if you need me."

"I'll be all right," she said. "Just talk to me now."

He told her about his day, and she told him about hers. It had been a really good day. Her family had gone to Carmel—the whole gang: her older brother and sister and their spouses, Tate, her younger sister and Tabby's boyfriend, her dad and his new wife. The only person missing was her real mom who had died six years ago in a car accident. But still, it had been a good day—the kind of day Danae knew her mom would want them to have without her.

Maybe that's why she had the dream tonight. She didn't blame her mother's death for the mistakes she had made. She knew what was right and what was wrong, and she'd made her own choices. But the pain and confusion associated with losing her mom at the tender age of seventeen hadn't been something she had dealt with in healthy ways. Her mom was gone. Her older sister was being too bossy and distrustful of everything she was doing. Her dad was hurting too much to talk to. Her friends were distant and walked on eggshells around her. God seemed nonexistent and a cruel reality at the same time. And so she'd found comfort in the only relationship that allowed her to escape the pain.

"I found out I don't have to work on Sunday," John said. "Do you think you can come back on Saturday instead?"

"Yeah, maybe," she said. "I'll ask Tate if he wants to. Oh, and Emma. I don't want to pull her away from her family a day early. I'll let you know."

"You and your empathetic heart. What am I going to do with you?"

"Just love me, John. I'm great at loving others for whatever crazy reason, but I can't always accept it for myself."

"Are you going to marry me one of these days?"

She didn't answer that. Yes, she wanted to marry John, and she had told him so when he asked her at Christmas, but she also told him she wasn't ready yet. Not for this summer like he wanted. She wasn't sure why she didn't feel ready yet, but she didn't.

"I love you, John. Please don't doubt that."

"I don't. That was a friendly reminder I still have a ring for you whenever you decide you're ready to wear it."

"I know."

"Tell me about the dream."

"It's the same, John. The same as it always is."

"Tell me," he said. "Get it out of your head so you won't have it again tonight."

"I don't want to tell you. I'll be all right."

"Tell me," he said again.

She gave in. There wasn't much to tell. The dream always began and ended in the same way with a few variations in between. She was kissing Evan. They were in her bedroom in her bed, the same room and bed she was currently in. It hadn't been the first time they'd had sex, but this time it ended differently with her dad walking in on them. She wasn't supposed to be home at that time of day, and neither was he. The dream always ended with the look of extreme shock, pain, and disappointment on her dad's face. It woke her without fail.

But her memory didn't end there. It had been real. Her dad had left the room without saying anything. She had laid there for what felt like an eternity, trying to figure out what to do. She had eventually asked Evan to leave, and he had. She'd gotten dressed, gone downstairs, and saw her dad sitting in the kitchen drinking coffee and staring at nothing.

She walked into the room and apologized for skipping school and for what he had seen. He hadn't said anything, and she'd left the house and gone to the beach for the rest of the day, just sitting there watching the waves roll in and out and feeling more alone than she had ever felt in her life.

"Does your dad know you have that dream?" John asked.

"No. I've never told him about it."

"I think you should."

Danae thought about that. Her relationship with her dad was much different now. Back then they hadn't really known each other. He was busy. She was busy. After her mom died they were both hurting but couldn't seem to talk to each other. It hadn't been until three months later she had gone to him to admit her need to start seeing the counselor she had refused to talk with much after her mom died.

She had broken up with Evan by then, and she was trying to find her way back to wherever she was supposed to be as a young Christian woman, a pastor's daughter, and a child of God; but it was too hard. She was too depressed and felt too alone.

The counseling had helped. Good friends had helped. Her family had helped. She considered her dad to be her biggest fan now, but the pain of hurting him was still there.

"Maybe you're right," she said. "But I don't know if I can. That's behind us. I don't want to dredge up old memories."

"He would want to know, babe. Just talk to him. Somehow I think he can handle it. Your dad is the strongest, most caring, most spiritually-stable man I know. He loves you. If you need to talk to him about it, he'd want that for you."

\*\*\*

On Wednesday morning Josiah woke up with the feeling he was being watched. Rolling over from his stomach, he saw Rachael sitting on the edge of his bed, and he smiled cautiously.

"What are you doing in here?"

"Watching you sleep," she said.

He pulled the blankets up to cover more of his torso and laughed. "I'm not sure that's too wise of an idea with me not dressed and you sitting there looking so beautiful, even at—" He glanced at the clock. "Eight-thirty in the morning."

"I've got breakfast for you, and I'd hate for it to get cold." She rose from the bed and went to his desk where she had set a tray of food. Turning back, she brought it over to him with the most delightful expression on her face.

"You made me breakfast?" he said, putting his pillow against the headboard and sitting up. "Just how early did you get up?"

"About an hour ago," she said. "I woke up and couldn't go back to sleep." She set the tray down on the blankets covering his lap. "When I went downstairs your mom was making breakfast, and she asked me if I wanted some. But I told her I could make my own and some for you too."

"Did you already eat, or are you going to eat with me?"

"I already ate since you were still sleeping, but then I couldn't stand to not see you for another minute, so I decided to bring it up to you."

Josiah smiled. She was acting very—he couldn't describe it. Sort of like a little girl and a young woman at the same time. Not like a giggly teenager, but not like his mom either. Just very sweet and genuine.

Leaning forward, he kissed her gently on the cheek. "Thank you," he said. "I have a surprise for you today too."

She smiled. "I like surprises."

"I know.  That's why I planned one."

She sat there and watched him eat for a moment. He felt self-conscious.  He didn't have a shirt on, and he wasn't exactly a buff guy.  He was on the skinny side, and he had almost no muscle definition. Certainly not at all like Gabe or his roommate Chad. Man, he'd kill for a body like that, but he wasn't big enough to get there even if he worked out every day.

But Rachael seemed completely oblivious to his scrawny arms and chest.  Her eyes were on his eyes, and he had learned that was the best place to keep his eyes on her also, so he did.

"What did I do, Rachael?" he asked, taking her hand and stroking her skin gently.  "How did I end up with you?  Look at you.  Look at me.  This is insane."

She smiled, but she didn't agree.  Leaning forward and giving him a kiss on the cheek, she whispered something to him.  "This is *right*, Josiah."

She rose from the bed and let herself out.  He sat there for a minute thinking about her, and he wondered how she saw him.  Was she attracted to him on a physical level, or was she settling for him because he was a nice guy?

Once he finished eating, he got out of bed and ready for the day, meeting her downstairs and telling her what she needed to bring for what he had planned.  While she went to get a few things from her room, he went into the kitchen and saw his mom watering the plants beside the breakfast nook.  His dad had left for work, but he'd already asked him this question last night, so he went ahead and asked his mom this morning.

"What do you think of her, Mom?"

His mother smiled.  "She's beautiful, Josiah. Inside and out."

"Do you think we fit together?"

"I think only you and Rachael can know if you fit together, but there's nothing imaginary about the love you have.  I can see that plainly."

His parents already knew about his plans for today, so when Rachael returned, he told his mom good-bye and the time he expected them to be back. Once they were outside, he told Rachael about their destination and how they were going to get there.

"You don't hate boats, do you?" he asked.

"No," she said.  "And I've been to Friday Harbor before.  Our marching band and dance team went there."

"So, this is nothing special then?"

Her expression turned more serious, and she hugged him.  "You're special, Josiah.  You don't have to do special things for me.  Just being you is enough."

"And you didn't have to make me breakfast this morning, but you did."

"I know," she said, stepping back and looking at him.  "But it wasn't an effort because I wanted to."

"And today isn't an effort for me, Rachael.  And you know why?"

"Why?"

"Because I'm in love with you."

He felt like he was putting his heart on the line by saying that, even more so than when he said, 'I love you.'  He could love Rachael and care about her without being in love with her, and she could love him and care about him without being in love with him.

But he was in love with her, and he wanted her to be in love with him.

"What does that mean to you?" she asked. "That you're in love with me?"

He knew how he felt, but he took a moment to put it into words. He was worried she would reject him for it. He wanted to ask if she was in love with him before he said it, but he took the risk.

"It means I never want to stop loving you, Rachael. I want to marry you. I want to have kids with you. I want to spend the rest of my life with you."

She smiled.

"I hope it doesn't scare you for me to say that."

"It doesn't."

She didn't say anything else, and that was okay. He pulled her close and held her, and he knew this was going to be a good day. Rachael made everything special and beautiful, and he hoped he made the world a brighter place for her too.

## Chapter Twelve

Mandy had been dreading spending a whole week without Matthew, but it wasn't as difficult as she had been anticipating.  As Matt had said, Amber was home, and she was able to have time with her, just the two of them.  Seth left on Monday afternoon to go spend time with his family, and she slept over the next two nights.

Amber didn't talk about the decision she had to make concerning Elle, but Mandy knew she was thinking about it.  Not occasionally, but a lot.  Mandy spent most of Wednesday helping Amber and her mom with addressing wedding invitations and making hair clips she and Amber's other bridesmaids were going to wear.  Her mom had come up with the design, and she and Amber were trying to copy her pattern, but they weren't the most crafty helpers, so it took them awhile to get all four of them done.

But it was fun, and Amber seemed in better spirits. Mandy stayed for dinner, and then Amber and her mom followed her back into town because Grandma had called and said Amber's dress was ready to try on again.  She had done so on Sunday, and Grandma had made a few adjustments.  She wanted to make sure it was okay before she went on to the next step.  Amber looked really happy as Grandma helped her with putting it on, and it seemed to fit perfectly.

On Thursday Amber came back into town and they went shopping together for things she needed to get for the wedding and honeymoon. Mandy helped her with selecting new clothes, a new bathing suit, and some pretty lingerie. Amber was planning to have dinner at Grandma's, and Seth met them there.

Mandy hoped everything was all right between Amber and Seth, but she couldn't help but notice the dramatic mood shift in her cousin between the time he arrived and when they left to go back to the house later in the evening. Amber had seemed down over the weekend when Seth was here, better after she had been away from him for twenty-four hours, but back to her uncharacteristic self now that Seth was back.

On Friday Mandy drove out to spend part of the afternoon with them as Amber had invited her to do. She tried to find a moment when she could ask Amber if she was all right, but Seth was constantly at her side, and she had the feeling she wouldn't be as honest with him there. Amber was trying very hard to disguise her sadness from him, and maybe she was fooling Seth, but she wasn't fooling her.

She remained through dinner, but then made up an excuse to go home. She couldn't watch Amber be like this, and an unthinkable concern entered her heart. When Amber walked her to the door, she asked if she could talk with her outside for a minute.

"Sure," Amber said, stepping out behind her and closing the door. "What's up?"

"I was going to ask you the same thing."

"What do you mean?"

"Something's wrong, Amber. I can see it. What's going on?"

"Nothing."

She waited for her to be honest.

Amber laughed. "What? Nothing's going on."

"I don't believe you. You're not yourself. Are you trying to keep something from Seth, or are you and Seth trying to keep something from us?"

Amber stared at her. "What do you mean by that?"

Mandy could feel her heart pounding. She hadn't really planned to say this, but now it was all spilling out. "You know what I mean."

"We don't have anything to hide," she said. "Is that what you think?"

"I don't know, Amber. I just know you're not yourself. I'm not trying to accuse you of anything, I'm just—"

"Yes, you are. That's exactly what you're doing."

Mandy felt like crying. Amber had never spoken to her this way, and she felt bad to be making false accusations, but she knew there was something Amber wasn't saying.

"Are you having doubts about getting married?"

"No."

"Is Seth?"

"Not that I know of."

"Okay, never mind. If you say you're fine, I believe you. I'm sorry, maybe I'm missing Matt more than I think, and it's making me see things that aren't there."

Amber didn't respond, and she didn't seem to have anything to say, so Mandy told her good-night and turned away, saying she would see her later.

"Mandy," Amber said before she made it to the stairs.

She turned back.

"I'm sorry I snapped at you. I know you're just looking out for me like I've always asked you to do. But we're fine, really."

"I know," she said. "I believe you. Good night."

"Good night. I love you.

"I love you too."

***

Amber watched Mandy drive away. She wasn't sure what that had been about and what Mandy thought she was seeing, but she supposed her cousin hadn't been around her much lately and was taking a little mood swing too seriously. Going back inside, she rejoined Seth on the couch and enjoyed a quiet moment with him as everyone else had left the room momentarily. They were all planning to watch a movie together.

"Is everything okay? Mandy all right?"

"Yeah, she had something to ask me. Privately," she added before Seth could ask her what. She wasn't sure why, but she didn't feel like telling him what Mandy had said.

"Are *you* all right?" he asked. "You've been quiet today."

"Have I?"

"It's fine if you're fine. I'm just wondering."

Taking into consideration what Mandy had said, she thought before answering Seth so quickly. Ben returned to the room, and Hope joined him. Ben asked if they had made a decision about camp.

"We're going," Seth said. "But we haven't decided about the other thing. And I forgot to tell you," he said, speaking to her, "Michaela decided she's going. She told Kerri when she saw her at church on Sunday."

Amber felt her guard going up. "Michaela? From school? I didn't know she was thinking about it."

"Oh, that's right, you're not in our class. She's been talking about it since January, and she sent in the application, but then she was debating."

"How does she know she's going if they haven't sent out the acceptance letters?"

"She applied to be a senior counselor. She's worked at another camp the past three years. I think she'll make a really good one, and you'll have a lot of fun working with her, don't you think?"

Amber didn't answer that. "What class do you have with her?"

"Drama. She's playing the lead role opposite me in the play we're doing next month. I thought I told you."

"No, I don't think so," she said. "I would have remembered that."

"What's that mean?"

Amber did not want to have this conversation. She had never said anything to Seth about her negative feelings toward Michaela, but they were there, and the thought of having Michaela at camp this summer made her not want to go.

"Nothing," she said. "Never mind."

"It doesn't sound like nothing."

Amber really did not want to have this conversation, especially with Ben and Hope in the room too. "It's nothing," she said. "Forget it."

She excused herself to go use the bathroom, trying to act casual about her exit. She tried to collect her emotions before going back, but she couldn't, and she didn't feel like facing anyone, so she snuck out the front door to get some fresh air.

Once she was outside, the reality of the pain she was feeling became overwhelming. She went down the steps and walked toward the creek trail. She had started to cry, and the deep-seated pain continued to make the tears flow. She couldn't stop, and at the same time she didn't know why it all hurt so much.

\*\*\*

"Where did Amber go?" her dad asked.

Seth had begun to wonder the same thing. She had been in the bathroom for at least ten minutes now, unless she'd gone upstairs.

"I don't know," he said to her dad who had returned to the room along with her mom. "I'll go check."

When he saw the bathroom door open, he went upstairs, but she wasn't anywhere up there either. He began to have an uneasy feeling. This wasn't like Amber to get up and leave the room and then disappear, and his suspicions were confirmed that she had been upset earlier when he talked about Michaela.

"Did you find her?" Hope asked, meeting him as he came down the stairs.

"No. I'll go check outside," he said, hoping to find her on the porch swing, one of her favorite thinking spots. But when she wasn't there, he hoped she hadn't chosen her other favorite thinking spot. It was getting too dark to be walking down to the creek. Going to his car, he got a flashlight, and Ben and Hope came out. He told them where he was headed.

"We'll look in the barn and around here."

Seth was grateful for their help, but he felt stupid for letting this happen. He was usually better at reading Amber's mood, and he knew he shouldn't have let her comment about Michaela go. Doubts about whether he was ready to get married and take care of her crept in, but right now he just wanted to find her. And he knew it was a stupid thought, but he wanted to be the one to find her, not someone else.

It was dark enough once he entered the dense forest and headed down the trail for the flashlight, and he turned it on. He'd gone about thirty paces when he heard her voice.

"I'm here, Seth."

He turned toward the sound and shined the flashlight onto the hillside where there was a small clearing and a big rock they sat on sometimes when it was too cold or wet to go all the way down to the creek. She remained in place, and he went to her, sitting down and holding her close without saying anything or demanding an explanation. He was relieved she was safe.

She had on jeans and a t-shirt with short sleeves. She felt cold, and he told her to put on the hoodie he had with him. She did, and she wasn't crying, but she appeared lost and broken in a way he had never seen before.

"What's wrong, sweetheart? Please talk to me."

"I'm sorry. I don't know why I'm upset. I had to get away to think."

"Think about what?"

"I don't know. Everything."

"About us?"

"I don't know, Seth. I feel messed up inside. Something isn't right."

"Is this about Elle?"

She shrugged. "That's part of it."

"And Michaela? What was that about?"

She didn't answer.

"What happened, sweetheart? Did she say something to you?"

"No."

"I know you don't hate people for no reason, Amber."

"I don't hate her. I don't even know her."

"But you got upset when I told you she was going to be at camp. Why?"

"She reminds me of Elle."

Seth let that sink in, not making the connection. He had known Michaela for a long time, and she was nothing like Elle. He'd never dated her, but one of his friends had, and she had dumped him because he couldn't keep his hands to himself. She was very sweet, a lot like Amber, not Elle. Kerri knew her better than he did, and he had never heard Kerri speak poorly of her.

"How does she remind you of Elle?" he asked.

"Do you seriously not know?"

"No," he said. "I'm sorry, but I'm not making the connection."

"Then maybe I shouldn't tell you. I don't want you to feel like you have to avoid her for my sake."

"Why would you want me to do that?"

She told him, and he could see what she was saying. He didn't believe Michaela had inappropriate intentions, but he knew that feeling of seeing other guys interacting with Amber sometimes and wanting to make sure they knew she was already taken.

"I know it's mostly in my head, but I was relieved when we didn't have a class with her this semester. Hearing you say you have a class with her I didn't know about threw up a sea of red flags for me. It was like last summer all over again when I found out you had been keeping something from me about Elle."

Seth regretted his lack of honesty with Amber, but he thought all that was behind them. Telling her Michaela was in his drama class had never occurred to him as being something she would care about one way or the other. He wasn't attracted to Michaela. He thought she was a beautiful girl, but he hadn't picked up on any improper flirting on her part. Michaela was that way with everyone: bubbly and sweet. But Amber had mistaken her behavior, and he could see how she might.

But to think Amber didn't trust him to be around other girls broke him up inside. He hated Elle for causing a division in their relationship, but he hated himself for his own mistakes more.

"It's not you, Seth," Amber said as tears began to fall from his eyes. "And it's not Michaela. It's me.

I'm sorry I feel this way. I'm sorry I can't get over what Elle did. I have tried so hard," she said, beginning to cry also. "But I can't."

Seth held her close and didn't say anything. He didn't know what to say. He didn't know how to fix this. He had tried and thought he succeeded, but he obviously hadn't. He didn't know what else to do.

He began to doubt the goodness of God. How could He let this happen? They had done everything right. They had upheld a pure and right relationship for two and a half years. He had done everything he could to guard their time together, and Amber had been right there with him in all of their good choices and commitments to one another.

They had been volunteering their summer for the benefit of others when it had all unfolded. In a week's time, their relationship had gone from near perfection to having this huge blemish on it that wasn't their fault. Even in keeping Elle's inappropriate behavior to himself, he had only been doing that to protect Amber, not because he had anything to hide. This had been Elle's doing, and God had done nothing to stop it.

Seth knew he should be praying for them right now, as he often did in stressful or uncertain moments, but he couldn't. He didn't have the strength. Hearing footsteps and seeing streaks of light coming down the trail, he waited to see who it was and shined his own light on Ben and Hope when they came into view.

They came over to join them, and Ben gave Amber a hug. "We were worried, Jewel," he said. "You okay?"

Amber didn't respond. Ben looked at him.

"Is this something you need to talk out on your own, or can we help?"

Amber still didn't respond, and he didn't know what to say or do. He felt at the end of himself. Did this mean they shouldn't get married? Was Amber thinking she couldn't be in this relationship with him anymore? Did they need to take a break, or a step back? He had no idea. He didn't want that, but maybe they needed it.

He decided to ask Ben to do what he didn't have the strength for. "Could you pray for us?"

"We can do that," Ben said, reaching for Hope's hand and keeping his other arm around Amber's back.

Seth took Amber's hand, and she squeezed his fingers tightly. Ben prayed, and Seth found his words comforting. He was reminded of God's presence here with them. They didn't have to figure this out for themselves. They could trust Jesus to guide them and give them what they needed, and he was reminded of the one good thing to come out of Elle's behavior and lies.

"Thank you, Ben," Amber said when he was finished, giving him a hug and holding on for a long time. "I miss you so much."

"I miss you too," he said. "Do you want us to stay, or can I leave you with this guy?"

She smiled and leaned into him, and Seth thought it seemed like a more genuine smile and display of affection than he'd been getting this week. "You mean this guy sitting out here without a coat on?"

"Yeah, him. The city-boy."

"You could leave us, but I think we'd better head back to the warm house. We can talk more there."

Ben and Hope went first, and Seth let Amber take the lead with how much affection she wanted right now. Something had changed while Ben was praying. He could feel it in her touch and see it written all over her peaceful expression, but he didn't know how close her thoughts were to his until they returned to the house and went upstairs to her bedroom for a few minutes of privacy together.

"I'm sorry, Seth," she said, wrapping her arms around his neck as he held her in the middle of the messy room. He wondered how someone could be home for a week and make such a big mess, but he didn't say it. This was definitely not the time for such a comment.

"Sorry for what?" he asked.

"Forgetting you always take care of me. What Ben said about us trusting each other reminded me how you took care of me last summer, and you've been doing the same thing all year at school. I'm sorry I lost sight of it."

Seth had been thinking about that too. He remembered a letter Amber had written him, thanking him for taking care of her that week and being someone she could always trust, and it had been a highlight for him in their relationship. Taking care of her had always been his top priority, and he knew he needed to do that now with the decision they were currently facing. And for the first time in over a week, he was pretty sure he knew how to do that.

## Chapter Thirteen

Amber enjoyed Seth's sweet kiss, and she realized she hadn't been doing that this week. Mandy hadn't been imagining things. She'd been feeling and acting different with him, and it changed who she was with others too. The reality she could trust him hit her afresh, and it was amazing what a difference it made to simply let that truth sink deep into her weary and confused soul.

"I think I know what we should do about the summer, Amber. If I'm way off-base, just tell me, but I don't think it should be us making the decision about whether Elle is there or not. It's too much responsibility on our shoulders, especially yours."

She silently agreed and waited for him to continue.

"I think we should tell Dave we're coming, but leave the decision about Elle up to him. If he thinks she should be a part of the team, we'll respect that and trust Jesus to carry us through the summer."

She knew he was right, and she nodded in agreement. That decision gave her peace. She could trust Dave, Seth, and Jesus to protect her.

"And let me say one more thing regarding Michaela and any other girls you feel threatened by for whatever reason: I don't see them, Amber. Not the way I see you. I love you. I'm in love with you. I'm satisfied with you—more than satisfied. I don't need to go looking elsewhere, and for the last two and a half years I've only had eyes for you. That is the absolute truth, and I hope you believe it."

"I do."

"I love you, Amber," he whispered. "Do you still want to marry me in two months?"

"Yes, I can't wait."

He kissed her and they enjoyed a few moments of sharing their mutual affection. She was thinking about the setting they were in, but she was surprised when Seth voiced his similar thoughts.

"I'd love to lay down on that bed with you and do this all night, Amber."

He gave her another kiss and then added something she was thinking too.

"Of course, we would have to find it first."

She laughed and tickled him. "I knew you were going to say that."

He let her get him back for his words but then pulled her into a gentle hug and held her in a possessive and loving way. She cherished the feeling of his closeness and was honest about her current thoughts.

"I can't wait, Seth. I can't wait until the night you can do that."

"Me neither," he said. "I will wait, but I wish it was tonight."

Amber felt incredibly loved. Seth wanted to be with her. She could feel his desire in the way he held her, but he would wait until the time was absolutely perfect for them.

They went downstairs, and everyone seemed to get she was okay now and didn't ask any questions. She snuggled into Seth during the movie, and she could feel the wholeness she had been missing. It amazed her how she could feel so close to Jesus and to Seth, and then suddenly feel so distant from one or both of them, even if she didn't do anything specific to create a problem.

She could be doing everything right: Reading her Bible, praying daily, making the most of her relationships; but things beyond her control came along, and her only defense was to keep believing what she knew to be true:

God loved her. She could trust Him in everything. Seth loved her. She could trust him too. She was living the right way. The pure and right way. She was seeking her God and loving Him, and she had to trust in that.

After the movie she went upstairs, feeling happy and in love. Hope knocked on her door after she was in her pajamas and asked if she could talk to her for a minute. Hope stepped inside, and she cleared a space on her bed for them to sit. She had wedding stuff everywhere. Once they were sitting down, Hope shared what was on her mind.

"I was thinking this week about something you once told me that helped me a lot when I was having a difficult time with my mom and never feeling like she trusted me or forgave me for the mistakes I made."

Amber had told Hope a lot of different things, so she wasn't sure what she was referring to.

"I had been praying she would change her attitude toward me, and that I could change mine toward her, but it didn't seem to be happening. And then you told me about praying for difficult people in your life and how you were wishing good things for them and how that had changed your perspective somehow. I started praying that way for my mom, and it did the same thing for me. I know you've prayed for Elle a lot, but have you wished good things for her?"

"No," Amber said. She hadn't prayed that way for awhile. She had gotten out of the habit, but she remembered it seeming like a powerful way to pray and seeing a lot of good results come out of it— including "wishing" for Hope's complete healing.

Having Hope sitting here, knowing she was happily married to Ben and appearing so peaceful, reminded her of how much Jesus could transform a lost and hurting heart. She didn't know what was causing Elle to be the person she was, but she knew there had to be something going on beneath the surface: a bad relationship she had suffered, a way she had been hurt by someone, difficult family issues; it could be a lot of things, but she doubted it was nothing.

With the decision about Elle not being on her shoulders anymore, Amber felt more free to pray for her, and after Hope left the room, she did. Taking out her journal, she wrote what brought freedom to her soul as she wished good things for her enemy.

*I wish Elle happiness and joy. I wish her healing and grace. I wish her more of you, Jesus. All that she truly needs. I wish her peace and rest in whatever has brought her pain in the past. I wish her a summer of healing, wherever she ends up spending it. I wish her an honest and pure heart—one that can only come from you. She needs your love, Jesus. And she needs mine and whoever else can give her some. I wish her love.*

\*\*\*

Emma heard her phone ring, and she reached for it on her night table. Seeing it was Danae, she supposed she was calling to let her know when they were heading back on Sunday.

"Hi, Danae."

"Hi, Emma. How's your week been?"

"Good," she said. "How's yours?"

"Fine. I was calling to ask if you might possibly be okay with going back tomorrow instead of Sunday? I know this is really late notice, and if you have plans for tomorrow or just don't want to, I totally understand, but something kind of came up and it would be good if I could be back by tomorrow night."

"What time do you need to leave?"

"Not until noon or so. If you can't, it's fine, really."

"That would be fine," she said, seriously not minding. An extra day to get resettled before classes began on Monday was fine with her.

"Really?"

"Yes."

"Okay. Evangeline still isn't heading back until Sunday, so I'll come pick you up tomorrow. Or, you could just go with her, I suppose. I didn't think of that. She's picking up Pam and Katy in San Mateo, but they would still have room for you."

Emma knew she would prefer to ride with Danae. Evangeline and the others were all nice, but she felt more comfortable with Danae. "No, that's fine. I can go with you, if you don't mind."

"Why would I mind? This was my idea, remember?"

She laughed. "I know. Tomorrow's fine, really. And I could get a ride to your house so you don't have to come down here to Monterey."

"Okay," Danae said, giving her the address and saying around noon would be fine.

Emma wondered what she had to get back early for, and Danae told her before she let her go. "Thanks so much. Really, Emma. My boyfriend stayed on campus this week because he needed to work, but he doesn't have to work on Sunday, and I really miss him."

"Not a problem," she said. "I like having someone to go with instead of driving all the way by myself, and getting back a day early is better for me anyway. I'll sleep better on Sunday night."

"You're a sweetheart. See you tomorrow."

"Okay, bye."

Emma hung up with a good feeling in her heart and an intense longing for something. After spending a year with her difficult roommates and a lack of close friendships, she had begun to have feelings of self-doubt and scrutiny like she hadn't ever felt before. Danae thought she was sweet, and she wanted to be that way. She wanted other people to see her as a nice and loving person, because she was.

But she had begun to question if that was enough. Maybe she should be more like Abby and Elissa and

Tiffany. Deep in her heart she knew that wasn't true, but they made her feel so socially backwards all the time, it was just hard.

She wanted friends like Danae who thought she was sweet and smart and pretty. She wanted friends she could talk to, not just to be talked at. And the following day turned out how she expected. Danae was her usual chatty self, but she didn't dominate the conversation either. Emma would have been happy to sit in the back, but Tate offered her the front seat, and she took it, and it was just as well because Tate wasn't much of a conversationalist, and it would have been more difficult for Danae to talk to her if she was sitting in the back.

About halfway there when they stopped to use the restroom and get snacks at a mini mart, Danae said, "Oh, did you notice my brother is with us?"

Emma looked back at him following them into the store, and she smiled. She thought he was really cute, but she hadn't expected him to be so quiet. He had seemed more talkative and outgoing during cross-country, but with only his sister and some girl he didn't know to talk to, what did he have to say?

He smiled in return and stepped ahead of them to get the door. They both thanked him, and after she and Danae had used the restroom, bought their purchases, and returned to the car, Tate was there waiting for them.

Emma didn't feel comfortable mentioning her hopes of getting new roommates next year in front of Tate, but when they arrived at the school and Danae walked with her to where they would part to go to their separate dorms, Tate was no longer with them, and she mentioned what Evangeline had said last weekend.

"Oh yeah, Lauren," she confirmed. "Are you interested?"

"Yes, definitely. The roommates I have right now are so not like me."

"Okay. I'll be seeing Blake on Monday. I'll let him know."

"Thanks. And thanks for the invitation to ride with you. I had a lot of fun."

"Me too," she said, stopping to give her a hug. "Stay sweet, Emma. It will take you a lot further in life than you think."

She smiled and headed for her room, feeling relieved when she stepped inside and found it empty. She did a little studying, mostly reading ahead for her classes to know what would be coming up next week, and then she went to bed early. In the morning she went to church like usual at the small country fellowship down the road, and since she was one of the few college students who attended there, it wasn't much different than a normal Sunday.

Returning to the campus, she went to the cafeteria to have lunch, sat alone, and was headed back to her dorm when she saw a familiar face coming toward her. She smiled, and he smiled back.

"Hi, Tate," she said.

"Hey," he replied. "I think my sister is looking for you."

"Where is she?"

"She was going to check your room and see if you were there."

"Okay. I'll probably see her then. Bye."

"Bye."

Emma kept walking, but Tate's voice stopped her.

"Oh, Emma?"

"Yeah?" she said, turning back to face him.

"I um, was wondering if—if you ever go running? You know, like to stay in shape for next season? Or are you planning to do cross-country next year?"

"Yes, I am, and yes, I run every day—outside as long as it's not raining, and I use the treadmill when it is."

"Do you run by yourself?"

"Yes."

"Do you prefer it that way, or would you like company sometimes?"

"I like company," she said. "Especially when I run on the road. Why? Do you know someone who's looking for a running partner?"

"Yes. Someone really lazy who only stays in shape when he has to."

"He?" she asked.

"You wouldn't be comfortable with that?"

"Running with a guy? I don't know, maybe. Who is he?"

Tate smiled. She wondered if one of Tate's friends from cross-country liked her, and this was Tate's way of doing a favor for him. She couldn't imagine why else some guy would want to run with her.

Tate had been the initiator of this conversation as well as the most talkative one, a side of him she hadn't seen before, but he suddenly went silent on her and acted like the quiet guy she had been around yesterday.

## Chapter Fourteen

Tate wanted to find the nearest exit. An exit out of this conversation and away from this beautiful girl who obviously had no interest in him whatsoever. This had been a really bad idea. He had thought of it last night but hadn't expected to run into Emma like this today when the idea was still fresh enough in his mind to act on it.

"Tate?" she asked again. "Who is he, and why are *you* asking me instead of him?"

"He is. I mean, it's me. I'm asking for me."

"Oh," she smiled, appearing intrigued. "You want to run with me?"

Her surprise made him feel bold again. "Yes," he said, cracking a smile and taking a step closer. "I'm serious about being lazy. I like being on the team and competing, but I'm not much into conditioning like I should, and I was thinking running with you would be good for me, but if you're not comfortable with that, it's fine. I'd probably slow you down anyway."

She smiled. "No. I'd love to run with you. I don't run for speed in the off-season, just endurance and to stay in shape."

"How far?" he asked, not wanting to hear the answer.

"However much time I have," she said. "Forty-five minutes some days. Others, an hour or more."

He could handle an hour at his pace, but he wasn't sure about hers, even if she was running "slow".

"What days do you have less time?"

She laughed. "Tuesdays and Thursdays."

"In the morning?"

"Not always. On Saturdays I run in the morning, but other days I can go before classes or in the afternoon. If I feel like sleeping another hour, I do, and if I don't, I get up and go."

"What time?"

"6:30."

He thought about his schedule and what would be best for him on Tuesday. That was a little early because he didn't have class until nine. He was about to ask when she ran in the afternoons, but he decided to take the plunge. This wasn't about running or his schedule, and if he had any hope of this turning into something more, he was going to have to give it his best effort.

"That works for me. Are you sure you don't mind?"

"No, not at all. Where would you like to meet?"

"I can meet you at your dorm. Are you in Priscilla?"

"Yes."

"Okay, six-thirty on Tuesday. I'll be there, and if you feel like sleeping in, don't worry about it. If I'm up that early, I won't have anything better to do, and I'll go anyway."

"Okay," she said.

Tate saw his sister coming toward them, and he wanted to escape again. Talking with Emma and working out this arrangement had become more comfortable, especially since Emma didn't seem to have any clue he was attracted to her, but he knew his sister would see through his plan in a heartbeat.

But it was too late, and he went ahead and pointed Danae out to Emma. She turned and saw her, and they both waited for his sister to meet them.

"Did Tate tell you I was looking for you?" Danae said.

"Yes," Emma replied.

Tate held his breath to see if Emma would say what else he'd told her, but she remained silent and waited for Danae to speak.

"This is my boyfriend, John," Danae said. "John, this is Emma, the girl who was sweet enough to let me come back a day early."

"Nice to meet you, Emma," John said. "I'm indebted to you for life. I was really happy to see her today. I know it's only a few hours, but when you're in love, that's an eternity."

Danae gave John a sweet expression, and Tate knew he would give anything in the world for Emma to look at him that way.

"Anyway," Danae said, turning her attention back to Emma. "I was looking for you because I saw Lauren, Blake's sister, at church this morning, and I told her about you. She's really excited about meeting you, and I told her I would try and bring you to lunch. Are you on your way there, or did you eat already?"

"I just ate," Emma replied. "But I can go back. I don't have anything else to do right now."

"Great," Danae said. "Let's go."

They all walked together toward the cafeteria, and Tate kept expecting Emma to say something to Danae about them running together, but she didn't. And she seemed oblivious to his presence once again, which was fine with him, so he didn't do anything to draw attention to himself.

Once they were inside the cafeteria, Danae took Emma over to the table where Lauren and Adam were already sitting, and John waited for Danae to return. Tate went ahead and got in line and began loading up his tray with what looked good today. He got to the table before Danae and John, and he sat beside Adam, who had become one of his best friends this year. Adam was dating Blake's sister, and they often worked in food service together. Adam and Lauren had come back yesterday also because Adam had to work the dinner-shift tonight. Tate wasn't working until lunch tomorrow.

Emma and Lauren seemed to be hitting it off fine, which didn't surprise him. Lauren was the kind of girl he could stand being around for more than five minutes, and he often envied Adam for having such a beautiful and sweet girlfriend.

"Hi, Tate," Lauren said after he and Adam had talked for a few minutes. "How was your break?"

"Fine," he said.

"Have you met Emma?"

"Yes."

"Oh, that's right. She rode down with you."

"We're in cross-country together too," Emma said.

Tate felt his body going tense once again. *Don't say it.*

140

"Uh oh," Lauren said, looking back at Emma. "Are you a runner? You're not going to talk me into going jogging with you every morning when we're roommates, are you?"

Emma smiled. "No. I don't mind running alone, and I hate running with people who hate running."

Lauren laughed. "That's definitely me, so don't ask."

*Don't say it.*

"I have a running partner," Emma said. "At least some days."

"Does she like to run?"

"It's a he, actually, and I don't know yet. We're starting this week—If he shows up like he said he would."

Neither Adam nor Lauren asked who it was, and Emma didn't say his name. But she glanced at him and winked. Tate almost passed out right there at the table.

\*\*\*

Danae opened the door and saw John standing there in the hallway as she expected. She had been feeling anxious to see him since returning to campus last night, and the sight of him was more joyful than she anticipated. He was really handsome. Sometimes she forgot that on a daily basis, but not seeing him for a week always reminded her of what a beautiful man she had managed to get herself—Inside and out, he was beautiful.

"Hey, handsome," she said, sparing him the more feminine adjective, even though she felt it was more accurate.  She stepped into his arms and felt his familiar touch, breathed-in his familiar smell, and lifted her face to kiss his familiar lips.

*Yes, John, I want to marry you.*  She didn't say it yet, but she planned to sometime today.

"Hey, babe," he said, giving her a gentle kiss.  "I missed you."

"I missed you," she said.

"You ready?"

She knew he was referring to being ready to head into town for church, but she thought of his words in another sense and answered that one too.  "Yes, I'm ready."

She got her Bible and her purse and met John in the hallway.  They took the elevator to the first floor. Often Evangeline and other friends rode along to church with them, and she never minded that, but it was nice to have time alone with him this morning.

Although John had suggested she talk to her dad about her recurring dream, she didn't expect him to ask if she had or not.  John wasn't that way.  He didn't pester her about things.  If he made a suggestion about something, he left it up to her whether or not she followed his advice.  The only things he kept after her about were the things she asked him to, like if she had been having consistent times with God and if she had been letting others do things for her instead of giving all the time.

On the way to church she told him about the last couple of days.  He did ask if she had slept well, and she said she had, but she didn't comment further for now.  What she had to say she didn't want to say in the car or when they only had a limited amount of time to talk.

She enjoyed the church service and was glad she had come back a day early to have today with John, but she also missed her dad this morning and would have liked to hear him speak at their church back home.  Her dad had a unique way of talking about God, especially in recent years, and after talking with him for a long time on Thursday about her dream and other things regarding the past, the present, and the future, she understood why.  Her dad was close to God. Very close.  Like she wanted to be.  And like the guy sitting beside her.

She often wondered what exactly had appealed to her so much about John.  He was handsome certainly with a pair of blue eyes to die for.  But beyond that, there had been something special and unique about him.  Something that had kept her interest after a few dates, and after he told her he wanted to hold off on kissing her until he felt ready.  He had waited a year, but she hadn't minded.  She wasn't sure why at the time, but she understood it now.  And she also understood why she'd felt cautious about marrying him.

After church they went back to the campus for lunch, and she went to Emma's room to see if she wanted to come to lunch with them so she could introduce her to Lauren, but she wasn't there.  She found her talking to her brother on the way to the dining hall, and she introduced Emma and Lauren once they arrived.

When she and John were both finished eating, she told him she wanted to talk to him about something, and they left the others they were sitting with to go for a walk. She had been walking with her dad on the beach when she talked to him on Thursday, and being with John had a similar feel except she didn't feel unsure about how John would react to what she had to say.

"I talked to my dad about the dream," she said.

"You did?"

"Yes," she laughed. "Don't sound so surprised."

He didn't apologize for his skepticism. "What did he say?"

"Something I never expected."

"What? That he loves you and forgives you and sees the beautiful woman you are now, not the lost and confused girl you were then?"

"No," she smiled. "I mean, he did. But I expected him to say that."

"What else did he say?"

"I told him how I felt so bad for disappointing him and for the extreme pain I know I caused him, and how that look in his eyes is what haunts me the most, and he said, 'I wasn't disappointed in you, Danae. I was disappointed in myself. I walked out of that room thinking, 'My kids need me, and I'm not being here for them.' The look on his face wasn't about me, it was about him.

"And I never knew this, but that was a huge turning-point for him. He had been trying to go on with his life as it had always been when my mom was there, but it wasn't the same life, and he realized it wasn't supposed to be. I actually helped him overcome his pain instead of causing him more. Isn't that crazy?"

"Not that crazy," John said, stopping his casual stride and pulling her close to him. "You've done the same thing for me, remember?"

John had told her before she had helped him to overcome his pain. When she first met him he had gotten out of an unhealthy relationship with his high school "sweetheart" who hadn't turned out to be so sweet. They had been dating off and on since they were fifteen, and she had basically used and abused him for three years. She would tell him she wanted to just be friends and then go out with someone else, get hurt, and then come back to him and beg him to take her back. He loved her, so he would, and then she would do it to him all over again.

During the summer between their freshman and sophomore year of college, John had decided to come here in the fall. They were together at the time, but he told her he didn't want them to remain together while he was at another school. He hadn't broken it off with her permanently but wanted to take a break for a year and see where they both were the following summer and if they wanted to be together at that point.

In spite of all the times he had taken her back after her flighty decisions, she had become very bitter toward him and abused him emotionally for the remainder of the summer.

Being away from her had turned out to be the best thing for John, and it hadn't taken him long to realize that, but it took him longer to decide if he wanted to be in another relationship after meeting her here during Fall Semester.

He knew he was attracted to her, and he tried to deny it, and she tried to tell herself she wasn't ready for anything either, but then they kept spending time together. By Christmas they were officially a couple, but they kept it a relationship of friendship where they both bared their souls to one another on a regular basis.

Danae had never had such a close friend, and it scared her, but she hadn't wanted to end it because John didn't kiss her or because she was afraid of what might happen between them if he did. She had learned to take it one day at a time—their relationship and her life. And eventually he had kissed her at the right time for both of them, and they'd had a pleasant and steady relationship ever since.

But when he proposed to her on Christmas Eve three months ago, she felt like if she said yes, she wouldn't be able to live that way anymore. That it would become about planning their future together and she wouldn't be able to handle the change. What they had now would be spoiled, and she didn't want anything to spoil this. It was too perfect. He was too perfect.

"Thank you for telling me to talk to my dad," she said. "I never thought of that, and even if I had, I don't think I would have had the courage on my own."

"I wasn't there, Danae. You did it on your own."

"No, I didn't. You were there, John. You're too much a part of my heart to not be wherever I am."

He kissed her, and there was a longing in his touch that sometimes scared her, but not today. Not anymore.

"I want to marry you, John. I want to start planning our future together."

He pulled her close and seemed afraid to breathe for a moment. She wondered how she could have waited so long. He picked her up off the ground, and she laughed.

"Danae, Danae, Danae," he said. "I love loving you."

He had told her that before too. Many times. The first time had been after their first kiss. John had realized what was missing in his relationship with his previous girlfriend. He had cared about her, so he kept taking her back. He loved her, but he wasn't enjoying it.

He told her that on their one-year anniversary and said, "I'm enjoying loving you, Danae. And I want to celebrate that joy by kissing you tonight. Is that all right?"

She felt the same way. Her relationship with Evan had been confusing and filled with shame, but with John she felt free. She loved loving him too.

He set her down and smiled. "How soon, Danae Morgan? How soon can I have you?"

"Well, there is this little matter of us finding jobs," she said. "Maybe we'll have to wait and see how that goes."

He was still smiling. "Guess what?"

"What?"

"Boeing called me this week. They want me to come for an interview."

"That's great! Why didn't you tell me?"

"Just waiting for the right moment.  It might not mean anything, but at least I have a shot at it.  Are you sure you want to move up to Seattle with me?"

"I'll go anywhere with you, John.  No matter what's going on around us, when I trust you to take care of me, you always do."

## Chapter Fifteen

Mandy was glad Matthew was flying in this afternoon, especially after having to say good-bye to Amber last night. She knew she would be happy to see him anyway, but the special times she'd had with Amber this week, along with hearing what had stolen and restored her joy, had reminded her of how close she and Amber had become, and how much she missed her.

Thinking of never having those really close times with her cousin again made her feel sad. Not to the point she wished she and Amber didn't have Seth and Matt, but she wished she could have it both ways. A special guy to share her life with and a really close girlfriend to confide in sometimes too. She'd come a long way in sharing her heart with Matthew, but there were still some things that were easier to talk about with Amber.

Seeing Matt coming toward her through the crowd of travelers in the airport terminal, she could see him searching for her, and when their eyes met, the look on his face brought tears to her eyes. He seemed really glad to see her.

Scooping her off the ground as soon as he reached her, Matt didn't speak, but his body language said it all. He had missed her. Bad. Matt wasn't afraid to show emotion, and he cried quiet tears as he held her close and whispered loving words.

"Never again, Amanda. I'm not going to be away from you for that long ever again."

She didn't voice her thought, but Matthew was supposed to be gone for a whole month this summer. He was scheduled to be a part of the youth mission team going to Mexico in June, and she hadn't been dreading it because her family was going to be on vacation for two of those weeks, and the other two she was planning to live with her sister and help Melanie with her baby due in May. She knew she would miss him, but she would deal with it.

"I'm not taking the job," he said, setting her down and giving her a kiss on the forehead. "And I'm taking this summer off to be with you. I talked to Pastor John about it on the trip, and I told him I'm trying to divide my time between you and everything else, and I can't do that right now. I think we should go to Lifegate like we were planning—go to school and be together instead of me being so busy all the time. I need you, Amanda. I need you every day."

She smiled and didn't feel like arguing with him, so she didn't. He kissed her, and she cherished it. She cherished the intensity of his love for her, and his fearlessness to show it.

They went out to dinner and then she drove him to his house. She was planning to say good-night to him in the driveway, but he didn't want her to go. He talked more about his decision, and she knew he was serious. This wasn't something he was considering; he was doing it.

"I support you in anything you want to do, Matthew, but you're not deciding this because you're scared, are you?"

"Scared?"

"Scared of failing? Scared of not being ready for so much responsibility? Because I know you can do it. Seth said you've never failed at anything when your head and heart have been in the right place, and I've seen that too."

He smiled. "No, Amanda. I'm not scared. Not about the job. This is about us. I want this for us. I want time with you. What I'm scared of is waking up one day a year from now and realizing I've been investing time and energy into everyone around me except you."

"I don't feel like you're doing that."

"I just spent ten straight days with the people on that team, but when was the last time I did that with you?"

She didn't answer that.

"I'm doing it, Amanda. And I watched my dad do the same thing, neglecting my mom and his marriage and his boys to try to save everyone else, and I don't want to be that kind of husband and dad. I want to meet the needs of those closest to me first—the ones God has specifically entrusted to me, and then I'll do more as He leads me, but I'm not sacrificing you on the altar of busyness for the kingdom.

"And Pastor John agrees with me. That's not God's Kingdom. He doesn't run it that way. That's our kingdom where we convince ourselves we can do everything, and if we don't, a whole bunch of people are going to end up in hell. I don't believe that. I believe we're creating our own hell right here on earth and bowing down to the wrong king."

She smiled. "You really should be a preacher."

He smiled and kissed her. "I'll practice on myself first."

He kissed her more, and she enjoyed it, but she had a question on her mind, and she asked it.

"Do you think it was a mistake for us to stay here this year? I thought we were following God in this."

"We were. And it hasn't been a mistake. God had something to show me, and I believe this is part of it. I learned a lot, and I had time with my parents that we both needed, and I balanced my time with you well. But next year you're not going to be my girlfriend, Amanda. You're going to be my wife, and I take that seriously, and I want to live like it, not just say so."

His words reminded her of something Amber said yesterday when she told her about why she hadn't been herself this week—how she had allowed the burden of Elle's poor choices to be put on her own shoulders and forgetting she could trust Jesus and Seth to take care of her. When she'd said that, Mandy had realized how much she had come to trust Matthew and how much she felt that this week.

There were very pretty girls who had gone along on the mission trip, both college-age girls in leadership and high school students, and Matt was around them all the time at church and on youth group activities too, but she never worried about Matthew cheating on her. She had to trust him in that, and she was.

"I trust you, Matthew. I trust you to take care of me."

"You are such a crazy girl," he said, kissing her tenderly once again. "And I really don't want to say good-bye to you right now."

"I noticed that. We've been standing out here for thirty minutes."

"Take me home with you," he said. "I don't have to be at the church until Wednesday night. I had a couple of things I was going to do tomorrow, but they can wait. Let me go home with you tonight, and we'll go to school tomorrow, spend the afternoon and evening together, do it all over again on Tuesday, and then you can drive me to the MAX station after school on Wednesday."

He went to pack a few things, and she got in the car and waited for him. Often when they drove places together, Matt would drive, but she knew he was tired from the trip, so she drove and he stayed awake for about twenty minutes but then fell asleep. When they arrived at the house, she woke him with a gentle kiss, and there was something about the way he looked, all sleepy-eyed and happy to be with her, that made her say something specific to him.

"You need someone to take care of you too, Matthew. Do you trust me to do that?"

He smiled. "Why do you think I asked you to marry me? I've been trusting you to take care of me for a long time, Amanda, and don't ever doubt for a second how much I need you. When I asked Jesus to get me out of the pit I was living in, He gave me two things: His Spirit to strengthen and empower me, and very good friends to love me—most of all you."

"What do you need most from me?" She didn't have a clue what this incredibly special, talented, caring, and self-sufficient guy needed from her. He may have been in the pit at one time, but he certainly wasn't anymore.

"What you've been giving me all along, Amanda: You never let me forget I am loved and worth something to an Almighty God. And if I have that, I have everything."

*** 

Amber was happy to see Colleen again. They had both been home last week but hadn't seen each other except on Sunday at the pizza place. Welcoming her inside the dorm room, Amber gave her a hug before asking the question foremost on her mind. They were the only two here at the moment.

"How did Blake's interviews go?"

"Good. All three places want him. Now it's a matter of him deciding which one, or if we really want to be up there. I think he feels more confident now he could find something around here if we decide to stay."

"What do you want?"

"I don't know, to be honest. It was nice being home, and I can imagine being happy as long as Blake is there too, but I know I'd be happy here, or anywhere with Blake. I keep telling him that, but he doesn't seem to get it."

They shared more about their time at home and what they had coming up. They didn't usually talk much here because Colleen and Blake worked on the nights she and Seth had free, and the nights when Blake was at the church and Seth was working at

Tony's, they both knew they needed to study and wouldn't get anything done if they tried to study together. That had never worked for them.

Amber told Colleen about her major breakdown on Friday and the peaceful solution she and Seth had decided on. "I know it won't be easy, and I was pretty bent out of shape over it all week, but then I remembered I can trust Jesus and Seth to take care of me."

"I'll pray for you," Colleen said, giving her a hug. "You're a lot stronger than I am. I'd never go for it."

"I think you might. Especially if you trust Blake like you keep telling me."

"I suppose that's true."

When Lauren came in from being out with Adam this evening, Colleen knew it was time to go because Lauren usually went to bed around nine. But Lauren had something to tell her before she left, and Amber listened to the news.

"I think I found a roommate for next year. It's a girl one of Blake's friends knows. She's a freshman too, and she's in desperate need of new roommates. I know I told you not to count on rooming with me next year since I was considering living in town and working, but I've been asking God for direction on that, and I think this is His answer. So, if you and Blake end up staying local, you could be our fourth roommate."

"Okay," Colleen said. "I'll add that to my list of options. Although, I really do feel like this is up to Blake and where he decides he needs to be. When you see him, can you try and convince him I mean that? He's not listening to me."

"I'll try," Lauren said.

Once Colleen was gone, Amber asked Lauren about her week while she was getting ready for bed, and she said it had been nice to have extended and uninterrupted time with Adam. Amber told her the news about them going to camp and Elle possibly being there too, and Lauren said similar things that Colleen had about praying for her and not knowing if she could do it.

Amber didn't say so to Lauren, but one of her main concerns about having Elle there again wasn't so much for herself, but for other couples Elle might try and break up so she could have the guy for herself, and she knew Adam could be one of the guys she would be after. She decided to talk to Seth about it later, knowing he would be fine with talking to Adam and giving him the heads-up on everything that had happened last summer. Everyone knew about the false accusations, but only a few knew about Elle's inappropriate advances on Seth also.

She thought about sending an email to Dave, letting him know her concerns in that area and also for the girls Elle would be counseling, but she decided against it. Dave had likely already thought of those factors himself, and she knew she needed to leave it completely in the hands of others and God. That was the only way she had peace.

# Chapter Sixteen

On Tuesday morning, Emma felt ready to get up and go for a run. After running for many years, but mostly alone, she welcomed the chance to have someone to run with. The beach was her favorite place, but up here the forested setting of the Redwood Coast was nice too, especially on the highway running through the mountains.

The only thing she didn't like about it was the secluded setting where some crazy person could easily stop along the road and attack her without anyone seeing or hearing her scream. She tried not to worry about it and believe God would protect her, but it was often in the back of her mind. So having someone to run with, especially a nice guy, would give her a better feeling about it.

From the moment she met Tate in front of her dorm and they began running toward the front gate of the campus, she felt comfortable being with him, and they ran her normal stretch down the highway and back. Tate seemed to keep up with her pace easily and didn't try to push them any faster. She hadn't paid a lot of attention to how well he had done this season, and she asked him. His results sounded good for someone who didn't keep in shape during the off-season, but the thing that surprised her was how much he seemed to know about her performance.

It wouldn't have been too surprising for him to know she had placed first in several of the meets, but for him to know exactly which ones? That seemed a little suspicious. If she didn't know better, she would think he had a crush on her, but she knew that couldn't be. She again wondered if he was doing this for one of his friends he would eventually invite to run with them.

They parted in the parking lot between the girls' and guys' dorm areas, and Tate said his legs were killing him, but he didn't appear winded.

"I hope I wasn't slowing you down too much," he said.

"No, not at all. But I need to go or I'm going to miss my chance at a shower. Do you want to go again on Thursday?"

"Sure, if you don't mind."

"I don't mind. See you then."

She jogged all the way to her building and up the stairs to her floor. Stepping inside the room, she saw her roommates were still sleeping, and she took advantage of the free bathroom and then went to grab breakfast before class. Her thoughts remained on Tate throughout the morning, and in the back of her mind she knew she had a major crush on him. She had been feeling that way ever since last weekend, but she wasn't allowing herself to go there. He was a year older than her and too cute to ever be interested in her.

But running with him this morning had been fun, and she did allow the happy feeling to remain with her until sometime that afternoon when she slowly forgot about it. She met him again on Thursday, and she had an equally fun time. He was sore from Tuesday, and it was foggy, so they didn't run as far, returning with enough time to spare that she didn't have to rush off right away. He asked about running with her on Saturday, and she said that was fine. They decided to meet at eight instead of six-thirty. Neither of them had to be anywhere.

"Is that church we run past the one that you've been going to?"

"Yes."

"I heard you telling Danae about it on the drive. Would you mind if I went there with you this Sunday?"

"Why would I mind?"

"I know you like it because it's smaller and you can have a more personal time with God there, and I wouldn't want to disrupt that."

"It's fine," she said. "I'd like to have a friend to go with, I just don't right now."

"I feel the way you do about college groups sometimes being too big. If you haven't noticed, I'm not an extremely social person, and when I go to church here it's often more about which group I can manage to work my way into that week than connecting with God and learning anything."

"I definitely don't feel that way there. Everyone is really nice. Older people. Young families. It reminds me of my church back home, and the pastor is easy to listen to. Very down to earth and practical about God."

"He sounds like my dad."

"Is your dad a pastor?"

"Yes."

"I didn't know that."

"Yep."

"Do you like that, being a P.K.?"

"I don't really think of it that way. I think about my dad being my dad."

"Is that what you want to do? Be a pastor?"

"I don't know yet. Maybe. The social side of it scares me. My dad is more of a people-person than me."

"What else interests you?"

He smiled.

"What?"

He suddenly seemed embarrassed about something, and she wondered what other professions he was thinking about that would cause such a reaction from him.

"I don't know," he recovered. "Teaching maybe, or something with computers like making video games."

She laughed.

"I know. I'm hopeless. Twenty years old tomorrow, and I'm clueless about my life."

"Your birthday is tomorrow?"

"Yes."

"What are you doing to celebrate?"

"Nothing really. My family had a thing for me last week when I was home."

"Tate, you have to do something. Twenty? That's a big deal."

"I'll take the day off from running."

"You'll do that anyway," she laughed. "Come on, get your roommates to take you out for pizza and video games."

"Two of them are working, and the other one is more boring than I am."

"You're not boring. You're quiet. There's a difference."

"My roommate is boring, trust me. All he ever does is study."

"This is college," she laughed. "That's a good thing."

"Is that what you do on Friday nights? Study?"

"Yes, mostly."

She expected him to say something about setting the two of them up and wondered if his roommate was the one behind this 'wanting to run with her' thing, but how would his roommate know her? *Okay, Emma. Stop trying to over-think this. He just wants to run.*

"Any desire to change that?" he asked.

*Okay, so maybe I'm right.*

She shrugged, not really knowing how to respond to that. If a guy liked her, she wanted to know that, or maybe she didn't if he didn't have the courage to talk to her himself.

"Would you go out with me, Emma?"

Her eyes snapped back to Tate's face. She had no idea how long it took her to respond, trying to process his words and figure out if she heard right.

"Me? With you?"

"Yes."

She could see the nervousness in his eyes now and knew he was serious. Why on earth this good-looking, nice, funny, and sweet guy would want to take her out for his twentieth birthday, she had no idea, but she couldn't imagine saying no. She had been waiting all year to be asked out on her first college date, and rejecting Tate with that insecure look in his eyes—she didn't have it within her.

"Sure. I'd love to."

"You would?"

She smiled. "Yes."

He relaxed and let out a relieved sigh. "Okay, I get it. So this is why you wanted me to run with you, Emma? You were just looking for a date?"

She laughed and felt very special. He hated running, but he had faked it for this. "This was your idea," she reminded him.

"Was it?"

"Yes."

He smiled. "Yeah, I guess it was."

"Did your sister put you up to this?" she asked.

"No. And this is way overdue."

"Overdue?"

"You'd better go, or you're going to miss your shower," he said, obviously trying to escape this conversation.

"Tate? What do you mean, overdue?"

He sighed. "I should have done this in October."

"October?"

"Yeah, but I couldn't even talk to you then, so asking you out would have been a little difficult. Sorry. I'm not very good at this 'letting a girl know I like her' thing."

She wanted to ask why he liked her, but she did need to go. That question would have to wait until tomorrow.  "Okay," she said, stepping away.  "Should I meet you tomorrow, or—?"

"No.  I'll come all the way up and knock on your door like a normal person.  Is five-thirty all right?"

"That's fine."

"Pizza and a movie?  Or is that too boring?"

"It's your birthday."

"Okay, maybe I'll try and be a little more creative."

## Chapter Seventeen

"I don't feel like going home tonight," Matthew announced on the walk to the car following their last class on Thursday afternoon.

"You can come to my house," Mandy said.

"Amanda Smith," he teased. "Do you have a crush on me?"

She laughed and let go of his hand to put her arm around his waist. "What gave it away?"

He pulled her close and stopped to give her a sweet kiss. "I don't know if I'm ready for a girl like you."

"Ready or not, you're in love with me."

"Yes, I am," he said. "And I'd love to come to your house this evening."

"And sleep over?"

"Yes, I'll do that."

At dinner he told her parents about his revised plans for the summer, and about them going to Lifegate in the fall. He had received his acceptance letter too, and he hadn't wavered from the decision he made on the trip. He called Seth after dinner and told him also, and Mandy felt like it was all settled. She was more in love with Matthew than ever, and August suddenly seemed very far away.

They had originally chosen the date in mid August for their wedding because of Matt being gone during June and part of July, and also because if they went to Lifegate, they could come home from their honeymoon, have a few days with family, and then move into their apartment together on campus without having to find another place to live.

As much as she wanted to, she didn't see how they could change it now that he had decided not to go on the mission trip.  Even if they could get everything together to get married in June, where would they live for two months?  Matt was quitting his job.  She had very little money.  And she didn't think living with his family or hers would be better than waiting until August to have the wedding.

But the thought had been on her mind, and she mentioned it to Amber when Matthew passed the phone over and left the room, saying he had something to ask her dad.  Amber reminded her that Kevin and Kerri's apartment would be available for six weeks this summer, beginning in mid June and up until two weeks before they would be able to move onto the campus.  She also mentioned another option.

"This won't have you married any sooner, but you and Matt could spend the summer at camp with us and be a part of our crew team.  We'd make sure you have lots of time together.  And to be honest, I feel like I could really use you there with me, Mandy.  It's a selfish thing, I know, but will you think about it?"

"Yeah, I will.  I hadn't thought of that.  I knew I didn't want to be away at camp all summer without Matt there too, but that could work.  Are you still doing okay?"

"Yes. I've had a really great week, and this news just makes it even better."

"I know. I realized last week while you were here how much I've missed you, and I feel better about getting married, knowing we'll be down there with you and Seth instead of up here on our own."

Matt returned to the room, and before she let Amber go, he asked to speak to Seth again, but he took the phone and went outside to talk to him. She knew something was up, but she didn't have any idea what it could be. When he returned with a certain look in his eye and a sweet smile on his face, she asked, but he wasn't telling.

He'd been that way all week. Very playful and sweet. He had always been one to tease her in a loving way that made her smile, but lately he'd been busy and stressed about work, so it was nice to have the carefree and spontaneous Matthew back.

She mentioned Amber's idea about them spending the summer at Camp Laughing Water, and he liked the possibility. They would have to miss the last week or two because of the wedding, but Amber didn't think that would be a problem.

They spent the rest of the evening together studying, and Matt did stay overnight. He had a busy weekend coming up, and he invited her to spend it with him. The youth group was going to a concert tomorrow night and helping with a fund-raising activity on Saturday. He gave her until tomorrow to decide, and on the drive to school in the morning she told him she wanted to go. The only reason she had for saying no was spending time with his family, especially overnight, wasn't her favorite thing, but she knew she would rather endure that than not see Matthew again until Monday.

"I'm glad you're coming," he said, kissing her tenderly before they got out of the car. "I've enjoyed having so much time with you this week, Amanda. It's convinced me I'm making the right decision. I don't just like having time with you, I need it."

She smiled. "You know what I need?"

"More kisses?" he teased, giving her several before she could respond.

"Besides that."

"What?"

"For you to be happy. When you're happy, I'm happy."

"And when you're happy, I'm happy. I love you, Amanda."

"I love you too. And I'm so thankful for you. I didn't say anything to you, but a few weeks ago when you were really busy and I didn't see you for several days, I got a call from one of my friends in Eugene. She asked me to pray for her because she had been involved in a destructive relationship, lost her virginity, and had spent about a year lying to her family and friends before she finally got out of it and confessed everything to her parents; and I remember thinking, 'Okay, so maybe Matthew is a little busy right now, but at least I'm not having to deal with something like that.' It reminded me of how good I have it and how much you are an answer to all the prayers I've prayed about the kind of man I want to marry someday."

"Thanks for praying for me, Amanda. I'm convinced that prayer is the reason I am who I am now."

"Thank you for listening to Seth and Pastor John and whoever else helped you to get to this place, because I am convinced that I'm the one who will benefit the most from who you have become."

*** 

On Friday Emma only had two classes: Chemistry lab from nine to eleven-thirty and Calculus from one to two. She often ran in the afternoon instead of the morning, and she had decided to do that today because she was going out with Tate tonight, and she knew she would be nervous.

She ran around the track and the outskirts of the campus and back to the track for a few more laps before stopping at four o'clock to go get ready for her date. Walking around the backside of the Chapel, past the guys' dorm area, and across the parking lot to the stairs on the other side, she saw Danae coming from the other pathway, and she joined up with her.

"Hi, Emma. How are you?"

"Good," she said, wondering if Danae knew about Tate asking her out tonight. "How are you?"

"Great," Danae said. "Guess what?"

"What?"

"I'm engaged!"

"You are? That's great. When did that happen?"

Danae filled her in on John proposing to her at Christmas but her reluctance to say yes and how that had come to an end last week.

"I was thinking of calling you this evening and seeing if you wanted to do anything. Evangeline and I were talking about going to see a movie. Do you want to go?"

"No. I mean, thanks, I'd like to, but I have other plans."

"We could wait and go tomorrow. Are you free then?"

"I should be."

"What are you doing tonight?"

Emma smiled. "I guess he didn't tell you."

"Who?"

"Tate. He asked me out."

Danae appeared surprised, but she smiled. "For tonight? On his birthday?"

"Yes."

"When did he ask you?"

"Yesterday. After we went running."

"Running?"

Emma smiled. "He didn't tell you that either?"

"I haven't seen him since Wednesday. When did he ask you to go running?"

"Last Sunday. We went on Tuesday too."

Danae appeared shocked, and Emma began to get an uneasy feeling. "Does he usually tell you about the girls he hangs out with?"

Danae laughed. "What girls?"

Emma smiled.

"I don't want to scare you by saying this, but Tate doesn't do this, Emma. He doesn't date on a whim. He doesn't date period! As far as I know, you're the first girl he's ever asked out."

"Ever?"

"Ever."

She smiled again.

"What's that smile for?"

"I haven't dated anyone either."

"Does he know that?"

"No."

"You should tell him."

"What else should I do?" She laughed. "I have no idea what I'm doing or why he asked me out."

"He asked because he sees something special in you. Something he's been waiting for. And all you have to do is be yourself, Emma. Have fun, and be yourself."

"Okay. I think I can do that."

Continuing on to her room, Emma took a shower and then went to her closet to decide what to wear. As far as she knew, they were just going to dinner and a movie, so she chose jeans and one of her favorite tops that was nice but not too dressy. Going back to the bathroom, she dried her hair and then heard one of her roommates come in.

"Who's in here?" Abby said, thumping on the closed door. "I need to go."

Emma opened the door and stepped out. "Go ahead. I'm finished."

"Wow. You look nice," Abby said, scanning her from head to toe. "Are you going somewhere?"

"Yes," she answered, feeling both shy and triumphant. Finally, *she* was the one going out on a Friday night. "I have a date."

"With who?"

"His name is Tate. He's a sophomore."

"Where are you going?"

"I'm not sure. It's his birthday, so I told him he could decide."

"How do you know him?"

"I know him from cross-country, and I also know his sister. That's more how I got to know him."

"Huh," Abby said, as if her curiosity had been satisfied. "I hope you have fun."

"Thanks."

"But, you might want to think about wearing something else," she added. "Something that shows a little more skin. Guys like that, especially someone who's having a birthday," she chimed in a suggestive way. Closing the bathroom door behind her, Abby left her standing there.

Emma didn't dress like Abby and her roommates. The only clothes she owned that showed a lot of skin were those she wore under other things, not by themselves. She didn't take Abby's advice, nor Tiffany's when she came to the room to drop off her things before leaving with Abby for dinner, but when Tate arrived to pick her up, she suddenly felt very self-conscious.

"Hi," he said.

"Hi. Happy Birthday."

"Thanks. Are you ready?"

*Why? Don't I look ready?* "Yes," she said, stepping into the hallway and closing the door behind her. Tate asked about her day, and she spoke as she always had with him, but she felt guarded and not free to be herself.

When they got to the car, Tate appeared concerned. "Are you all right?"

"Yes."

"Do you still want to do this?"

"Yes. Do you?"

"Sure.  Why wouldn't I?"

"Umm, am I dressed okay?"

He smiled.  "You look great to me."

"Did you decide on something besides pizza and a movie?  Because I can go change if—"

"You're fine," he said.  "I did decide on something else, but nothing fancy."

"But you look nice."

"So do you."

He opened the door, and she got into the car. Once he was seated beside her, she told him about seeing Danae this afternoon.

"Did you tell her we were going out?" he asked.

"Yes."

"What did she say?"

"She was surprised.  She said you don't date much."

"At all, Emma.  I don't date at all."

"Why not?"

He laughed.  "Because I would have to talk to girls to do that."

"You don't talk to girls?"

"I talk to girls I like as friends, but whenever I'm strongly attracted to someone, I don't.  I can't."

"So, you just like me as a friend?"

He smiled.  "I didn't say that."

## Chapter Eighteen

Tate didn't feel as nervous with Emma as he thought he would.  He had been more nervous about seeing her all day than he was now.  She seemed nervous, and that gave him a feeling of boldness.  She needed him to be confident, and he was confident about wanting this kind of time with her.

He had decided to keep the evening relaxed and casual but more special than pizza and a movie.  He didn't have any specific expectations.  He just wanted to be with Emma and see what happened.  Driving down the hill and arriving in town, he pulled into the parking lot at Tony's but took one of the five-minute parking spaces and told her to wait in the car while he went inside to pick up the pizza he had ordered.  They had it waiting for him, and Tony told him to have a nice time.

"That's my plan," he said.

Returning to the car, he put the pizza in the back seat.  Emma was smiling at him.  She had the best smile.  Taking her to the park, he found an open picnic table to sit at.  He set the pizza down and pulled paper plates from a sack along with drinks.  Emma watched as he set everything out, and once he had it all arranged, he looked at her and returned her warm smile.

"I want us to get to know each other tonight, Emma. And I thought we might be more open with each other here. Is it too cold out?"

"No, I'm fine," she said. "Our other two dates have been outdoors, why not this one?"

He smiled. It was the first time she had spoken tonight in a spontaneous way, and it was perfect. Innocent, teasing, and honest. They were sitting across from each other, but the table seemed ten feet wide, and he wanted to be closer to her. Getting up from the bench, he slid his plate over to her side and walked around the table to sit beside her.

"Is it all right if I sit here?"

"Fine with me."

He could still detect a bit of shyness on her part, and he didn't want that. He wanted the girl he'd watched talk to his sister for hours in the car, the girl he had gone running with, and the girl she had been with her teasing comment. Slipping his arm around her waist, he leaned close enough to smell the scent of shampoo coming from her hair, and he spoke softly.

"I like the Emma I went running with this week. You don't have to be nervous."

She turned her face and looked into his eyes. "I'm sorry I've been quiet. This is my first date too. I'm not used to dating either."

"You'd better get used to it because at the end of tonight, I'm going to ask you again."

"I don't think you're supposed to tell me that until later."

"Like I'm supposed to go out with lots of girls before my twentieth birthday?"

"Yes," she laughed. "Why me, Tate?"

"Because when I look at you, Emma, I never want to look away."

Lifting his hand to her face, he touched her smooth skin and kissed her gently. She smelled nice, and her lips were soft. He felt like a different person than he saw in the mirror every day. He felt confident with her and so alive.

"I'm sorry," he said, pulling back and remembering something. "I was supposed to ask permission before I did that."

She smiled.

"May I kiss you, Emma?"

"Yes."

He kissed her again, and it was amazing. He couldn't believe he was doing this less than an hour into their date. Their pizza was getting cold, and he'd had a more private and romantic spot in mind to possibly kiss her for the first time, but this was honest and real. This is why he'd asked her out. Not just to talk and get to know her—he could do that while they ran together. But to kiss her and hold her and be close to her, he had to be her boyfriend for that.

*** 

Tate didn't kiss her for a long time but enough for Emma to know she liked it. He pulled away from her slowly, and she opened her eyes to see him looking at her in a way she knew he liked it too. Who was this guy, and what was he doing in her life? How had she ended up on a date with him, and what did he see that made him want to kiss her?

"Is this your first kiss?" Tate asked.

"Yes."

"Mine too."

They smiled at each other and then began eating their pizza. "Is this where you work?" she asked, pointing to the Tony's Pizza box.

"Yes. Just two nights a week. Tuesdays and Saturdays. I do deliveries."

"Do you have any sisters besides Danae?"

"Yes, two. Grace is older than Danae, and Tabitha is younger than me. She's a senior in high school."

"Any brothers?"

"One older. Drew. He's married, and his wife is going to have a baby later this year."

Emma had four siblings too, but they were all younger: two sisters and two brothers. Tate already knew that because Danae had asked about her family on the drive up last weekend, and she wondered what else he already knew about her. She couldn't remember everything she and Danae had talked about, but she knew he had heard most of it.

"What's it like to have pesky little brothers like me?" he said.

"Peter is only eighteen months younger than me, and we used to fight a lot, but not much the last few years. And Josh is only eleven, so he's been like a permanent baby-sitting job for me along with my youngest sister. Those two fight all the time too."

"I want a big family," he said. "Do you?"

She took a moment to let that sink in. Not because she didn't want a big family, but because he was talking about that already. "Yeah, I think so," she said.

He laughed at himself. "Sorry, I didn't mean that the way it sounded. I was just making a comment, not trying to plan our future."

She laughed but had a warm feeling pass through her at the thought of being married to Tate someday. She could spend a lot of time with him and enjoy it very much. She didn't understand why he would feel shy around anybody, especially her. He was the type of guy anyone would like instantly, and in less than an hour he had chased all of her insecurities away.

***

On Friday afternoon, Rachael hung around the OSU campus after her final class. She was taking Digital Photography this term, and their first assignment had been to get some campus shots that were due on Monday. She had taken a few on Wednesday, but they had been of the main buildings and common outdoor beauty spots. Today she was in search of less prominent features that would make good and more unique photographs.

Her mom and dad were going out of town this weekend, so she stopped at Taco Bell on the way home to get dinner and arrived at the empty house at six-thirty. She didn't have any plans tonight except for calling Josiah. She'd had a good week, considering how much she missed him. Talking to him tonight for an extended amount of time would help.

After eating her burrito at the kitchen table and looking at her mom's list of what she needed her to

179

do, she went upstairs to transfer her pictures onto her computer and see what she could do to improve them. Most of them looked good on their own without any digital enhancements, and she saved the ones she especially liked.

Hearing the phone ring, she knew it probably wasn't Josiah. She had told him she would call him tonight, and if he did beat her to it, he would call her cell phone, not the house. Picking up the extension in her room, she expected it to be for her mom or dad.

"Hello?" she said, quitting her photography program with the click of the mouse at the same time.

There was a slight pause, and then she heard someone say her name, but she couldn't place the voice. It was a guy, but she didn't think it was Josiah.

"Rachael?"

"Yes," she replied.

"Hi, um, this is Gabe."

Rachael froze. She hadn't talked to Gabe in almost a year.

"Don't hang up," he said. "I-I need to talk to you."

"Okay," she said cautiously.

"I'm here. In Corvallis. Can you meet me somewhere?"

Her heart started beating really fast. "You're in Corvallis? Why?"

"To see you. I really need to talk to you, Rachael. I know I've been an idiot, but nothing has been right since you've been out of my life. I skipped my classes today to come see you. I had to. Please?"

She didn't want to see him. "What do you want, Gabe? Just tell me over the phone."

"No, I want to see you. The things I have to say can't be said over the phone. That's why I'm here."

Rachael supposed it wouldn't do any harm to see him, but since her parents weren't home, she didn't think having him over to the house would be a good idea. Meeting him someplace where she could leave and drive away would be better.

"How about if I meet you at Starbucks?"

"No, someplace more private. Someplace where we can talk."

Gabe had always been able to get her to do things his way, but not this time. She went with what her instincts were telling her. "I'm not comfortable with that."

"Okay, how about the parking lot of Starbucks? We could talk in the car."

Rachael told herself to think. This didn't seem like a good idea. Why would he come all this way? There was only one explanation for that, and she had no desire to get back together with him.

"How long are you here for?" she asked.

"I don't know. I haven't thought that far ahead."

"Will you still be here tomorrow? Could I meet you on the OSU campus in broad daylight?"

"I'm not going to hurt you, Rachael. I just want to talk."

"I can't tonight," she said. "If you want to talk, it will have to be tomorrow."

"Just make up some excuse to get out of there. You're nineteen, Rachael."

There was a time such a comment would have made her give in to his wishes, but not anymore. "This isn't about my parents, Gabe. This is about you.

I'm not comfortable meeting you like this. If you want to talk to me, you can come here tomorrow and ask for my dad's permission."

"Okay, I'll meet you at Starbucks," he relented.

Rachael almost went for it, more out of curiosity than a desire to see him, but she didn't want to talk to him tonight. Not until she had a chance to talk to Josiah. Gabe knew they were together now, and she found the idea of him going behind his best friend's back to meet with her disturbing.

"I'll meet you at Starbucks tomorrow. There's one on the highway, right near my house. Eleven o'clock."

"Ra—"

She hung up on him.

The phone rang again, but she didn't pick it up. Going downstairs, she checked to make sure she had closed the garage door so that if he came by he wouldn't see that her parents weren't here. Gabe wouldn't have the guts to come knocking on the door, she felt certain.

Going back upstairs, she called Josiah. He answered on the second ring and sounded happy.

"Hey, Beautiful. It's not eight o'clock yet."

"I know. I need to talk to you now."

His voice changed to one of concern. "What's wrong?"

"Gabe is here."

"He's there, with you now?"

"No. In Corvallis. He just called me. He wants to meet me somewhere and talk."

"Where?"

"I suggested Starbucks, but he didn't like that idea. He wanted someplace more private."

"Like where?"

"In the car outside of Starbucks." She laughed. That was so Gabe.

"Are you going?" he asked nervously.

"No. I told him he could come over here tomorrow and ask for my dad's permission."

"Aren't your parents gone this weekend?"

"Yes, but he doesn't know that, and I wasn't about to tell him."

"What does he want? Did he say?"

"No, but I could take a guess."

"To get back together with you?"

"He said nothing has been the same since I was in his life."

"That's the truth, I'm sure."

"Josiah! What am I supposed to do?"

"What do you want to do?"

She thought about that. What did she want? "I guess I'm curious about what he has to say, but—"

She heard the doorbell ring.

"Oh, my God."

"What?"

"He's here."

Josiah didn't respond, and she didn't know what to do. Going across the hall to her brother's room that overlooked the front yard, she peered out the window and couldn't see him, but there was a car in the driveway she didn't recognize.

"What kind of a car does he have?"

"A Jetta."

"It's him! What am I supposed to do?"

"What do you want to do?"

"Not have this be happening!"

"Calm down, Rachael. Go open the door. He's not a serial killer. See what he has to say."

"Will you stay with me?"

"Yes, I'm right here."

"Okay," she said, leaving the room and going downstairs with her heart beating wildly in her chest. The doorbell rang again when she was almost there. Unlocking the door, she opened it, and there he was. Gabe. Her first love. Her first heartbreak.

She waited for him to speak.

## Chapter Nineteen

"Hi. Is your dad home?" Gabe asked somewhat seriously.

"What are you doing here?"

"I decided I didn't want to wait until tomorrow, and if asking your dad for permission is what it's going to take, then here I am."

His cocky tone annoyed her, as if this was all her fault and he was the innocent one. "My dad isn't here," she said.

"May I come in?" he asked.

If Josiah wouldn't have been on the phone, she would have said no, but since he was, she allowed it.

"Sure," she said, stepping to the side.

He came inside, closed the door, and whispered, "Who are you talking to?"

She held out the phone to him.

He took it from her. "Your dad?" he asked.

"No. Say hi."

"Josiah?"

"Yes."

He handed it back to her. "No, thanks."

She lifted the phone to her ear and relayed the message. "He doesn't want to talk to you."

"No surprise," Josiah said. "You're better than him, Rachael. Don't stoop to his level."

"Am I?" she challenged him.

"Don't go there, baby. He cheated on you before you cheated on him."

"But I didn't know that."

Rachael felt tears stinging her eyes. Gabe couldn't hear Josiah's end of the conversation, and she knew Josiah had never told Gabe about Steven. Gabe may have hurt her, but she hadn't been completely innocent in their relationship. She had allowed him to do things to her physically because she wanted it and then had been mad at him later, and she'd justified being with Steven when she shouldn't have been.

"Let me talk to Gabe," Josiah said.

"I'll call you back later," she said, clicking off the phone before she could change her mind. Walking to the stairs on the backside of the foyer, she sat down on the second step and looked up at Gabe. He came to sit by her, and she waited for him to speak. Her phone rang, and she answered it.

"Baby, don't hang up on me," Josiah said. "Let me be there with you."

She didn't respond.

"I'm sorry, Rachael. I shouldn't have told you to let him in. Let me talk to him."

"I'm all right," she said. "I'll call you back."

Clicking off the phone once again, she turned off the ringer, set the phone aside, and turned to face Gabe. "You came to talk. Let's talk."

He reached for her hand. "I miss you, Rachael. I miss you so much, it hurts. I'm sorry for what I did.

Please forgive me. Let's go back to the way it used to be."

She removed her hand from his. "What about Sienna?"

"I don't love her."

"It's your baby, Gabe. You need to take responsibility for that."

"She told me she was on birth control pills. She was the one who wanted it. I was confused and I missed you so much. It shouldn't have happened."

The house phone rang, and Rachael smiled. She let it ring six times but then got up to go answer it, hearing it ring another three times before she got to the kitchen.

"Hello?"

"Rachael, listen to me," Josiah said.

She waited for him to go on.

"Are you there?"

"Yes."

"I'm not losing you. I didn't do all of this and see you come to a place of healing for you to go back to Gabe and get hurt all over again."

She smiled and let the tears fall.

"Please, don't do this."

"Do what?" she asked gently.

"Go back to him because you don't feel worthy of me. Maybe that's not what you're thinking, but if you are, stop it. I love you. I need you. You're mine, and I'm not ashamed to beg."

She laughed. "You don't have to, Josiah."

"I don't?"

"No. I don't deserve you, but I need you. And I love you. I'm all right. I'm going to talk to Gabe for awhile, but I'll kick him out if I have to."

"He's a smooth-talker, Rachael."

"I know that. I know that better than anyone. Just pray for me. I'll turn my phone back on, but give me at least ten minutes before you call me, okay?"

"Okay."

"I love you. You're my hero."

"And you're my princess. Don't forget that."

"I won't."

She hung up the phone and went back to the stairs, only Gabe wasn't there. He'd gone into the living room and made himself more comfortable on the couch. She went into the room, but she took a seat in the chair beside the couch.

"That was Josiah," she said. "He said you can't have me."

"And what do you say?"

"The same."

He started to say something, but she interrupted him. "I have something to tell you."

"What?"

"I cheated on you too."

His eyebrows went up. "Oh?"

"Over the summer, before I ever knew about Sienna. I was hurt because you were being distant, and I let someone else comfort me in that."

"Who?"

"Just this guy I know. It's over now."

"Why are you telling me?"

"I think you have a right to know since technically we were still together then, and I need to admit I made mistakes in our relationship too. I let you do things to me I shouldn't have. I tempted you, and I shouldn't have done that either. And I'm sorry it didn't work out for us."

"Come here," he said. "Don't sit way over there. It can still work for us, Rach."

She shook her head. "No, it can't."

He got up and came to her, holding out his hand and pulling her to her feet. He tried to kiss her, but she turned away. He took her into his arms and held her close.

"Rachael, please?"

She was a little surprised she felt absolutely nothing at his touch, but she knew he was in a space he simply didn't belong anymore. "Let go, Gabe."

"You don't mean that."

"Yes, I do," she said calmly. "Let go."

He released her and sighed. "I came all this way, Rachael. For you. For us. Doesn't that count for something?"

"No. It's too late."

"Because of Josiah?" he asked like Josiah was the problem.

"Yes," she said. "Because of Josiah. We're in love."

He laughed. "I'm sorry, Rachael, but I'm not seeing that. You and Josiah? It's sweet, but you don't belong with him."

"Yes, Gabe. I do. He's the kind of guy I prayed for. He's the one who loved me when I didn't deserve to be loved. He's the one who makes me feel whole and right and beautiful all the time."

She let the tears flow freely at the thought of Josiah's love for her. And Gabe seemed to get he couldn't argue with her. He stood there for a moment and then stepped away. She let him go and didn't follow him. When she heard the front door open and close, she sank into the chair and cried from the deepest part of her soul. Not for the pain Gabe had caused. Not for the mistakes she had made. But for Josiah's love for her.

She didn't deserve him, but he was here, and she didn't have to let go. No one could tell her she had to do that. And she wasn't going to—ever.

***

Josiah forced himself to wait fifteen minutes before calling Rachael back. He usually had the room to himself on Friday nights because Seth, Chad, and Adam were either working or out with their girls, giving him the privacy to talk to Rachael freely, sharing whatever was on his heart. He couldn't always do that if others were in the room, and his cell phone didn't work here, even if he went outside. Dialing the number, he waited for her to pick up, and she sounded calm.

"Hi," she said.

"You all right?"

"Yes."

"Is he still there?"

"No."

"What happened?"

She told him everything, and he was proud of her for telling Gabe the truth, and touched by what she said about him. He didn't feel proud of himself for the way he loved her, but he knew he was being the man she needed him to be. He couldn't control the mistakes of others, but he could do what was right.

"Would you like me to come up tomorrow?" he asked. "I could be there by noon if I leave early."

"My parents aren't home."

"I'm not coming to see them."

"You know what I mean."

"Yes, I know. That's probably not a good idea, but I don't want you to be alone."

"I could call Casey and have him stay with me."

"Do you want to call him now?"

"Yes, I'll call you back."

Rachael let Josiah go and called her brother. He was at his apartment, and she told him about Gabe showing up and asked if he could sleep here tonight.

"Josiah doesn't like the thought of me being alone right now."

"I'll be over in a few minutes."

"Thanks, Casey."

"Not a problem, sis. Anything for you."

She went downstairs to wait for her brother, and he didn't live very far away so he was there in ten minutes. He said something encouraging she hadn't thought of, but she knew why he saw it as a big deal.

"I'm proud of you for calling Josiah and me, not just trying to handle Gabe yourself."

"Yeah, I've been down that road before. It doesn't work too well. And I'm glad I have such a great boyfriend and brother to turn to."

"He is pretty great. Josiah, I mean. You know that, right?"

"Yes, I know."

"I never liked Gabe too much. I didn't trust him. But Josiah is different. I knew that from the moment I first met him."

Calling Josiah back, she went up to her room to talk to him, relaying Casey's words about trusting him with his little sister. They talked for another two hours about their respective weeks, about her new classes this term, about their individual times with Jesus, about Gabe and their mutual concern for him, about their hopes for the summer and next fall, and about him possibly coming up to see her over Easter Weekend. He didn't have classes on either Friday or Monday, so he could spend those days driving while she was at school, and they would have two full days together. She wanted him to come. Easter was in three weeks, and they would only have four more weeks of separation to go after that.

"What was it like for you to see Gabe again?" he asked. "Was there a part of you that wanted to take him back?"

She took his question seriously and thought for a moment. "I think if I didn't have you in my life, I might have felt that way. But I'm glad I do because I know that wouldn't be the right choice for me. We had a passionate relationship I missed when it was over, but we had problems, Josiah. Major problems we tried to cover up and pretend we didn't have."

"Do we have problems, Rachael? Problems we're sweeping under the rug and ignoring because we don't want to deal with them?"

"I don't think so," she said, wondering if he thought differently. But she honestly couldn't think of a single thing wrong with their relationship.

"I guess if loving each other isn't supposed to feel this good, and I'm not supposed to be missing you terribly and thinking about you at all hours of the day, and we're supposed to be fighting all the time and having major problems and letting our physical desire take over, then we're in big trouble."

She smiled. "Don't let go of me, Josiah. I won't let go if you won't."

"I won't."

"How would you be feeling if you were Gabe right now?"

"Like I threw away the best thing that ever happened to me."

"Would you be hating your best friend?"

"You mean, do I think Gabe hates me?"

"Yes."

"No, I don't. He was wrong, and he knows it. He doesn't hate me, or you. He hates himself."

That thought made Rachael feel sad, but she didn't think there was anything she could do about it. Except pray for him, and maybe one other thing.

"Would you mind if I wrote him a letter? I feel like I have things to say that could help him—things I've learned about how God heals us and leads us into a deeper relationship with Him through our shortcomings. Things he might be willing to hear from me since I've been in the pit too—more so than from his perfect best friend."

"I'm not perfect, Rachael."

"No, but I'm sure Gabe sees you that way."

"That's fine if you want to write him," he said. "You're probably right."

"Probably?"

"Always. You're always right."

"No, I am not! Don't ever let me think that about myself."

"And don't let me think I'm perfect, Rachael. I just want to love you the best way I know how, so I try hard and ask God for lots of help."

"Are you saying I'm high-maintenance?"

He laughed. "Are you trying to pick a fight with me?"

"I'd say it's about time. We've been together for three months and we haven't had one yet."

"That's fine by me," he said. "If you haven't noticed, I don't handle conflict and stressful moments too well."

"You were pretty adamant about not losing me. I think you actually raised your voice."

"Sorry, I panicked."

"Don't be sorry," she laughed. "I liked it. I like you being possessive of me."

"I'm not making you feel trapped, am I? Like you want out of this, but you don't want to hurt me?"

"No," she said.

Closing her eyes, she imagined something she had thought of often this week. When Josiah had been here on Saturday, they were watching a movie together. Her parents were here, but they were alone in the family room, and Josiah had invited her to lie beside him.

She had been wary of it because she'd done the same thing with Gabe and Steven in the past, and it always led to inappropriate touching. She told Josiah she didn't know if that was a good idea, but he promised to be good and just hold her. She had decided to trust him and told herself to not keep lying there if she didn't feel comfortable with it. But Josiah had simply held her close to him, and she relaxed into it, and for the next hour while they watched the second half of the movie, she'd had the most amazing feeling of being safe and protected in Josiah's arms. He had been a perfect gentleman and continued to hold her after the movie ended, telling her everything he liked about her.

"Are you sure, Rachael?" Josiah asked, referring to his question about if she felt trapped in this relationship.

"I'm sure, Josiah. You don't make me feel trapped. You make me feel free. I feel like I belong to you, but in a safe way, not a confusing one."

He let her go shortly after that, and she clicked off the phone. Remembering something she had written in her journal either yesterday or today, she took the notebook from the drawer of her nightstand, and she flipped the pages looking for it.

At the end of her prayer from yesterday, she read these words:

*Am I meant to be with Josiah? Now? Forever? I want whatever You want for me, Jesus. Please show me if he's the one.*

She had forgotten about that until now, and He had answered her in a way she didn't expect. By reminding her of the difference between Gabe and Josiah.

*Yes, he's the one, Rachael, and you know it. Don't let go.*

## Chapter Twenty

"I just realized I don't know something," Tate said.

Their date was coming to an end with him walking her from the parking lot to her dormitory building, but Emma felt confident this wouldn't be the only time she went out with Tate. He hadn't asked her about any definite plans, but he had confirmed they were going running in the morning.

"How exactly did you meet Danae?"

"She didn't tell you?"

"No, she just said she offered for you to ride with us when I saw her at breakfast, and at the time I was so panicked about seeing you in another twenty minutes, I didn't think to ask how she knew you."

Emma smiled. "You were panicked about seeing me?"

He reached out and took her hand. "I've always gotten nervous before I knew I would be seeing you."

Emma felt in awe any guy would feel that way about her, especially someone as good-looking and sweet as Tate. "I'd actually just met her the night before," she said. "I'd gone to The Oasis with my roommates, but then they were going to the rec room to meet up with other friends and I didn't feel like tagging along, so I was walking back by myself, and

Danae and her friends were ahead of me. Danae turned around and saw me, and she recognized me from cross-country."

"But you'd never spoken to her before then?"

"No. I couldn't believe how she pulled me into her circle of friends like that and then was offering me a ride home a minute later."

"Yeah, she's always been like that. My mom was the same way."

"Was?"

"Oh, I guess I assumed you knew, but if you just met Danae two weeks ago then you probably don't. Our mom died six years ago. Car accident."

"Oh, I'm sorry," she said. "No, I didn't know that. How old were you, fourteen?"

"Yes."

Emma had met Tate and Danae's dad last Saturday when her mom drove her up to their house for the ride back to school, but she had assumed their mom wasn't there, not that she had died.

"Do you miss her?" she asked. "I mean, I'm sure you do, but is it still hard now, six years later?"

"Yes and no. There are times when I really miss her a lot and wish I could talk to her or go home and have her there. But it's been easier since I've been away at school, and my dad remarried four months ago, so that makes it a little better—to think of him not being alone without her."

"Do you like his new wife?"

"Yes. She's a lot like my mom. I haven't gotten to know her very well yet, but my dad loves her, so that's the most important thing to me."

They reached the patio area in front of her dorm, and Tate stopped walking, turning to face her and appearing to still be in thought about their conversation more than their time together coming to an end.  Almost as if he was so used to being with her, this was the end of many other such nights they'd had.

"I had a nice time, Emma.  Did you?"

"Yes.  You were very creative.  I liked it."

He smiled.  "I actually got the idea for the dance lesson from my dad."

"You asked him for ideas?"

"No.  He used to tell us about the first time he took my mom out.  It was a sappy story about how he'd asked her to this dance at school, and she said, 'Andrew Morgan, I don't believe you know how to dance.'  And he said, 'You're right, I don't.  Want to take lessons with me?'  She agreed, so they took some from my grandmother before the big dance and fell in love with each other before their first date."

"Did he take your mom running too?"

He laughed.  "No, for him it was getting a job working on her daddy's farm.  My grandma always served lemonade on the back veranda to those hard-working boys and usually sent her daughter to give them refills.  My dad used to pour his out in the bushes just so he could be the last one to leave."

She smiled and Tate stepped closer.  He hadn't kissed her since they'd been at the park, and she had been hoping he would do so again.  He remembered to ask permission this time.  His tender lips felt the same, but he took his time with ending the kiss, taking her someplace she had never been before physically or emotionally, but he ended the affectionate moment with a gentle hug and words that stayed with her long after she stepped inside and went up to her room. Getting into bed before her roommates were back from their Friday night dates, she laid her head on her pillow and remembered his tender words in the quietness of the room as if he was right here whispering them to her.

"You're becoming very special to me, Emma. I don't know what I was so afraid of. What are you doing with the rest of your life?"

She'd stepped back and smiled, not feeling threatened by his words. He was being honest, and she responded likewise.

"I don't know, Tate Morgan. Maybe you'll get to find out."

***

When Seth returned from a pleasant evening with Amber, Josiah was still up studying, but he appeared disturbed about something.

"You all right?" he asked, hoping nothing had gone wrong between him and Rachael. They usually talked on the phone on Friday nights, putting him in a more happy state than he seemed to currently be.

"I've been better," he said, confirming Seth's concern.

"What happened?"

"Guess who showed up at Rachael's house tonight?"

Seth only knew of one person Josiah had serious negative feelings about. "Gabe?" he guessed.

"Yep."

Seth sat down to hear this story. "Why?"

"He wants her back. Drove all the way to Corvallis today just to beg her for forgiveness and a second chance."

"Is she considering it?"

"No, thank God."

Josiah went on to tell the whole story, and Seth could sympathize with Josiah's agony of having to endure even a few minutes of thinking he was losing her.

"So why the long face, man? That sounds like good news to me."

"It is, I just wish I could go see her tomorrow. I don't like the thought of her being alone this weekend. It might hit her more tomorrow."

"Why don't you?"

"Her parents are gone. I don't think it would be a good idea."

"Maybe Amber and I could go along. Are you interested in that?"

"Sure," he said.

"Adam or Chad could probably take my shift at Tony's on Sunday afternoon. They're always looking for more hours."

He asked the first one who entered the room twenty minutes later, and Adam said he could do that. He had already called Amber, and she was fine with it and had suggested they could all go to the beach after they got to Corvallis.

"Are you going to call Rachael and tell her we're coming?" Seth asked.

Josiah smiled. "No. I think I'll surprise her."

Seth thought that was a good idea until the morning came and Josiah seemed quieter on the early drive up to Oregon than he would expect from a guy who was going to be seeing his girl in a few hours. Both Josiah and Amber had slept for the first stretch while he drove, and then once Josiah was more awake, he offered to drive. Seth sat up front with him because Amber was sleeping in the back, but he wasn't very talkative.

"You all right?" Seth asked.

"I should have told her we were coming. What if she's not there?"

"You could always call her."

"That's not what I meant. Before Gabe showed up at the house last night, Rachael told him she would meet him this morning. Maybe he stayed in town overnight and will talk her into seeing him again."

"Then you'll get to rescue her from making the biggest mistake of her life."

"I'm not good with this stuff. I hate conflict."

"You don't win battles in times of conflict; you win them in times of recovery and peace."

"What do you mean?"

"I doubt there's anything Gabe could say to Rachael now that would make her forget who you've been to her these last four months. Believe in that. Believe in what you've given to her. You didn't have to be there last night to get her to choose you. And the whole thing made you shine more brightly in her eyes."

Josiah glanced at him and cracked a smile. "That was poetic. No wonder that girl back there fell for you."

Seth turned around and looked at Amber. Her eyes were closed, but her ears were open.

"You've got that right, Josiah," she said, opening her eyes and smiling at him. "And if I was Rachael, I'd choose you too. No contest."

***

Blake had an interview with a church in Eureka on Saturday morning. It was a large church with a full-time youth pastor, who was currently running ministries for middle and high school students. He was overloaded and was looking to hire a person to work specifically with the middle school students so he could devote more time and energy to the older ages.

It was an ideal position for him. He could remain close to Lifegate, and Colleen could continue to attend school there. He would be working under an experienced youth pastor rather than having to go it alone. And they already had a great group of energetic volunteers, so he could step in and use his strengths of planning, discipleship, and teaching.

Another thing that appealed to him was the youth pastor already had the summer planned with taking kids on mission trips and to camps, so he wasn't actually looking to bring someone on until August, giving Blake the option of having time with Colleen and his family this summer rather than having to start right after graduation. He had a week to think and pray about it, but when he returned to the campus and told Colleen everything, he knew he wanted to take it.

"Is that okay?" he asked. "Us staying down here?"

"Yes. I've told you that, and I think I've settled on a major Lifegate offers, but I didn't want to say anything until I knew where you were going to be."

Blake decided not to scold her for thinking that way. He wanted to know what had captured her interest. He asked, and it wasn't what he expected. She had always leaned toward the math and science side of things. Her dad was a math genius and her mom was a nurse and health educator, but this was more in line with his career choice: youth counseling.

"What made you decide that?"

"Being a counselor at camp started it, and the roommate I had last semester in Oregon was having major problems, things I haven't personally had to deal with, and yet I was able to help her and others I've met here. I can listen to someone for a short amount of time and pinpoint their need."

"Have you always been that way?"

"No. I used to hate to give anyone advice because I had no clue—either because they were going through something I couldn't relate to, or because I had the same problem but had no idea how to fix it, but God has taught me to think differently about myself and my life, and youth counseling makes sense if I'm going to be married to a youth pastor."

They had gone for a walk, but he stopped and pulled her close to him. "I'll support you in whatever you decide, but I can see you doing that."

"Thank you," she said.

"And what's this about marrying a youth pastor? Do you have a specific one in mind?"

"Yes."

"You know I'm ready for that anytime you are."

"I know."

"Are you ready?"

"No, not yet. I'm happy, Blake. Not that I wouldn't be if we got married anytime soon, but I just want to enjoy this for now. Is that okay?"

"Yes."

"Are you sure?"

"I'm sure. I'm happy, Colleen. Being married will be great for us someday, but just having you in my life is great. I have everything I could want and need and good things to look forward to."

"I feel that way too. And it's funny because I surrendered myself to whatever God wanted for me, and for us. If you would have found a job away from here and my family, and you wanted to take it but felt like we should get married first: I was okay with that possibility. But neither you or God is demanding that of me right now, so I'm content to wait."

"I love you, Colleen. I love you being in my life and knowing you're not going away."

"I love you too, Blake. I love being in your life and knowing that's enough right now. And that you're not going away either."

# Chapter Twenty-One

When Rachael woke up on Saturday morning, she realized she had slept in later than usual. Probably because it was so quiet, she reasoned, recalling the events of the previous evening and her brother's presence overnight, which had allowed her to sleep peacefully. She knew she wasn't here alone, and Casey wasn't a noisy person.

Getting out of bed, she wondered if he was still here but assumed he was. Last night he told her he didn't have to be at work until one o'clock. Taking fresh clothes out of her drawer, she headed for the bathroom and could feel a hot shower calling her name. Things had turned out well last night, but the stress of it had affected her while she slept. Her back and shoulders ached, and she hoped the warm water would help relax it away.

Just as she was about to turn on the shower, she heard the doorbell ring. The possibility of Gabe showing up today, and her uncertainty about Casey being here made her instantly tense up. She waited to either hear the doorbell again or her brother opening the door. She heard the latter, and she relaxed. If Casey was here, she would be okay, and when she heard what sounded like a positive greeting of whomever it was and muffled chatting, she assumed it was one of his friends.

Stepping over to the bathroom door, she opened it a crack so she could hear what they were saying, just to be sure, and she heard Casey say, "I think she's still sleeping, let me go check."

She heard Casey's footsteps on the stairs, and she opened the door fully to step into the hall and see what this was about. Casey spotted her, and an instant smile came to his face.

"Hey, you are up," he said.

"Barely," she said. "Who's here?"

"I think you should come see."

She was still in her pajamas. "I'm not dressed."

"Get your robe and come down. Trust me, he won't mind the sleepy-eyed Rachael."

"He?"

"Josiah, and he didn't drive all this way to see me."

"He came? He told me he wasn't going to."

"I guess he changed his mind."

Rachael went to her room and grabbed her robe. Following Casey down the stairs, she wasn't sure she believed it until she saw Josiah standing there in the foyer. He smiled at her, and she felt so loved. She stepped into his arms without saying anything, and he spoke first.

"I didn't want you to be alone today."

She couldn't speak, but she didn't cry. She felt too overwhelmed to do either.

"I brought friends," he added. "We're kidnapping you to the beach for the day."

"What friends?"

"Seth and Amber."

Josiah had talked about them often. Rachael had been looking forward to meeting them whenever that time came. If Josiah had come here alone, she would trust him to protect their time together, but knowing he brought reinforcements reminded her whom she was dating.

Not the guy who had come here last night trying to steal her back and wanting to meet with her secretly, but the one on the phone who said, 'I'm not losing you, Rachael,' and not just saying it, but showing up today to prove how serious he was.

"Give me ten minutes?" she said.

"Take your time," he said. "We can wait."

She smiled and gave him a kiss. "I can't. I'll be right back."

***

Seeing Tate waiting for their Saturday morning running date, Emma stepped toward him and felt many of the same emotions she had experienced last night. He surprised her with a sweet good-morning kiss. She had been expecting his shy nature to take back over until he had a chance to get comfortable with her again, but he didn't seem at all embarrassed or shy about what had happened between them last night, making her feel instantly comfortable also.

They ran for a long time, and their conversation flowed easily and constantly, making a ninety-minute run feel like half that. Tate was in better shape than he gave himself credit for. He hadn't been running every day since their cross-country season had ended, but he was active in other ways. He was currently taking two P.E. classes: racquetball and indoor soccer, and he also went swimming at the campus pool a couple of times a week. He had been on the swim team during high school, and he would be here too if they had a team, but they didn't.

"Why did you decide to come here?" she asked after they had returned and were stretching by the raised flower beds ablaze with spring color along the front of Priscilla Hall. "Why not to a school with a swim team or in a more competitive cross-country division?"

"That's why," he said. "I was too caught up in all of that during high school. It was a good outlet for me, better than other things I could have been involved in, but I realized during my senior year that sports had become a substitute for God. A good substitute—something that others praised and I could feel good about, but I was worshipping sports, not worshipping God through sports. You know what I mean?"

She wondered if she was doing that, or if she had in the past. She hadn't thought about it before. One of the things that had saved her last semester with being away from home for the first time, having difficult roommates, and not having a boyfriend like she wanted, had been her involvement in cross-country. Running every day and competing in meets each week had become her god. Her savior from the loneliness and pain and hurtful words of others.

"What made you realize that?" she asked.

"It was something my dad said during one of his messages. He was talking about himself and the different ways he had substituted people and things for God during his lifetime. For him it was a bunch of little things, and nothing bad. The greatest example was actually ministry. That got worse after my mom died, but it was also what made him realize he was doing that."

"Was that true for you too? Was sports your way of dealing with her loss?"

"Yes, but it was also my way of dealing with life in general. Searching for significance, the stress of being a teenager, the need to succeed—sports was my answer for all of that, not Jesus."

"So, you decided to come here where you knew you wouldn't have any of that?"

"That was part of it. I also wanted to be closer to my sister and be in a Christian environment—maybe meet a nice girl," he said, stepping closer and putting his hands on her waist as she finished the last of her arm stretches.

She smiled. "But none of that is a substitute for God?"

"No. It's part of the way God wants to bless me and those around me, but my relationship with God is what I keep at the forefront every day, no matter what I'm doing or not doing."

Emma wasn't certain that was true for her, or how she could make it more that way. She was taking the required Bible classes, and she went to church every Sunday, and she read her Bible a few times a week, and she attended Chapel like she was supposed to, and she helped out with the midweek children's program every Wednesday evening, and she prayed every night before she went to sleep; but she suddenly felt like maybe she was missing something.

Tate kissed her sweetly several times, and she enjoyed his touch immensely. She had enjoyed spending the morning with him, and when he suggested they part for now to take showers and get a little studying done but then meet up again for lunch and spend the afternoon together, she didn't argue.

On the way up to her room, she thought more about what he said, and she whispered a prayer to God. "Am I doing that, Jesus? Am I using people and things as a substitute for you? Do I really know you like I think I do?"

***

It was a beautiful day at the beach, and Amber soaked up the familiar sounds, sights, and smells of the Oregon Coast like a distant friend she hadn't seen for awhile. The beaches of northern California had their fine points too, but it wasn't the same as being home.

Sitting on the large blanket she and Seth had brought to share, Amber enjoyed watching the various people walking along the shore, tossing Frisbees to one another, flying kites, and splashing in the cool water. She felt content to relax with Seth while Josiah and Rachael were on a romantic walk together, but watching others filled her thoughts with memories of times she had been with family and friends doing similar things.

Seth was lying beside her, doing his reading. She knew she should probably get one of the books out she had brought along, but she didn't feel like it. Being away from school today felt nice, and she wanted to think about Josiah and Rachael and how sweet they were together, about her own relationship with Seth, getting married in two months, and about the enjoyable times she had with her family last week.

She was lost in thought when Seth sat up and pulled her toward him. He asked if she was all right, and she answered honestly.

"I'm fine. I'm really glad we had an excuse to come here today. I know we had time away from school last week, but it was a little stressful. This is nice."

"And how are you doing with the decision we made about camp? One week later—do you still feel the same way?"

"Yes. Do you?"

"Yes, but if that changes for you, I want you to tell me, okay?"

"Okay, but I don't think it will. I have peace about it, and that's what I need."

# Chapter Twenty-Two

"Where have you been all day?"

Emma glanced at her roommate and answered the question casually.  Tiffany had still been in bed when she left to meet Tate for lunch.

"With Tate."

"Is that the same guy you went out with last night?"

"Yes."

"Where is he now?"

"He has to work tonight."

"Where does he work?"

Emma answered her question along with another string Tiffany fired at her for the next five minutes. She was surprised at her roommate's interest.  Tiffany had never been too interested in anything about her before, but she was fine with sharing about Tate—until Tiffany asked a question that was too personal, in her opinion.

"Has he kissed you?"

"Yes," she said without adding any details, but Tiffany wanted them.

"How was it?"

"What do you mean?" she asked, going to her desk and taking her *Calculus* book from the shelf.  She wasn't used to having her Saturday afternoon so tied-up, and she had a lot to study tonight.

"Is he a good kisser? Did he do more than that? Did you like it?"

Emma didn't feel like answering that. She might share details with her best friend, someone like Christy back home, but Tiffany didn't fit that category, and her aversion to the question only made Tiffany more curious and jump to the wrong conclusion.

"He did?" she asked, appearing both surprised and impressed she would let a guy do more than kiss her. "How far did it go? Were you in his room all afternoon?"

Emma knew she had to answer now or Tiffany would have the totally wrong idea about Tate and their relationship. They hadn't been in his room or anywhere something could have happened, and he hadn't even kissed her much, just some brief ones throughout the afternoon and a slightly longer one when she told him good-bye beside his car.

"He only kisses me," she said. "And yes, he's good at it, and I like it."

"So, why didn't you just say so?"

"I'm not used to sharing stuff like that."

"Is he your first boyfriend?"

"Yes."

"Okay, Emma. Put that book away and come here. I can't let you go into this being totally naive. I can tell you everything you need to know about handling your first boyfriend. I didn't do so well with mine, but I've learned a lot since then."

Emma wouldn't mind advice about having a boyfriend for the first time, but she knew she wasn't going to get good advice from Tiffany.  "Thanks, but I need to study.  I think I'll be all right."

"I would have said the same thing my first time, but trust me, you need to hear this."

Emma didn't respond, but Tiffany went ahead and started talking.  Before coming here, Emma never would have imagined a girl saying the things she told her on a Christian college campus, but knowing Tiffany and her other roommates like she did, it didn't surprise her too much.  And Emma wasn't sure what to believe and what to dismiss as totally ridiculous.

A couple of times she said, "Tate isn't like that," but Tiffany would say, "Don't be so naive, Emma, all guys are like that," or something similar, so she stopped responding.  After about twenty minutes, Abby returned to the room, came back to say hello when she heard Tiffany's voice, and then Abby joined the discussion, pretty much confirming whatever Tiffany said.

It made her angry.  It made her feel stupid and wondering how much of what they were saying might be true.  It made her afraid of what she was getting herself into and yet longing to see Tate again.  She wished he was here on campus so she could go knock on his door and ask if they could talk, but she didn't think she could repeat to him what her roommates were saying.

After ten minutes of Abby being there too, she got up from her desk where she had been pretending to study and listening to them at the same time, suddenly remembering she hadn't had dinner yet.  She couldn't concentrate on her math, but she didn't want Tiffany and Abby to know that.  Grabbing her meal card from her desk, she said she was going to the dining hall, hoping they wouldn't decide to come with her.

They said they had already eaten, and she didn't comment on anything they said one way or the other. Tiffany offered to "talk more later", however.

"Okay, bye," Emma said, leaving the room and not looking back. She took the stairs and stepped into the cool evening air. Walking toward the dining hall, she had every intention of going inside until she was almost there, but then she realized she didn't want to see anyone right now or have to sit alone in the busy cafeteria like she often did.

Bypassing the entrance, she continued walking down the path toward the main campus area. Stopping at the amphitheater outside the library, she sat down on the concrete steps overlooking the empty courtyard below. She felt numb and wished she had thought to bring her books so she could go to the library and study for the rest of the evening.

Turning her thoughts from Tiffany and Abby's words, she recalled the afternoon she had spent with Tate. It had been good, just like all of the other times they'd spent together. He was really funny without being crude or saying bad things about other people. He made fun of himself more than anything, and he had a unique view of the world that often made her smile. He took life seriously, but not too seriously.

The only thing that made her a little uncomfortable was what he said this morning about substituting other things for God. She again wondered if she was doing that. He hadn't asked her about it then or this afternoon, but she imagined him asking her and how she would respond. It wouldn't bother her if he asked—like she didn't think he had a right to be asking her something so personal—but it bothered her she didn't know what she would say.

Opening her heart to God, she prayed silently, asking God to show her if she was doing that. And then her prayers turned to other things.

*Am I too naive, God? Is Tate as nice as he seems, or is he just putting on the charm right now, and in a few weeks I'll see that everything Tiffany and Abby were saying is true? I don't like being alone. I want to have a boyfriend, but am I ready for it?*

Her insecurities about herself and the fear of the unknown brought tears to her eyes and a lost and confused feeling to her heart. She wished she had someone she could talk to, but there was no one, and that made her feel depressed. She remembered Danae's offer to go to the movies tonight, but she hadn't talked to her since yesterday afternoon, and she supposed Danae and Evangeline had already gone. She didn't know which room they were in or have their phone number here, so she dismissed that possibility as well.

She felt cold and hungry. She went to The Oasis and ordered a sandwich but left as if she had someplace to be. Eating on the way back, she decided to take a chance her roommates had gone somewhere, but she intended to get her books and leave immediately either way. They weren't there, but she didn't want to take the chance of them returning anytime soon, so she went down to the lounge and spent the rest of the evening studying there.

She felt powerless. Powerless to end things with Tate—she didn't want that and didn't think she could lie to Tate and tell him she did, but she also felt powerless to have this relationship be everything she hoped it would be. Studying took her mind off of it, but when she returned to the empty room at ten o'clock, got into bed, and tried to go to sleep before Tiffany returned, all the fears and insecurities mixed with her hopes and dreams were still there.

In the past when she felt lonely, she had been able to shake it off and dream about someday with someone, but she couldn't shake this off and dream a different reality. She was in the middle of this and had no idea what to do. In the morning she was going to be seeing Tate, and as far as she knew, spending most of the day with him. That's what he had suggested to her before they parted this afternoon, but now she didn't know if she could make it through the morning, let alone an entire day with him.

Wishing it wasn't dark out so she could go for a run, she knew that would be a good escape from her insecurities. She could get dressed and go use one of the treadmills, but Tate's words about letting sports be his savior instead of Jesus came to mind, and she knew this was a perfect opportunity to reach for a different way of rescue. And she heard Jesus calling her to do that.

*Give it to Me, Emma.*

She didn't know how.

*Let Me carry you in this.*

Her thoughts returned to something that had happened last night. She had been feeling insecure about seeing Tate after what Abby said to her. It had been a really sick feeling of suddenly not wanting to go on the date and be a hermit in her room like every other Friday night this semester.

*Oh, Jesus help,* her spirit had groaned. Tate had arrived a few seconds after that, so she hadn't had time to think about it much, but she remembered it now.

She cried out to Him again, more consciously this time. *Help me, Jesus. I don't know what to do.*

A bit of peace entered her heart, followed by a calming thought. *I can't do anything about it right now. I'll have to wait and see what happens tomorrow.*

She gave it to God then, and the feeling of powerlessness left her. She didn't have power over much, but she had the power to give all of her worries and fears and uncertainties to Him. She had always thought of Jesus as being her Savior, but He really became her Savior in this now.

The phone rang two minutes later. She answered it, expecting it to be for Tiffany, who was still out, but it was Tate, and she smiled.

"Did I wake you?" he asked.

"No."

"I tried to call on my break earlier, but you weren't there, and I wanted to make sure you were okay."

"I'm fine," she said. "I was downstairs in the lounge."

"How has your evening been?"

She hesitated to answer. "Okay," she said.

"Are you sure about that?"

Again she hesitated, but she was more honest this time. "No. I'll tell you about it tomorrow. It's too much to get into right now. It's just my roommates."

Recalling the amount of time she had already spent talking about them earlier today, she lost her peace momentarily. Tate was probably sick of hearing about it, but now she had committed to telling him more tomorrow.

*What am I going to say? I can't talk to him about that stuff.*

*Don't take it back, Emma. Give it to Me.*

It was too much for her to carry. *Okay, Jesus. I'm not going there. I'll let You take care of tomorrow.*

"You could move in with me," Tate teased her. "You can have my bed, and I'll sleep on the floor."

She played along. "Okay. I'll be there when you get back."

"I'm sorry I couldn't have spent the evening with you and kept you away from whatever happened," he said seriously. "I know this is easier to say than do, but try not to worry about it, okay? Get some good sleep and remember that I think you're a very special person, Emma. Don't go by what Abby and Tiffany say."

"Okay. I'm sorry if I talked about it too much today."

"I want you to talk to me. About whatever. I'm sure that's a really tough thing, and if you need to talk about it, then do. I want to be your friend, Emma, not just the guy you're dating."

She wanted to believe that.

"Have I been doing that so far?" he asked.

"Yes."

"Do you know that's what gave me the courage to ask you out? After running with you twice, I already felt like we were friends. I always expected to be tongue-tied when I got up the nerve to ask you, but then it was easy."

Emma knew the same had been true for her. She'd worried her first date would be uncomfortable and awkward, but it hadn't been. Being with Tate was an easy thing. Her roommates made her feel socially inept and confused, not Tate.

He made her feel alive and safe and valuable.

They talked for the fifteen minutes he had to give her, mostly about his night rather than hers, and then he restated their plans to go to church together in the morning and spend time after that with each other also.

"I'm really looking forward to it, Emma. I hope this doesn't sound too needy, but you're kind of the best friend I've got right now."

"I know the feeling," she said softly. "I missed you tonight."

"I missed you too. I'll see you tomorrow."

"Okay. Bye."

"Good night, Emma. Sweet dreams."

***

Tate clicked off his phone and said a brief prayer for Emma. She was so special. He didn't want to think of her having another difficult evening with her roommates. Some of the things she had told him today—how could anyone treat someone as sweet as Emma that way? It made him angry, and he wasn't a person who angered easily.

Going inside, he went back to work and made four more deliveries before the busy night was over, but he was thinking about her the entire time. He knew he was already falling in love with her, and he hadn't expected that. He hadn't expected to feel this way. He couldn't even describe how he felt. Last night had been great. Today had been amazing. He could have spent another six hours with her so easily. And since he didn't have to work tomorrow, he had every intention of spending the entire day with her. He couldn't imagine going to his room to study all by himself if she was just across the parking lot in her own dorm room doing the same thing.

Like they'd probably been doing every Saturday and Sunday all year.

*God, I was such an idiot! How did you let me go so long without her? I could have been there for her all these months while her roommates have been criticizing her qualities instead of praising them. I know, I know, I wouldn't even be with her now if you hadn't stepped in and intervened, but why did you wait so long?*

He didn't get an answer on that. Not that he was blaming God for his own shortcomings, but how could Jesus lead someone to go to school here and then have that kind of situation waiting for her? He'd had exactly the opposite thing happen to him. His experience here had been great—couldn't have been better, unless he would have let Emma know how he felt much sooner than now.

When he got back to the campus he'd never had such a feeling of wanting to get in bed and go to sleep, just so tomorrow would come. Fortunately he felt tired and fell asleep easily. He woke up at nine when his alarm went off, took a shower and got dressed, and went to the dining hall for a quick breakfast before going to meet Emma. They had to be at church at ten-thirty, and he arrived at her door at the time he said he would.

One of her roommates answered the door. He hadn't met any of them yet. She said a cheerful good-morning to him and introduced herself.

"Hi, I'm Abby. You must be Tate."

"I am," he said, noticing the very strong scent of different perfumes coming from the room. "Is Emma here?"

He saw her coming toward the door then, and his eyes went to her. She looked stunningly beautiful and was a sharp contrast to Abby and another girl who popped over to say hello. They were both wearing tight clothing and low-cut tops, and had on a generous amount of makeup and perfume.

Emma was wearing her hair loose and long, and she had on a feminine looking, almost old-fashioned white blouse and a pale blue skirt with delicate flowers on it. She looked like something from another time, and he couldn't resist saying so right in front of the others.

"You look beautiful," he said, giving her a kiss on the cheek.

"Thank you," she whispered.

He didn't have to ask to know something was very wrong and she was anxious to get out of there. He stepped to the side to let her go before him, and he followed her.

Abby said a saccharin good-bye to both of them and closed the door. Emma had stepped ahead of him toward the stairway, and as he took the steps to catch up with her, he could hear an outburst of laughter coming from behind the closed door.

## Chapter Twenty-Three

Emma had never felt such a mixture of anger and pain in her life. She had never known the feeling of actually hating someone until now. Even with as difficult as this year had been and the other things Abby had said to her, she had always been able to let it go and not let anything get to her too much.

But the last twenty minutes had been the most humiliating moments of her life, and she was so tired of it. She wanted to go home. She wanted to go back to high school where she had learned at home, had nice friends, spent a lot of time with her family, and was never criticized for being who she was.

The only thing keeping her from waiting until her roommates left for church and going back and packing her things was Tate. Not because he was here and she couldn't imagine telling him what the last twenty minutes had been like, but because she liked him. She really did, and unless he was completely lying to her, she knew he liked her too. She couldn't run from that. She had been waiting too long to run from it.

She planned to hide her pain and go on with the morning. Maybe this afternoon when she told him the things Tiffany and Abby had said yesterday, she would mention the events of this morning too, but she didn't know if she could tell him, or what difference it would make anyway.

But somehow Tate knew something was up, and once they were in the stairwell, he stopped her with a gentle hug.  His touch was so comforting and so needed that it brought instant tears, and the deep pain she had buried and hid from her roommates surfaced fully. Everything inside of her was saying, 'Stop, Emma. Those girls don't deserve to be cried over. Just forget about it.  And don't cry all over Tate; you're going to drive him away.'  But she couldn't stop.

She couldn't because they hadn't said anything untruthful.  They had managed to dredge up and expose all of her physical and emotional insecurities about herself in ten minutes flat.  And they were right. She wasn't like them.  She didn't know how to dress. She had no figure.  She was a simple, hometown girl who had been sheltered from the real world.  She hadn't been kissed or had a boyfriend until she was nineteen, and she had no guarantees that Tate was going to really love her or stick around for more than a week or two.

But he was here now, and she clung to him.  She couldn't help it, and maybe she was clueless about guys, but she couldn't imagine him letting her go without an explanation.  Maybe a lot of guys were indifferent to the needs of their girlfriends, like Tiffany had said, but so far Tate had not struck her that way, and right now he was being exactly what she needed without saying a word.

He didn't speak until she had calmed down, and then his voice was so caring and gentle she knew she had to tell him everything now, not wait until this afternoon. He wouldn't let her wait, she felt certain, even if it meant them being late for church or not going at all.

"What happened, Emma?"

She stepped back and wiped her wet cheeks. "Can we go outside?"

He took her hand and led her down the stairs. She put on her sweater once they were in the cool springtime air, but Tate retook her hand and waited for her to speak. She didn't know where to start, and she told him so.

"What happened this morning?" he asked. "Can you start with that, or is this related to what happened yesterday?"

"Sort of, but not really. Yesterday was about you. Today was about me."

"What about you?"

She decided to tell him everything. If he was going to reject her for who she was, she may as well let him do it now. "The way I'm dressed. The church I'm going to. The fact I have no friends, and it's my own fault, and how I'd better change really fast if I have any hope of hanging on to you."

He laughed. Taking her into his arms, he was adamant about his opinion on that. "Don't you dare change a thing, Emma. I like you just the way you are."

"Why?" she had to ask. "I'm not like them."

"That's why," he said gently. "I don't want you to be like them. Do you?"

"No, but they make me feel like I should."

"They're wrong, Emma. You know what I saw up there?"

"What?"

He stepped back and looked her over from head to toe. "A vision of true beauty coming to meet me. You're stunning. Like something from another time. Like something I don't see every day, even around here."

She told him a secret. "This is my favorite outfit. I wore it because we're going to church together for the first time, but then they made fun of it and called me Laura Ingalls Wilder."

Tate ran his fingers into her free-flowing hair. "I seem to remember Laura getting Almanzo without ever having to become like Nellie Oleson."

"You know those stories?"

"My mom used to read them to me and my younger sister."

She smiled. "I think you're from another time too."

"Are you calling me old-fashioned?"

"I don't know, are you?"

"I have morals. Is that what you mean?"

"Yes."

"Is that what yesterday was about?"

"Yes."

"Let me guess. They called you a naive virgin who needs to do certain things for me so you don't lose me to someone else who will?"

"Yeah, something like that."

"And you believed them?"

"No, but it made me wonder how much I'm ready for this and if I am being naive to think someone as sweet as you would actually be interested in me."

"You're beautiful, Emma," he said, seeing right through her insecurity about that. "I like you for your personality and the ton of inner beauty that I see, but I think you're physically beautiful too. I was attracted to that before I ever knew you."

He kissed her then, and she felt beautiful. She felt safe, and she felt cared for. Maybe too much. His tender lips and possessive touch on the small of her back as he pulled her gently against him made her feel things. She felt desperate to be loved, and she felt certain Tate could meet that need.

Tate ended the moment with a confession and a surprising decision. The confession seemed to have taken him by surprise, but the decision was one he had made a long time ago.

"Girls like Abby make me have desires for them by how they look and the way they dress; but you make me have desires for you, Emma, by what's in your heart. And I think that's twice as dangerous for me. I have morals that I believe in very strongly. I believe waiting for marriage is the right thing and the best thing, but that doesn't mean I'm not going to have any desire for you until then, and I'm not going to try and convince myself or you otherwise."

"I have them too," she admitted. "What are we supposed to do about that? I am very naive about all of this. How much is too much? How far is too far?"

"This is my limit, Emma. Just kissing. Do you want to do something besides go to church this morning?"

"What?"

"Go into town with me. I need to get my ear pierced."

Tate wasn't what Emma would consider to be "expressive" through the clothing he wore or his hairstyle or by having things like tattoos or body piercings. She didn't think there was anything wrong with guys who were that way in one form or another, but Tate wasn't. He was conservative and ordinary, so his suggestion seemed funny to her, and she laughed.

He laughed too, seeming to understand why she would be doing so, and yet he was serious, and he explained himself. "I know that doesn't sound like anything you would expect me to say, but my youth pastor back home had his ear pierced, and it's for a specific reason. I've thought about doing it for a long time but haven't had a need to until now."

"What reason?"

"As a purity symbol. Like the purity rings and bracelets some people wear, only mine would be in my ear. It wouldn't just be a piece of jewelry I wear, but something physical, like a sacred vow before God to follow Him in this area of my life, and something I would see every day when I look at myself in the mirror. Would that be all right with you?"

"Yes," she said. "I haven't heard of that before. Would it be something just between you and me, or something you would tell others about?"

"I would tell anyone who asks, but it's not about me making a statement to everyone. It would mainly be between me and God, and me and you."

"Can I ask you something?"

"Yes."

"Yesterday when Tiffany was telling me about her different boyfriends and all that, she kept saying things that sounded like a bunch of games to me. Like she says or does something to make a guy think a certain way about her, and how the guys do the same thing, and all this stuff about learning to "read" guys and "play them right". Can we not do all that? Can this just be real? You being you, and me being me, and if you're wondering something you just ask me, and I'll tell you the truth, and vice-versa?"

"I can't be anything but real with you, Emma. And I want you to feel like you can be the same way with me. If you ever get to a point where you're having to pretend or fake feelings for me or whatever, don't. I don't want this just to be with someone. I want this to be with you, and I hope you feel the same way, but if you don't, then tell me so, okay?"

"Okay."

"And so you know, I can't imagine losing the feelings I have for you anytime soon. Maybe we'll go our separate ways down the road, but I don't want it to be about not playing the game right. This isn't a game to me, Emma. This is my life, and I want you to be a part of it. Possibly a huge, life-changing part of it."

Emma had a thought and she continued thinking about it as they walked to Tate's car and drove into town. Going into this year, she had prayed for two specific things. She had asked God for a good roommate and for one specific close friend also. At the beginning of the year, she thought He had answered her. She had two difficult roommates, but she also had one good one, and Caitrin had become a good friend.

But this semester she felt like God had totally let her down. He had taken her only friend away and replaced her with a roommate who was as bad as the other two. But now suddenly, when she least expected it, she had Tate in her life who wasn't just a roommate or a good friend, but maybe someone much more special. Someone she might not need right now or see how special he was if she wasn't in the situation she was.

Tate decided to get his hair cut first at a walk-in place, and then they went to get his ear pierced, and in no time at all she was looking at the new version of Tate Morgan. Her boyfriend with a small diamond stud earring in one ear. What would her parents say? She hadn't told them about him yet, and she knew her usual Sunday night call home wouldn't be so usual tonight.

They went to the pizza place to have lunch, and it didn't take long for anyone there who knew him to see the change, both with the earring and with a girl at his side. Tate didn't say anything specific to anyone about the reason behind the earring until one of his friends came to sit with them while they were eating.

He introduced her to Blake, whom she learned was his roommate and worked here also, and to Blake's girlfriend, Colleen. They seemed nice and commented on the earring, but Blake already knew why he had it.

"He's been telling me he would do this when the right girl came along, but I honestly can't believe it. This guy didn't want to ride in the car with you two weeks ago, and now look at him—he's piercing his body for you."

Emma smiled, and Tate corrected his friend. "I wanted to ride in the car with her, I just didn't think I could be the guy she would need me to be."

"Yeah, I can see you're really letting her down there, bro."

"Hey, Colleen," Tate said then, changing the subject. "Have I heard you say there are only three girls in your suite?"

"Yep. It's me and me on one side, and two awesome roommates on the other. Charmaine and Kim. Why?"

Tate smiled at her, and Emma's heart started pounding, knowing exactly what he was going to say. "Emma's having a little trouble with her roommates. Would you mind sharing your side for the rest of the semester?"

Colleen looked at her. "You're Emma!" she said. "The Emma who's going to be rooming with Lauren next year?"

"Yes," she said. "How did you know that?"

"Lauren is Blake's sister, and my best friend's roommate."

"Would that be okay? If I moved in with you now?"

"Absolutely," Colleen said. "We don't have anything to do this afternoon. Do you want to go back after lunch? We can have you moved in by dinner."

"Yes, thank you," she said. "That would be great."

Colleen smiled at her, and Emma smiled in return, but she had tears in her eyes when she looked at Tate who had thought to ask initially on her behalf. He winked at her and reached for her hand, lifting it to his lips and kissing her fingers gently.

By that evening she was completely moved into her new place. They had dinner with Blake and Colleen and her other new roommates, who both seemed nice also. They helped her move, and the transition up to the fourth floor had gone quickly and smoothly. Tiffany came to the room while she was packing her stuff, and she seemed more disappointed than Emma expected her to be, but Tiffany's somewhat heartfelt plea for her to stay didn't convince her. She asked if this was about what Abby had said this morning.

"Yes, and some other things," she replied. "But it's fine. I'm moving in with Tate's roommate's girlfriend."

"Oh, that's nice. Hopefully you won't break up with him, or that will be awkward."

"I don't think that's going to happen," she said as confidently as possible, but feeling relieved when she heard a knock at the door. Tate had taken her suitcases upstairs while she was finishing up with her desk, but he was back, and he didn't leave her alone with Tiffany after that.

Blake and Colleen went into town after dinner to go to an evening service at church they often attended. Tate asked if she wanted to go since they had missed church this morning, but she felt tired and wanted to relax here in her new room.

"Can I stay too, or are you kicking me out?" he asked.

"You can stay, unless you don't think you should."

"I'll be all right as long as I don't start kissing you."

She was already sitting on her bed, leaning against the headboard, and he was on the floor, leaning against Colleen's bed where he had been sitting beside Blake. He remained in place, and they talked, but she knew she needed to call her parents. They usually called her on Sunday evenings, but she wasn't in that room anymore. Tate decided to go call his own family and said he would come back later and they could study downstairs for the rest of the evening.

"For some reason, I haven't gotten much of that done this weekend," he said, giving her a brief kiss before stepping away and heading for the door.

"Me neither," she said. "I'm usually bored by Sunday night."

She hadn't shared with her parents about her roommate troubles, so her mom was surprised she had moved in with someone else, but she understood and asked if she would mind a visit from them next weekend. They had been thinking about it, but hearing about her struggles seemed to give her mom more incentive to make it happen.

"If you do, it's fine," she said. "But I think I'll be all right now. If you can't come, don't worry about it."

Her mom talked of other things going on at home and church and around the neighborhood, and then she had something to ask her to pray about. Her younger brother was seriously thinking about starting college in the fall rather than waiting until he was eighteen. Academically her parents knew he was ready for it, but her mom wasn't so sure about him being ready to be away from home.

"I'm hoping he decides to go to community college for the first year, but I'm trying to leave it in God's hands and let him make his own decision."

"I'm sure he'll be all right, Mama. Even if he has to go through some tough things like I have, I'm the better for it, and God is taking care of me. He helped me find a new roommate, and He's also brought me a special friend I think I appreciate more than I might have otherwise."

"Oh? Your new roommate?"

"No. I mean, I think Colleen will be a good friend, but I'm talking about someone else."

"Who?"

"His name is Tate. He's Danae's younger brother, the girl I rode home with for Spring Break and then back again."

"Is he more than a friend?"

"Yes. We spent some time together this week, and we went out on Friday, and yesterday, and today."

Her mom was silent for a moment.

"I'm nineteen, Mama. You knew this day would come."

"I know, baby. I'm happy for you. Just a little nervous."

"He's very nice. You and Daddy will like him."

"I think we will come next weekend so we can meet him. Would that be all right?"

"Yes."

"Okay, love you, baby. Write and tell me about him if you have the chance, okay?"

"Okay. I will. I love you too, Mama."

# Chapter Twenty-Four

"I hope you don't mind me suddenly invading your space like this," Emma said. She and Colleen were getting ready for bed, and Emma could imagine how having all of this room for herself must have been nice.

"I don't mind," Colleen said. "I always shared with my younger sister, so I'm used to it, and I'm sure you're much neater than she ever was."

"I always shared until a couple of years ago when we put a small addition on the house. How old is your sister?"

"Two years younger in age, but three in school because she had to repeat first grade. She's a sophomore this year. How old is your sister?"

"I have two. Hannah is fifteen, and Sara is thirteen."

"And all three of you shared?"

"Yes."

"Then you are definitely entitled to share my space," Colleen laughed. "Are you the oldest, or do you have brothers too?"

"I have two brothers, but they're both younger. Seventeen and eleven."

"Was it hard for you to leave home, or were you like, 'Get me out of here!'?"

"Both," she said, pulling back her pink comforter and blankets and getting into bed. "I miss them, but it's nice to be away."

"I know what you mean," Colleen said. "I have two older brothers, and I remember the house feeling empty after they were away at school, but now I can see why they never seemed too sad about leaving."

Colleen had told her earlier she usually went to bed around ten, the same time she did, and that's the time it was now, but they kept talking for another half-hour. She didn't feel totally comfortable with Colleen yet, because she had just met her this afternoon, but she felt much better than she ever had with Tiffany.

In the morning she met Tate for breakfast. She was on her way to class after going for a run and getting ready for the day, but he had just rolled out of bed twenty minutes ago and would be going back to his room to shower and get ready for his first class that wasn't for another hour. Last night after they had spent time studying together in the lounge, Tate had made up a little schedule of the times they would be able to see each other every day.

He said he would be happy to run with her every morning if she wanted him to, but she said solo running-time was when she usually did her best thinking, and he was honest about not wanting to run every morning. He liked his sleep and usually stayed up later than she did.

He asked how her first night in her new room had gone, and she knew the look on her face probably said it all, but she shared something she had realized last night when she was talking to Colleen.

"Living with Tiffany and Abby made me become very careful about what I say and do. I could feel myself holding back with Colleen and having a fear that at any moment she was going to make fun of something I said, or say something I didn't know how to respond to. Girls talk about how stupid and rude guys can be, but girls can be ten times worse."

"You need to get going," Tate said, reminding her of the time. He was right, but she felt like she wanted more time with him. It had been twenty-five minutes, but it seemed like ten. "Come on, I'll walk you partway."

They took their trays to the dish-room window and left the cafeteria. He walked her down the path toward the academic buildings in the center of campus and commented on what she said about being guarded with Colleen.

"Give yourself time to heal. You've been hurt, Emma. If you had just gotten out of an abusive relationship with a guy, no one would be expecting you to start dating again the next day. Just be yourself, and I'm sure Colleen will see what I see. A very sweet person she likes being around whether you're talking or just sharing the same space in silence."

She turned toward him when they reached the street, and he gave her a light kiss. She hugged him and enjoyed the security of his embrace. "Thank you for getting me out of there."

As the week went by, that feeling of thankfulness only increased, as did her awareness of how much she had been emotionally abused by her former roommates. Most of it had happened a little at a time, but as she began to experience the freedom to be herself again, she could see how much control Tiffany and Abby had over her. Elissa had always been more neutral toward her, not saying anything to her directly as the others had, but not defending her either.

But now she had Colleen, who wasn't anything like that, and she had Tate, who was constantly telling her how special she was and how much he enjoyed being with her. She tried to open up to both of them as much as possible, but she didn't fake or try to force anything. On Thursday she saw Abby and Elissa on the way back to the dorm after her last class, and an instant feeling of panic came over her. They stopped to talk, saying they'd heard from Tiffany why she had moved, which was only partially true, but she didn't add anything to what they said.

"Oh, I saw Tate yesterday," Abby commented. "He was at the bookstore. I told him to say hi to you for me. Did he?"

"No," she said. "He must have forgot."

"Yeah, guys are really bad about stuff like that. Come by and visit sometime. Bye."

"Bye," she said, stepping away and continuing on to Priscilla Hall. The minute she had with them made her feel edgy and guarded, and she wondered why Tate hadn't mentioned seeing Abby yesterday. In her heart she knew he didn't see the need to mention it, but in her head she began to make other speculations about Tate secretly being attracted to Abby and wondering how long of a conversation they'd had.

She didn't say anything to Tate about it when she saw him at dinner.  They went for a walk afterwards, and that was nice.  She told him her parents were coming on Saturday and she planned to spend the whole day with them.  They were actually driving up tomorrow night and would be staying at a motel in town and then coming up after breakfast on Saturday.

"They want to meet you, and I said they could.  I hope that's all right."

"Sure," he said easily.  "Do you want me to only meet them or spend the day with you?"

"Either way.  Whatever you want."

"Whatever I want?  That's a no-brainer," he laughed.  "But I don't want to invade your time with them if you'd rather not have me there."

"I want them to get to know you, not just meet you."

"Are you asking me out?"

She laughed.  "Yes.  Will you go on a double-date with me and my parents on Saturday?"

He stopped walking and turned to face her.  She was already attached to his side, and their lips met easily.  "I thought you'd never ask," he teased.  "I've been waiting all year for you to get around to noticing me."

They spent the rest of the evening together in the lounge, and she made a pleasant discovery when he went to get them something to drink from the vending machine.  They had been tucked away in the corner by the windows, and she hadn't thought about Seth and Amber being here tonight until she heard someone talking to Tate, and she turned around to see them in their usual place near the fire.

Apparently Tate knew them, and she found out why a minute later when he came back and said he had people for her to meet. She went with him to the couches huddled around the fireplace, and he introduced her, saying he and Seth both worked at Tony's.

"Hi," she said, feeling shy because she had been secretly watching and admiring them for a long time. They both greeted her nicely in return, and she had a comfortable feeling once they chatted a bit.

"You're Colleen's new roommate, right?" Seth said.

"Yes."

"Blake was telling us about it when we saw him at lunch yesterday."

"Oh, you're Emma!" Amber chimed in. "Yes, Colleen has mentioned you every time I've seen her this week. She is thrilled to finally have a roommate, and she says you're really sweet."

"Like Mandy," Seth added.

"That's right, she did say that," Amber confirmed.

"Who's Mandy?" Tate asked.

"My cousin," Amber said. "She's not here. She lives in Oregon."

"The one who's marrying my friend Matt," Seth said to Tate as if Tate would know who that was.

"Oh, okay," Tate replied with understanding and then turned to her, pulled her closer, and added, "Yeah, I think I found a pretty special one. Even her name is beautiful and sweet, don't you think? Emma. Just like that."

Emma felt touched by Tate's words and a little embarrassed. Glancing at Amber, she half-expected to see her rolling her eyes at the mushy young-love comment, but Amber winked at her instead and leaned into Seth as if she was quite familiar with hearing sweet comments from her man.

"Colleen told me you're getting married," she said. "Congratulations."

"Thank you," Amber said. "I'm pretty excited about it. Less than two months to go. Right, sweet thing?"

Seth gave her a kiss on the forehead. "Fifty-eight days," he said.

They let them get back to their studying. Emma felt happier than she had all evening, and she had almost forgotten about seeing Abby today until Tate asked her on the way upstairs if she was all right.

"You seemed a little quiet tonight," he said. "Anything you want to tell me or talk about?"

The elevator door opened, and she said it as they stepped into the fourth floor hallway. "I saw Abby today. This afternoon."

"Did you talk to her?"

"For a minute."

"I saw her at the bookstore yesterday," he said, instantly dispelling her crazy thoughts about him trying to hide something from her, but she asked him anyway.

"Why didn't you tell me you saw her?"

"Somehow, 'I saw Abby today, and she said to tell you hi,' didn't strike me as something you would be excited to hear."

He had a point, and she appreciated his effort to guard her from any unnecessary comments about Abby. It was Abby who made it sound like they'd had more than a casual run-in.

"Why didn't *you* tell me you saw her?" he fired back gently.

She shrugged.

He pulled her into his arms when they reached the door, and she let the tears fall. She didn't know why she felt the need to cry, but she did. Tate removed the ponytail holder from her hair and stroked her loose hair gently for several minutes until she stopped crying and became completely silent.

"You can tell me anything at any time, Emma. I want to know what you're feeling so I can help."

"You help by being you, Tate. I didn't tell you anything was wrong, but you made me feel better anyway."

"Would kisses help too, or have you had enough loving-on for one day?"

"Kisses would help," she replied.

His tenderness and caring touch took her back to Sunday when he admitted his strong desire for her. This time he didn't end it like he wasn't sure what to do, he simply confessed his thoughts, reaching for her hand and lifting it to touch his ear as he spoke.

"I'm committed to this, but that doesn't mean it's going to be easy for me. I want to comfort you, Emma. I want to show you how beautiful and amazing I think you are."

"You did," she replied, feeling completely restored from her encounter with Abby today. It was going to take a lot of love to cover the deep hurt in her heart, but Tate was giving it to her. "You don't have to do anything else, Tate. This is enough. And not just the kisses, but the time you're giving me and the words you say."

"Then I won't stop," he said.

Going into her room, she was alone for a little while because Colleen worked on Thursday evenings and her other two roommates were out somewhere too. She expected to fall asleep, but she couldn't for some reason. One thing about the evening that stood out to her was meeting Amber and Seth and especially the way Tate had talked about her right in front of them.

Usually if anyone said something about her to someone else, it was, 'She's smart, she runs, or she's quiet,' but he hadn't said any of those things. He said, 'She's special, beautiful, and sweet—the one I found for me.' It was a side of herself that had been there all along, but Tate saw it as being for him, not just being there.

"Sorry, did I wake you?" Colleen asked. She had come in a minute ago and was getting ready for bed.

"No," she said, getting out of bed to go use the bathroom. "I can't sleep."

When she returned, Colleen was in bed but she asked if anything was wrong or if she wanted to talk. Emma didn't feel like anything was wrong, but she wanted to share about her day, so she did, telling Colleen about seeing Abby this afternoon and how Tate had known something was wrong even though she didn't say so. Colleen could relate, saying Blake was the same way, and she appreciated that about him very much.

"The guy I dated before Blake was terrible at knowing when something was bothering me, and even when I would tell him, he wasn't the best listener. At the time I thought all guys must be that way, but I've learned they're not. Sometimes I feel like Blake is more in tune with my needs than I am—or at least knows how to meet them better than I do."

"How do they do that? I don't feel like I can read Tate yet, but he's got me all figured out."

Colleen laughed. "I hear you, honey. That's been my world for the last eight months, even before me and Blake were dating. You want to hear my theory on that?"

"Sure."

"I haven't met a guy yet who is close to God, I mean really close to His Heart, who isn't also very aware of the needs of those around him."

An image of Seth and Amber came to her mind, and she told Colleen about meeting them tonight and how she had been admiring them for months. She didn't have to ask to know the answer, but she did anyway.

"Seth is that way, isn't he?"

"Oh, my God, yes. And Amber would be the first to tell you that. He's been that way for as long as I've known him, and everything about their relationship is real. What you see is what it is."

"I never prayed for any specific guy, but I prayed for a guy like that, and I'm almost positive God is giving me one."

"It sounds like He is," Colleen said. "And I know it's probably a little scary right now, but don't be afraid of it. Letting Blake take care of me is the easiest thing I've ever done."

## Chapter Twenty-Five

Tate felt nervous about meeting Emma's parents. Ever since she mentioned it on Thursday, he'd been running all the different scenarios in his mind of how things would go.  He didn't know them at all, so that left room for his imagination to go just about anywhere.  He knew her parents were Christians and had raised a smart and sweet daughter, but he also knew people sometimes had weird ideas about what it meant to follow God and could be very overprotective of their children.

Some were ultra conservative about everything and discouraged anything that seemed "worldly" to them, like modern dating, guys having earrings, and dancing.  He wondered what Emma's parents would think of him, and if after meeting him, they would discourage Emma from dating him.  That scared him because he knew Emma would have a difficult time going against their wishes, and he wouldn't want her to have to do that.

But when Saturday came and he met them outside of Priscilla Hall, he didn't get any kind of negative vibes coming from either Mr. or Mrs. Jones.  Emma's brothers and sisters hadn't come, so it was just the four of them.  They talked casually for a few minutes and then went to the car to ride together down the coast highway to the touristy town of Eureka. On the way, Tate answered a lot of questions about himself and his family, and he got the feeling having a dad who was a pastor gave him a little more credibility as being a good choice for their daughter, but otherwise he didn't feel like they were judging him in any way, just trying to get to know him.

They had lunch together in Eureka, did some window-shopping and wandering through the local attractions on the Eureka Boardwalk, and then went to the performing arts theater Downtown to catch an afternoon showing of a local theater group performing *Oliver Twist*. It was different than the way he would have spent time with his family visiting for the day, but it was nice, and he knew Emma was having a fun day.

The thing that spoiled the day for him wasn't anything he anticipated. He became aware of it late in the afternoon, but he couldn't say anything to Emma right then. Mrs. Jones said something about seeing him again this summer once school was out, and Emma made a comment about how great it was he lived so close to Monterey instead of meeting a guy at college she would have to be away from during the summer. He didn't have the time or the courage to tell Emma about his summer plans in that moment, but he knew he couldn't put it off for long without being dishonest and unfair to her.

By Sunday morning he felt more nervous about talking to Emma and telling her the vital information than he had about meeting her parents. No, nervous wasn't the right word. More like completely panicked and sick to his stomach. Everything had been going so great, giving him a strong feeling this was meant to be between them, but now that reality seemed to be in jeopardy, and he didn't like it. He wanted to give Emma a perfect relationship, but one week into it they were facing a major obstacle, and he was the one responsible.

He went up to her room to meet her, and they went to church together. He could see why Emma liked the smaller country church, but he had a difficult time concentrating and knew he wasn't being himself. He wavered back and forth about whether to tell her or to change his summer plans without her ever knowing the difference. He didn't have to go, but there was a part of him that wanted to, even if it meant being away from her for the summer. And he began to wonder if that was a bad sign.

Was he not as committed to being in a relationship as he thought? Had his six-month infatuation with Emma misled him during the time they had spent together? Did he really have feelings for her, or did he just *want* to have feelings for her?

On the way back to the campus for lunch, he could tell Emma knew something was wrong, but she didn't ask. *Oh, Jesus. I hate this. I don't want to deal with any problems. I just want our time together to be happy. I can't hurt her. You can't let me do that! Please help. I don't know what to do.*

Parking the car, he shut off the motor and asked Emma if she wanted to go have lunch now, or if she wanted to wait. He felt like he could use more time to pray, and he realized he could have been doing that for the past hour while they were at church, but he hadn't been. He'd only been worrying and trying to figure this out on his own.

"We can eat now," she said. "I usually do. It's more crowded later."

"Okay," he said and inwardly cried out a prayer from the Psalms he had relied on in the past.

*I call as my heart grows faint; lead me to the rock that is higher than I!*

"I have something I need to tell you first," he said, not getting out of the car.

"You didn't like the church?" she guessed.

"No, I did," he said, realizing now that confirmation while they were there would have been what she needed from him. "I'm sorry. I know I've been quiet this morning, but it's not that or anything about you. This is about me."

She looked scared, the same way she had for the initial twenty minutes of their first date. She hadn't looked at him with anything but trust since, and he knew she might not like what he had to say, but there were worse things: 'This isn't working for me and I want to break up.' He could see her thinking that, and he didn't want to prolong this any more than necessary.

"I want you to know before I say this I haven't been keeping anything from you intentionally, Emma. This has happened so fast between us I haven't had time to think, and it wasn't until yesterday when you were talking about me living close to Monterey that my summer plans occurred to me."

"What plans?"

"Every summer since I was fifteen, I've gone to Iowa to work on my grandpa's farm, and I was planning to go this summer too. I'm sorry, Emma. I should have said something before now."

She didn't say anything.

"I don't have to go," he quickly added. "It's my choice, but that's basically what I had in mind."

"Do you want to?" she asked. "I mean, is it important to you?"

"Yes," he admitted. "The first summer I went, it helped me to cope with my mom's death. Being there made me feel like she's still alive—In Heaven, I mean. And I like the work. It's been good for me."

She didn't respond.

"But I don't have to," he repeated. "It's not like my grandpa is counting on my help. It's always been my choice, and he fits me in somewhere, but the Andriessen Family Farm isn't going to go down the drain if his grandson from California doesn't show up."

"But you want to?" she asked seriously.

He reached for her hand and knew he wanted them to share in the decision, something he hadn't considered until now. "I want us to talk about it. What are your plans for this summer?"

"Other than thinking you would be close to Monterey, I haven't thought about it much. But I do sort of have a commitment for this summer too."

"And this is the first I've heard of it?" he teased.

She smiled. "Last year my youth pastor asked me to hang around for the summer as a student-leader for the group, and I went on the activities, a camping trip, and also to middle school camp for two weeks as a counselor. When I was home for Spring Break, he asked me if I was going to be around this summer and if he could count on my help again, and I said yes. I also usually help my mom with VBS and other children's programs going on."

Tate felt better about his oversight, but he wasn't sure how to handle this. He wanted to say he would stay here and do something else this summer, but there was another thing he needed to say if he was going to be completely honest. Deciding to get out of the car and tell her on the way to the cafeteria, he felt apprehensive but excited too. He liked talking to Emma. She was a good listener and didn't make fun of the things he said unless he was intentionally trying to get her to joke around with him. She could be really funny sometimes, but never at his expense.

"I have one more thing to tell you I've actually never told anyone. I started to think about it last summer, and it's been in the back of my mind all year, but this is reminding me of it because it's one reason I would choose to go back again—more so than because of my mom or because this is what I've had planned."

"What?" she asked, sounding as though she wanted to know, not like she was thinking, 'Would you just drop this and stay here!'

He slipped his arm around her waist. He couldn't believe he was about to say this. Other than having a few casual conversations with Grandpa Tate about it last summer, he hadn't mentioned this to anyone.

"Last summer I started to seriously think about moving to Iowa permanently after I graduate from college and being part of The Farm there—like as my career. I love the work, the atmosphere, being around my family roots. Two of my uncles pretty much run things there now with my Grandpa getting older, and one of my cousins works there on a permanent basis too. If the business is going to stay in the family for another generation, I could definitely see myself being a part of that."

"What do you like about it?" she asked, and he told her. And he didn't speak in generalities. Once he started talking about the different jobs he had done there over the last five summers, and those he would like to learn that took place at other times of the year, he couldn't stop, and he talked her ear off about it all through lunch. But she was a good listener, just like always, and he didn't sense that she was wishing they could drop the subject. He actually tried a couple of times, but then she asked him something else and it was never a quick answer.

He knew he was opening up a whole new side of him for Emma, but it wasn't a new side for him. Although, he wasn't sure he realized how much his time there had affected him until now, or the dreams that were in his heart for the future.

"Can you imagine doing that kind of work around here too, or is it about family as much as the work?"

"I think it's both. It's not specifically farming that interests me, but the whole package. Farming isn't just work for them, it's a way of life, and I've had a taste of that. I guess you could say I long for it every year."

"That sounds like something you should seriously consider then," she said. "Don't you think?"

Tate felt like he was dreaming. Emma had heard stories from Tiffany and Abby about the way guys could be, and he'd heard things from other guys about the way their girlfriends could be: manipulative, controlling, and whiny. But as far as he could tell, Emma wasn't anything like that.

She was happy with their relationship for what it was. She didn't complain or try to get her way. If anything, he had to pull things out of her to get her to speak her mind sometimes. She had asked him not to play games with her, and she wasn't doing that either. And now he was telling her something that could affect her summer plans and her life down the road, but she was being as supportive and interested in what he was saying as she could be.

He didn't want to be away from her this summer, but he knew this was important to him and something he did need to seriously think about, talk to his grandpa more, and pray about too. But he wasn't sure he could be excited about doing so if she was sitting here telling him, 'The Farm or me, you pick.'

"We can talk about it more," he said. "I'll call my grandpa and let him know what I'm thinking, but I think that's where I'd like to be this summer. Is that okay? Really? Be honest with me, Emma."

She smiled. "As long as you come back."

"I'll come back," he promised her, sealing that promise with a kiss. "I'm becoming very passionate about something here too, and I'll be longing for you while I'm away."

# Chapter Twenty-Six

Emma was feeling lost in Tate's kisses. She had been all week. Ever since last Sunday when he told her about Iowa, he had been more affectionate, and he seemed to be in control of his desires fine, but she had begun to feel weaker and weaker. She wanted things. Things she wouldn't ask Tate to do but wouldn't try to stop if he did.

Currently they were at his house. They had come down for Easter Weekend on Thursday afternoon and had been spending most of the time together, and with their families too, either at her house or his. They had dinner with her family last night and went to the Good Friday service at church. They had spent most of today with her family, decorating Easter Eggs this afternoon, delivering food baskets to needy families in the community, and coming up here to have dinner with his family and spend the evening at the house. Everyone was here, including Danae and John, and she liked being with his family, but currently they were upstairs, alone in his room, and she felt needy and weak.

They weren't doing anything except kissing, but she didn't think it was right for her to be having the thoughts she was having. If she was having the thoughts, they may as well be doing it. She had been keeping them to herself, but she didn't think that made it okay. And she needed to let Tate know this was getting out of hand for her. She didn't know how to control her desires.

Stepping away from him, she spoke before she lost her nerve. "I need to tell you something."

"What?"

"You're making me feel things, Tate. I can't—I don't know—"

"We can go back downstairs. I just wanted a minute alone with you."

"It's not you," she said. "It's not just now. I mean, I've been feeling this way all week."

He took her hands and held them gently. She felt ashamed. She felt confused. She felt thrilled about their relationship and scared to death at the same time.

"What are you feeling?" he asked.

She wasn't sure if she could tell him, but she needed a solution. "I want you to do more than kiss me. I want you to touch me. I want to lay down with you and feel you holding me close and kissing me places besides my lips."

"I don't think we should do those things," he said with a crooked smile.

"I don't either. But I want you to, and I don't know how to stop feeling that way. It's scaring me."

He didn't say anything.

"Do you feel that way too?"

"No. If I did, it would have happened by now."

She wasn't sure she liked that answer. "So, you don't have any desires for me?"

He laughed. "I didn't say that!"

"Then what *are* you saying?"

He kissed her gently and leaned his forehead against hers. "I don't think about those things. I can't or I'd do them, Emma. And I know I can't, so I don't think about it."

"What do you think about?"

"I think about you. Not your body, but you. I think about your smile and your laugh and the fun we have together. I think about how much I like being with you. I think about making you feel loved—maybe I'm doing too good on that one."

"But how do you do that?"

"I rewire my brain. I tell myself that while those things may be great in the future, right now they would be destructive to you, and me, and our relationship. I don't know that from experience, but I've heard enough people say so who've been there. And I'm choosing to listen to their stories instead of having to learn it the hard way."

She thought about what he was saying, and she said something she knew was true, even though she hadn't thought about it like that before. "So, in my mind I think it would be great, but the reality is it wouldn't be?"

"Yes, something like that. It might be great initially, but later we would regret it. We're not ready for that with each other. I'm not sure why, but it doesn't work, Emma. It's temporary. It's fleeting pleasure that doesn't last and destroys us from the inside out. The road to healing is there, but it's long. Danae has lived that, and I don't want that for you, or me, or us. I want what is good and right for now and will be the best for our future together."

She understood what he was saying, and she knew he was right. She'd heard others talk about the pain of sexually active relationships outside of marriage and the value in waiting, but now that she was in the situation, she felt like none of it would apply to her.

"I've heard the other stories too," he said, slipping his arms around her waist and holding her gently.

She leaned her head on his shoulder. "What stories?"

"The stories of true love. The stories of purity from those who have waited. From my mom and dad, my older sister, my brother and his wife, my youth pastor. That's what I want for us, Emma. Do you?"

"Yes."

He kissed her again, not as intensely as before, but it had an affectionate quality to it, and she thought about Tate. She thought about what a special guy he was, and how he was becoming her best friend, and the ways he made her laugh and feel good about herself, and the way he protected her.

There was a knock on the door, and Tate invited whomever it was to come in, but he didn't step away from her. Danae opened the door, and she smiled at them standing there together.

"We're all having pie and ice cream now," she said. "Do you two want some?"

"I'll have some," Tate said. "How about you, sweetheart?"

"Yes," she said to his sister. "Thank you."

Tate wanted to make sure she was okay and if she needed to talk about this more before they went downstairs, but she said she felt better, so they left the room. She had a thought when Danae handed her a plate of dessert, but she didn't act on it until the following day when she returned to Tate's house to spend the afternoon and evening with his family after they had spent the morning with hers.

They were all hanging out at the house and John had left because he had to work tomorrow. Danae looked a little lost without him, and Emma went to sit beside her while Tate was talking with his dad.

"Hi, Emma," she said, looking up from the mail-order catalog she was flipping through. "How was your Easter this morning?"

"Nice," she said. "It was nice to be home. I think that made it more special after being away most of the year."

"I always feel that way too."

"Could I talk to you?" she asked. "Privately?"

"Sure," Danae said, laying aside the magazine instantly. "Do you want to go upstairs?"

"Yes. If you don't mind."

"Why would I mind?" she said, smiling and leading the way up to her room. Once they were there, Danae closed the door and went to sit on her bed, and Emma joined her.

Emma didn't feel apprehensive about talking to Danae, but she wasn't sure how to bring up the subject. It seemed like a really personal thing to be asking someone she didn't know that well, and yet she knew Danae was very open about this. Danae had told her in general terms about the mistakes of her past a month ago when they first met, and she knew her much better now than she had then.

"Yesterday Tate and I were talking about keeping our physical relationship where it should be. That's been harder for me than I expected. Nothing has happened. Tate is very good about it, but I've found myself having some weak moments."

"I know how that is," Danae said. "It's a good thing John held off on kissing me for that first year, because I've had enough trouble handling his sweet affection ever since."

"He didn't kiss you for a year?"

"He had struggled with his desires in the past too, and it was a personal decision he made when we first started dating. I don't think either of us imagined him waiting that long, but it was good. And I'm glad he did. I needed that too."

"And now that he kisses you? How do you handle it?"

"I think about how he makes my heart feel, not my body. He can completely satisfy my heart with just a kiss. My body might want more, but my heart doesn't, so that's what I focus on. And I don't let John become a substitute for Jesus."

"What do you mean?"

"If my heart is feeling dissatisfied, I don't let John be the one to satisfy it. If I'm feeling lonely or depressed or hurt or regretting the past, that will usually lead to me wanting more physical affection from John, and I've learned to recognize that. If my heart is messed up, I need to let Jesus fix that, not John."

*** 

Danae was happy to have a chance to talk to Emma about her past mistakes, and she prayed from the depths of her soul Emma would take her advice and not choose the same path for herself. She knew her little brother had found someone very special, just like she had prayed for many times, and she wanted purity for both of them.

She knew God would forgive them for any mistakes they made and could bring healing. But she also knew it was a painful and long road, and she wouldn't wish anyone the healing process over doing things right in the first place. She knew from experience her relationship with John was so much better due to the choices she was making now. Good for her relationship with John and for her relationship with God.

God's ways were the right ways. She had learned that in this, and it helped her to follow Him in other ways too. There had been a time when she had questioned the Bible, feeling like it was out of date, for another time and another group of people, but not for her. But she didn't feel that way anymore. Maybe the books were written a long time ago, but the truth didn't change. God didn't change, and the human heart didn't change. If people five thousand years ago were hurt by premarital sex, adultery, dishonesty, and betrayal, then she would be too.

She talked with Emma for a long time, and she felt like she made a difference. She loved that feeling. God had allowed good things to come from her mistakes, and that was one of them. In another month she was going to be graduating with a degree in accounting, and she planned to find a job someplace to use her skills in that area. But her life wasn't going to be about her career. It was going to be about people: Letting herself be loved by those who wanted to love her, loving them in return the best she knew how, helping those in need either by things she said to encourage and teach them, or by helping them in practical ways.

She and John had talked about that many times, and he wanted the same thing. John wasn't going to be a youth pastor or involved in ministry as a career choice, but they planned to get involved at church and in their community on a volunteer basis, and do whatever they felt God leading them to do in their careers and family life. She had been down that road of making her life about everything besides God and the plans He had for her, and she never wanted to go down that path again. It was meaningless and unsatisfying and just plain painful. Jesus and John had rescued her from that, and she was never going back.

By the time Tate came up to see where his girlfriend had disappeared to, they were about finished, but Danae had one more thing she wanted to do, and she told Tate to give them a couple of minutes.

"No hurry," he said. "I was just checking."

"We're all right," Danae said. "And actually, you can be a part of this. Come here, little brother. I want to pray for you two."

Tate stepped into the room and closed the door behind him. He sat down beside Emma who was sitting on her daybed and leaning against the pillows. Emma smiled sweetly at him, and he gave her a look in return that gave Danae goose-bumps. She could usually spot a good relationship when she saw one, and she had been feeling that way about Emma and Tate.

Taking both of their hands, she prayed for them, asking Jesus to guard and guide their relationship and for them to seek God's best for their lives in every way. She cherished the moment, gave them both hugs when she was finished, and asked if either of them had anything else they wanted to ask her.

"Got any advice on how to survive time away from each other this summer?" Tate asked. He had told her and the rest of the family about his plans to return to The Farm this summer and to talk to Grandpa Tate about going full-time in a couple of years, and she was very excited for him. She could see him doing that and knew it would be a good life for him and Emma in their Midwest roots.

"My first suggestion, little brother, is that you don't make it a three-month separation. You have to come home for my wedding, so plan to be here for at least a week then. Right now we're thinking of mid to late July, so that would help you survive that last stretch before school starts."

"And the rest of the time?"

"We're all going there for two weeks in June. Invite her to come with us."

Tate smiled and gave Emma a light kiss. "Want to come to Iowa for two weeks this summer?"

"Okay," she said easily, and Tate smiled.

"And, the rest of the time," Danae continued, knowing this answer from experience also. She and John had spent quite a bit of time apart during the summers and on holiday breaks because his family lived in Washington. "You write letters, call each other, email, text, video chat: whatever you need to do to stay close. And then when you see each other again, it will only be all the better. I think John and I have grown in our relationship just as much during the times we've been apart as when we've been together. God has a reason for it. Trust Him in that."

## Chapter Twenty-Seven

After spending two full days with Rachael on Easter Weekend, Josiah met her for lunch on Monday also. She had two classes she needed to be at this morning, so he went to the library to study and then met her to have lunch before he needed to head back to California this afternoon.

Walking up the campus street to the large building on the corner, he saw her waiting for him. Some other guy was standing there talking to her, but he approached her confidently. He didn't feel confident, but he could fake it. The guy was an Adonis and Hercules put together. He didn't need to be a girl to see that. He was even better-looking and more buff than Gabe.

They were just talking, and he didn't feel like Rachael was being flirty with him in any way, but he could see plain-as-day the guy was attracted to Rachael. Most guys were, but some made him feel threatened by the way they looked and the way they looked at her, and he was definitely one of them.

Rachael saw him coming, and she politely excused herself from the guy she apparently didn't know well enough to introduce him to. Smiling at him in her usual way, she stepped into his arms and laughed, seeming completely giddy about seeing him. He held her close and glanced at the guy over her shoulder. He wandered off in the opposite direction, but he did look back, and Josiah tried to give him a look that said, 'Hands off, buddy. She's mine.' But the guy didn't look too apologetic nor threatened.

"Who was that guy?" he asked.

"What guy?"

"The one you were talking to."

"Oh, I don't know. He just walked up and started talking to me. I'm not usually waiting here for my boyfriend to come meet me for lunch." She released the tight hold she had on his neck and gave him a kiss. "I'm glad you decided to stay. I missed you already."

"I missed you too."

"But you know what I was thinking all morning?"

"What?"

"That today will be the last time I have to say good-bye to you like this. I'm really glad I got my acceptance letter to camp on Saturday so I could know that before you leave today."

"If I get accepted too," he said.

"Josiah! Of course you're getting accepted. If they are taking me, they're definitely taking you."

He knew she was probably right, but he had been in a weird mood this weekend. He felt afraid of enjoying himself too much and then having something go terribly wrong between now and the summer when they wouldn't have to be away from each other anymore.

They went inside the large building and got food from the deli counter on the first floor. Finding a table in the adjacent dining area, Josiah sat across from Rachael and saw the guy she had been talking to earlier a few tables away in his line of sight. He wasn't looking at them, just talking with his friends, but Josiah kept glancing his way.

"Who are you looking at?" she asked, turning around before he could answer, but she didn't seem to spot him.

"Nobody," he lied, realizing he'd been focused on someone who didn't matter instead of the girl he only had another hour with. "Do you always eat here?"

"Sometimes," she said. "For lunch on Mondays and Wednesdays this term because my morning and afternoon classes are all right around here."

He didn't look over at the guy again, but Rachael still called him on his distracted mood later. He felt really weird for some reason.

"Talk to me, Josiah. What's going on with you?"

"Nothing," he said.

"I don't believe you."

He looked at her for a moment. She was adorable even when she was accusing him of lying to her. She was right, of course, so that was no help. He smiled. They were both finished eating, and he asked if they could get out of here.

Once they were outside, he felt better, and he held Rachael close to his side, feeling determined to enjoy the short amount of time they had left. She was right about this being the last time they would have to say good-bye for an extended period, and that lifted his spirits. But she didn't let him get away with not telling her what had been bothering him in the crowded cafeteria filled with college guys who would jump at the chance to have Rachael for themselves.

They stopped along the path in a quiet area between two buildings, and she allowed him several kisses before making her inquiry. "Are you going to tell me what's bothering you, or are you going to leave here today keeping a secret from me and letting me think you're not happy and something is wrong and that I'm never going to see you again?"

He sighed and got it out in the open. "I'm scared of losing you."

"What makes you think you will lose me?"

"You're too beautiful. Too out of my league."

"Too promiscuous to trust?" she challenged him. "Is this about that guy?"

"No. I don't mean that. I trust you, Rachael. I'm just afraid of you getting tired of me and wanting to move on."

She took his concern seriously, wrapping her arms around his neck and holding on tight. He often felt like he held her, or they held each other, but she was definitely holding him, and it was a comforting feeling. She didn't have to say anything. Her body language said it all, but when she released him, she did have something to say.

"Do you remember when we were in Bellingham during Spring Break and you said you want to spend the rest of your life with me?"

"Yes."

"I felt like saying it back, but I decided to wait and pray and only say it if I knew I meant it."

"You don't have to say it just because I'm feeling insecure."

"I won't. I can't tell you things unless I mean them, Josiah. Gabe and Steven—I could tell them whatever I felt like they wanted to hear. I didn't intentionally say things I didn't mean, but I said a lot of things that later I knew I couldn't know yet. But I haven't done that with you, I promise."

"And I meant what I said that day, but I don't want—"

"Shh," she said, pressing her fingers on his lips. "Let me say this, and then you can speak, okay?"

"Okay."

"I've been thinking about it and praying a lot. And my initial thought hasn't changed. Not even for a second. Every time I've asked myself, 'Do I want to spend the rest of my life with Josiah? Do I love him?' The answer in my heart is always yes.

"But," she continued, "I was still hung up on the fact I have made some really bad choices, and I felt like I didn't deserve you. I had been trying not to feel that way, but it was always there, lurking in the shadows, you know?"

"Was?" he asked.

She smiled. "That ended for me yesterday. During the Easter service, it suddenly hit me: Jesus rose from the dead so that He could raise *me* from the dead. Not just someday after I die and He takes me to Heaven, but right now. Not accepting God's forgiveness and the way He's restoring me, or not letting you love me: it's like I'm staying in the grave of my sin instead of letting Him lift me up to the new life He has for me."

Josiah smiled. She was always saying stuff about her recovery process and how God was changing her view of Him and herself through it. Things that often encouraged his own heart and he needed to learn too. He knew he was going to be thinking on that one for the next several days and he wouldn't ever see Easter the same way again.

"I love you, Josiah," she said with confidence and joy. "I love you, and I believe you are the one I'm meant to spend the rest of my life with. And from today on, I want to believe I can. That it's okay for me to accept your love and have this relationship with you because you are a gift from God to me. A gift that says, 'I love you, Rachael. Don't stay stuck in the past. Move forward and live the life I have for you.'"

Josiah pulled her close to him. "I love you, Rachael, and I never want to let you go. Even saying good-bye to you today is excruciating for me."

They stood there in silence for a few moments, and Josiah could feel the beauty of their surroundings mixed with what was going on inside their hearts. The birds were singing happily above them, and the spring leaves were rustling lightly in the breeze. The sun was shining brightly today without a cloud in the sky, and he breathed in the sacredness of sharing it all with Rachael. Holding her in his arms and being in a relationship he never could have imagined six months ago when he first contacted her with a letter containing devastating news. He hadn't expected to hear back from her, let alone for it to be the beginning of something this amazing.

His heart was screaming something he wanted to say, and he took a moment to pray silently and search his heart deeply about whether he should or not, but he didn't see any reason why he shouldn't. He meant it with all of his heart. He felt that his motives were right. He had been feeling insecure five minutes ago, but he didn't feel that way now. And leaving here without saying it seemed like a waste of a perfect moment.

His heart started thumping wildly, and that made him know for sure he should. Whenever that happened and he said what was on his heart, it always turned out to be the right thing. If it was scary but he had the courage to say it anyway, then he knew he should.

Taking Rachael's hand, he laid her fingers over his thumping heart. "Do you know what that's for?"

"What?"

"For the way you're making me feel right now. For what I'm about to ask you."

She smiled like she knew what it was, and he kissed those sweet lips before whispering the words.

"Will you marry me, Rachael?"

"Yes," she whispered back.

He kissed her again, and he felt the world spinning. Beginning to feel lightheaded, he opened his eyes, held Rachael close to him, and let the dizziness pass.

"I don't a have a ring," he said.

"Yes, you do." She stepped back, took the purity ring he had given her off of her right hand and held it out to him.

He took it from her and got down on his knees. Taking her left hand, he slipped the ring onto her finger and kissed the back of her hand.

"I mean it, Rachael. I love you, and I'm promising you forever."

"I'm promising you forever too."

He stood up, and they held each other without saying anything until he reminded her she had a class to get to. They began walking that direction, and when they got to the building, he kissed her several times and honored her request to wait to leave until after she went inside.

"It's easier when I don't have to watch you leave," she said.

"I'll wait. And I'll call you tonight when I get there."

"Check your mail first so you can tell me the good news about camp."

He smiled. "I'll do that. And, I'll see you soon."

They shared one more kiss before she turned away. He remained in place and smiled when she turned around at the door and waved. He walked away slowly, returning to where they had come from, feeling in a daze until he reached the spot he had proposed to her.

Stopping for a moment, he felt the quietness surrounding him as most students were in class now rather than milling around enjoying the noontime break. The earth around him was still, but the heavens were not. His heart was overflowing with joy at what had just happened between him and Rachael and for the past six months. And things had begun even before that, he remembered. He first met her almost two years ago, five minutes from here, never suspecting what God had set in motion. He had brought him into Rachael's life then because He knew the pain she would suffer later and that she would need him like this now.

Feeling keenly aware of the excellence of God's plan and timing, he did something he hadn't done for a few months.  He'd found it increasingly difficult to pray for Gabe.  It was too frustrating to pray, get his hopes up that Gabe was on the verge of a major breakthrough, and then either not hear anything from him or only more of the same.

But as he walked back to his car, he allowed hope to well up in his heart once again, praying for great things for his friend and believing God could take the mistakes and turn them around for something good. Just like He'd done for Rachael.  Just like He always promised.

## Chapter Twenty-Eight

Emma couldn't believe her freshman year of college was over. In some ways it had seemed long, in other ways short, but either way, it had definitely been eventful and a time in her life she would never forget.

Taking the last of her things out to the car, she returned to help Colleen with cleaning the bathroom while their roommates dusted and vacuumed and got the rest of their things out of the room. Emma was glad she knew who her roommates were going to be next year: Colleen, Lauren, and Jessica, but she would have been happy to have Charmaine and Kim along with Colleen too. They had all brought healing to her wounded heart and been very supportive of her relationship with Tate. They thought he was so sweet, and they saw the value in that rather than ridiculing it or telling her it was too good to be true.

She had mixed feelings about the school year ending. She felt anxious to get home and have extended time with her family. But Tate would be leaving for Iowa in two weeks, and she knew that was going to be difficult. Fortunately she would be seeing him two weeks later when she went there with his family. He would be coming home for Danae's wedding in late July too, so they wouldn't have more than three weeks apart at any one stretch, but right now it was difficult to imagine being away from him for a day.

Meeting him for lunch once she was moved out of her room, they had a couple of hours together until the graduation ceremony being held at two o'clock. Along with Danae and John graduating today, Blake and another one of Tate's roommates were also. A lot of underclassmen had left yesterday and this morning, but Emma was glad she had an excuse to stay and be a part of the graduation festivities.

"I've had a lot of good times here the last two years," Tate said when they were walking to the car after having cake in the gymnasium. "But the last half of this semester was by far the best."

"Oh? And why is that, Tate Morgan?"

"Because of you, Emma Jones. Plain and simple."

"Are you calling me plain and simple?"

"Oh, no. You are definitely not plain or simple. You're beautiful and amazing."

He stopped walking and kissed her slowly and tenderly.

"I'm looking forward to being here next year and having the whole year together instead of just two months," she said, trying to focus on the positive.

"Me too. And I'm going to miss you this summer."

"Thank you for delaying your trip an extra week for me."

"I'm not doing that for you," he said, tickling her gently in the ribs. "I'm doing that for me."

"And what are we going to do for two weeks?"

"Lots of long walks on the beach, tons of time doing nothing at all, whatever. I'm staying just to be with you."

***

Amber knew her wedding was coming up in two weeks, but that reality didn't hit her until Monday morning after she was back home and she began sorting through all the things she had left to do before the big day. Her mom was there to help, along with Mandy and Colleen, although Mandy wasn't done with school yet, so she could only help in the evenings.

Seth spent most of the week with his family. They went to the beach for a few days, and Amber talked to him in the evenings, but mostly she was too busy to miss him. He seemed to be missing her a lot more, and by the end of the week he was more than ready to spend the weekend with her. They were going on a camp leadership retreat at a small conference center here in the foothills of Mount Hood.

They met Dave and the others there on Friday evening, and it was a good weekend of getting to know everyone they would be working with in leadership-roles this summer, hanging out with old friends, and getting some planning done for training week and the rest of the summer.

Seth stayed at the house after they returned on Sunday afternoon, and they went to the movies with her mom and dad that evening. It was fun and reminded her of how much she wanted her and Seth's marriage to be like her parents'. On Monday afternoon they walked down to the creek, and she shared that with him and asked what he liked about his own parents' marriage.

"The way they always trust God, no matter what. I didn't grow up learning about crisis. I grew up learning about having faith in the midst of crisis. They've always been very strong that way, and I want that for us too."

She agreed with that and also shared something she had noticed about them she liked. "They always seem to be on the same page about things. Even though they're both busy in different ways, they're supportive of each other's work and ministries."

Seth agreed. "They've taken their individual callings in medicine and counseling and figured out the perfect way to combine them with the pregnancy center, having girls in our home, and other things."

"They're best friends too, just like my mom and dad."

"And like we are," he said, putting his arms around her and pulling her closer to him. "Our marriage might not be officially beginning until next Saturday, Amber, but we've been laying the foundation for it for the last two and a half years."

"I know."

"How are you feeling about the summer?"

"Good."

"Even about having Elle there?"

"I have peace about it. I'm glad we had that talk as a whole senior-staff this weekend and that we talked to Michaela individually too. I feel like everyone is going to be watching out for us. I'm praying mostly that Elle won't do something hurtful to someone else."

"Are you mad that Dave decided to let her be there? Even a little?"

"No, I'm not."

"Are you mad at me for suggesting we let him decide?"

"No," she said, giving him a gentle kiss. "You were right about that, no matter how the summer turns out. Don't you dare carry any kind of burden about it. You made the right choice for us."

"You know, I actually did that because of something I remembered about my dad."

"What?"

"It was several years ago, before I knew you. I was probably fourteen or so, and we had a girl living with us who was really rebellious. She was okay for the first couple of months she was there, but then after she had her baby, it was like she changed her mind about wanting to keep it, and she would leave the house without her baby or telling anyone where she was going, and other things that were against the rules my mom and dad had set for all of the girls who lived there.

"My mom tried everything with her, but nothing worked, and she got to the point where she wasn't herself at all. She knew it wasn't going to work and they were going to have to let Miranda go her own way, but she couldn't bring herself to make that choice. And then one morning we were having breakfast, and Miranda had been out all night again, and my mom was crying, and my dad just took her in his arms and said, "We have to let her go. I'll take care of everything. You go to the center today and help those who want your help, and you let me take care of this."

Amber hadn't been there to see that, but she could picture it perfectly, not just because she knew his dad and had seen the way he interacted with his mom, but because Seth had taken care of her like that many times. The decision about Elle hadn't been the only one, just the most recent.

She told him that, and he kissed her. They enjoyed several minutes of sweet affection with one another. It seemed unreal that in five more days they would be free to enjoy each other in every way with no more lines to be drawn, and yet she knew it would be very real and amazing and something she could trust Seth in as much as anything else.

"I still want to be doing this with you twenty years from now," he said. "Kissing and being all lovey with each other in the middle of the day like your mom and dad."

She laughed. "That used to embarrass me so much, but now I know why they're like that. Twenty-five years of marriage, and they're still in love with each other. I want that, Seth. I want that with you."

"Me too, babe. I love you very, very much."

***

Mandy saw Amber and Seth down by the creek, and she stopped Matt from going any further as quietly as possible. They were kissing and talking softly to one another, and it was adorable to watch. Matt watched for a moment with her but then turned her toward him to kiss her instead.

282

"We can't let them have all the fun," he whispered.

They didn't give themselves away until Matt tickled her lightly, and she giggled.

"What are you doing here already?" Seth asked. "You're early."

"Amanda's piano student couldn't come today, so we decided to head over," Matt explained.

Mandy enjoyed a warm hug from her cousin she hadn't seen since last Thursday. And then she hugged Seth. She hadn't seen him since Easter when she and Matt went to California for the weekend as a surprise. Seth knew they were coming, but it was something he and Matt had arranged three weeks earlier, and she hadn't known they were going until the morning of Good Friday when Matt told her they were doing that instead of him having a busy weekend at the church like he'd led her to believe.

They told Amber and Seth that weekend they had decided to work at Camp Laughing Water this summer as a part of their crew-staff. Mandy wanted to be there for Amber and her potentially challenging summer, Matt wanted to be there so they could be a part of the ministry, and they both wanted to be there because of the accountability they knew they would have with Amber and Seth to spend most of their spare time with.

The four of them were getting together tonight just to hang out. They began the evening by staying down by the creek and chatting about the things going on in their lives. Amber's big news was that Seth had been corresponding with his old boss at the print shop here in Portland during the last few weeks about getting her books into print, and they had figured out the best and most cost-effective way to do it. Amber didn't have time to work on it right now with her wedding coming up, but she planned to spend her spare time this summer getting them formatted on the computer properly so they could be printed in book-form, and then Seth's parents were going to be helping with the cost so copies could be given to whoever wanted them. She was also looking into ways she could have them published as ebooks, and she was excited about the possibilities.

Mandy felt very excited for her. She had enjoyed the stories, and they had helped her view of God and her relationship with Matt, and she knew the same would be true for anyone who read them. Amber said she had been praying about it a lot this semester, and in addition to believing God was leading her to take this step in her writing, she was also planning to take fewer classes next year so she would have more time to write. She had already cut back this year, taking one less class than most freshman students did, but she still didn't have a lot of time, and she felt like the stories were backing up in her head because she didn't have the time to get them onto the computer unless she stayed up late and was dead-tired every day.

She had a cool verse to share with them she had memorized. It was from First Kings, Chapter Eighteen where Elijah was calling on God to answer him and show the ones who were worshipping false gods that their gods were useless but his God was real and powerful and listened to those who called upon Him.

"'Oh LORD, let it be known that you are God and that I am your servant and have done all these things at your command. Answer me, O LORD, so these *people will know that you are God and that you are turning their hearts back again.'"*

Amber went on to say she was almost one-hundred percent convinced she was meant to be a writer. God had placed this particular calling on her heart as both a ministry and a career choice. Lifegate didn't have a specific major for that, so she was following God's direction in what classes to take. He seemed to be leading her to have a more complete understanding of Him and the Bible rather than focusing on writing skills and techniques. Those things came naturally to her, and trying to formulate it only blocked her creativity and imagination.

Listening to her talk about it, Mandy began to have a vision for her own future. She knew she could do anything academically: math, science, English, music, history, geography, cultural and political studies: it all came easily to her. Her interests were more in life science, music, and history, but she couldn't grab on to any one thing and say, 'This is what I want to pursue.'

The two careers she had seriously considered this year were teaching and nursing, and yet neither of those grabbed her to the point she felt passionate about it like Amber did about her writing. But something Amber said stuck with her throughout the evening and into the following day. Matthew had to head back to Portland after their last class, and she drove him to the MAX station like usual, but she told him what she was thinking before he had to leave. She began by restating what Amber said about being amazed by how God had led her into writing, having no idea how much she would love it until she was fully immersed in the process.

Matt said he felt the same way about youth ministry. But Mandy hadn't felt that way about anything except something she had been doing since she was six.

"I feel that way about piano. It's so much a part of me that I almost don't recognize it as anything special. It's not something I have to pursue, it's something I already have."

"And you play beautifully," he said for the millionth time. "You can't play that well and not enjoy it."

"I know, and I love to play, but I think what I want most is to pass on that love to whoever wants it. I probably won't make a fortune as a music teacher, but I think that's what I want to do. I'm going to major in Music Education at Lifegate, and I know it might be hard to find a job since so many schools have cut back on that, but if all I do is teach kids to play the piano in my living room, I know that will be something I'll really enjoy."

# Chapter Twenty-Nine

On Wednesday afternoon, three days before her brother's wedding, Kerri went to the airport to meet Kevin. She hadn't seen him for a week and a half, but it seemed like much longer. Even though she had been with her family at the beach most of last week, a place where she was usually happy, it hadn't been the same without him.

She felt strange. She felt like she had become a different person since getting engaged to Kevin. She was the same, but different. She didn't feel like Kevin had changed at all, but she had. And she couldn't put her finger on how exactly.

Since returning from the beach, she had been busy with wedding plans, and she'd had a lot of fun with her mom and sister, bombing around town, looking for a dress, making final decisions about the flowers and decorations, and meeting with the photographer this morning to discuss what she wanted.

The only detail she planned to involve Kevin in was where they would stay along the beach for their honeymoon. She was more of an expert on the Oregon Coast than he was, but she knew at least two nights they would be on the California Coast, and she wanted his opinion on that, as well as what types of attractions he would want to visit during the day up here.

She was more of a "walk the beach" kind of sightseer with a little bit of shopping mixed in, but Kevin was into going to aquariums and viewing historic highways and bridges. She didn't care much about what they did during that time, but she wanted it to be an enjoyable time for him with as much structure and schedule as he needed.

Seeing him come into view, she could tell he was a bit disoriented in the unfamiliar location. She went to him, and he didn't seem to see her until she was right there, but then he smiled and welcomed her presence easily.

"Hi, Kerri," he said.

"Hi."

He kissed her, and it was a very needy kiss.

"I love you," he said.

"I love you, Kevin."

He held her for several moments.

"You okay?" she asked.

"I am now."

"Did something happen, or were you just missing me?"

"Just missing you," he said.

Kerri decided to do something she hadn't planned. She'd thought about it, but she had wanted to wait and see how Kevin was doing today. Going to her house and being with her family might be what he needed, or time with just her might be better. She knew which one it was now.

"Come on," she said. "I have a good place to take you."

He walked beside her to the escalators, and they headed for the parking garage. She didn't say anything about where they were going, and he didn't ask, which she considered to be a sign of his trust in her. He usually wanted to know details like that beforehand.

It was a bit of a drive, but time in the car was never something he minded. They talked a little but were mostly quiet, and she realized Kevin wasn't the only one who needed the quietness and relaxed pace. Once they were beyond the heavier traffic of the freeway and the Columbia River came into view, Kevin asked where they were going.

"Multnomah Falls."

She knew he had never been there. During Spring Break they had talked about going but had never got around to it. He'd seen pictures, and he had expressed his disappointment they hadn't gone after they were back in California, so she had planned to take him this time, but not necessarily today. She had been thinking it would be a good thing to do with her family, which is why they hadn't gotten around to going in March, but now it seemed perfect for today— just the two of them.

And it was. Kevin loved the beautiful waterfall and was completely mesmerized by it when they first arrived. Eventually he focused his attention on her, and the remainder of the week was similar. They went to the beach on Thursday and Silver Falls on Friday, and they spent Saturday morning at the house before driving out for the wedding.

When they had been together here before, her family getting to know Kevin had been important to her, but now she knew it wasn't necessary to force anything. They loved him and accepted him as a part of her life, and Kevin didn't need to get to know them any better than he already did. What he needed was time with her, and she gave it to him. She needed time with him too.

When they arrived at Amber's house, she did her part to find her brother and make sure he was okay, giving him a supportive hug and last-minute words about him being a special guy Amber was blessed to have. But then she let things be and focused her attention on Kevin once again. Her brother didn't need her today, he needed Amber. And Kevin needed her, and there wasn't anyone here she would rather be with.

They went to find their seats in the front row of chairs that had been set up in the large backyard of Amber's country home facing a beautiful white gazebo, and they talked softly with one another while they waited for the other guests to arrive and for the ceremony to begin. She told Kevin details for their own wedding she hadn't told him yet, and she also got around to asking him about his preferences for their time at the beach.

After he said, 'I don't care' for the third time, she called him on it. "Do you care about this wedding at all?" Her voice was playful, but she wanted an honest answer. How could he have their Alaska trip planned down to the smallest detail, and yet not care if they spent a night in Lincoln City or Newport on their honeymoon?

"I care," he said.

"You just don't care about the details?"

"No."

"Kevin, that's not like you.  Are you mad I'm planning so much of this on my own?"

"No.  I told you to."

"I know, but why?"

"Because you take care of me," he said simply.

"Is that what all your schedules and routines are about? You feel like you have to take care of yourself?"

"No, I just feel better when I know how things are going to be, except with you. With you, I like not knowing.  I like the way you surprise me."

"So if I start making the pizza at Tony's the way I want to, that would be okay?"

"No.  There's only one way to make the pizza."

She thought for a moment and then said, "How about at home?  Is it okay if I make you pizza there but do it differently?"

"That would be okay."

She laughed and linked her arm with his.  "I could come up with a Kerri's Special."

"What's that?  A pizza that's different every time?"

"Sounds like a great idea to me."

He gave her a look that told her she had reached a part of his mind and heart that wasn't always accessible, and he was happy to be there with her. She expected him to say, "You're silly," but he said something else.

"I'm glad we will be together every day then."

She gave him a tender kiss.  "I wish this was our wedding."

"Me too."

Standing with his mom and dad, greeting guests as they arrived for the wedding, Seth didn't feel especially nervous. He felt anxious to see Amber and get this thing started, but otherwise he felt mostly calm and in a good mood. His parents received several good-natured comments from extended family-members and friends about "getting this one married-off so young", but family and friends of the Wilson family were more gracious, saying things like, "Craig and Carol think the world of your son. We're so glad he and Ammie found each other."

"Me too," he always said. Up until now he had been thinking about getting married being the next logical step in their relationship, but today he found himself looking back at all that had brought them here. The way they met when neither of them were really looking. The way Amber had captured his heart without even trying. Their times together from those early days of getting to know one another and only seeing each other on the weekends, to their summers at camp, and this past year at school.

He had fond memories of it all. He knew he could take any one moment or phase of their relationship and relive it over again with the same joy. Even the difficult moments had only drawn them closer, and while he probably wouldn't choose to relive them, he wouldn't wish them away either. All of it was a part of who they were and what they were doing today.

"How are you doing?" Matt said, coming over to check on him. "Do you need anything? Some water?"

"That would be good."

Matt went to grab a bottle for him, and he greeted a few more guests before Matt returned. Two of them were Adam and Lauren, and he felt touched they had come all this way. They seemed surprised he was surprised.

"What are you talking about? We wouldn't miss this day. You and Amber have been two of the best friends we've ever had."

Seth gave Adam a hug and Lauren too, and they both thanked him—"for everything", and he was reminded of the many times he had talked to Adam about his relationship with Lauren and how to make it the best it could be. He had never talked to Lauren in that kind of personal way, but his words for Adam had affected her. And he knew the same was true for Matt and Mandy.

Matt returned with his water, oblivious to his current thoughts, and Seth thanked him.

"I owe you a lot more than that, brother. You need anything else?"

"No, I'm good."

Seth felt humbled in that moment. Yes, he had helped his friends through difficult moments, and he'd had a positive effect on their relationships, but only because he had so much to give. Jesus had given him so much: from his upbringing, to good youth leaders and friends, and especially the beautiful woman he was marrying today.

He was so blessed, and all he was trying to do was pass that on. Somewhere along the line he had learned to live right and cherish all God had for him, and he wanted that for everyone else—especially those he called his friends.

## Chapter Thirty

Amber gazed at herself in the full-length mirror in her parents' bedroom, feeling a mixture of nerves, excitement, and absolute joy for what this day would hold. Her wedding dress had turned out better than she ever imagined. The top was fitted to her shape, but the bottom flared out into a full gown that made her feel elegant.

"You look beautiful, sweetie," her mom said, draping the string of pearls around her neck and securing the clasp in the back. Amber didn't have to hold her hair up out of the way because it was already pulled back and gathered at the base of her neck in a French twist with small white roses clustered together delicately in her brown hair.

She had chosen not to wear a veil because she thought the dress looked better without one. It was slightly off the shoulder with tightly ruffled lace all around the top edge in both the front and the back. The lace had small silk roses sewn into it, and a veil just hid all that, so she had opted to have flowers in her hair instead. Her mom and grandmother had tried to talk her into wearing a small tiara, but she didn't think that was her. This is the way she wanted to look for Seth today, and she was glad she had stood her ground during these last few days when she had more decisions to make than she'd ever made in her life.

"Are you nervous?" her mom asked once she had secured the necklace and come back around in front of her. She took her hands, and Amber realized her fingers were cold. The sun was playing peek-a-boo today behind scattered clouds, but it wasn't supposed to rain. Her dress had long sleeves, and the satin fabric was very warm, so she didn't think the weather had anything to do with her skin temperature.

"I'm excited, but nervous too. Being in front of a lot of people has never been my thing."

"Are you nervous about seeing Seth?"

"Yes. I still get nervous about seeing him on special occasions or when I haven't for a few days. Isn't that funny?"

Her mom smiled. "And how about tonight? Are you nervous about that?"

"I'm trying not to think about it." She laughed, knowing that didn't sound right. "I mean, I have to make it through the wedding, and then I'll think about being with Seth tonight. Everything seems very unreal right now."

"It's all going to be fine. I remember on my wedding day I was really nervous until I was standing with your dad, and then I realized we were still Carol and Craig: two people in love with each other. And it was the beginning of a new day for us, but we were still the same. I think you'll feel that too. In a few minutes, and tonight. He's still Seth, and you're still Amber, no matter where you are."

"Thanks for praying for us, Mom," she said, giving her a hug. "I feel so safe. Seth has taken such good care of me for the last three years, I know I can trust him to do the same today and for the rest of my life."

Her mom held her, and when her dad stepped into the room, she hugged him too. Amber had been feeling thankful for her parents these last few years, but no more so than today. They had trusted Seth and had never given him a difficult time about dating their daughter or seen him in a negative light, but they had also kept a close watch on her and their relationship for any signs of distress she may be reluctant to tell them about. She had always known that, and Seth had too, and she knew it had made a difference in the overall well-being of their relationship.

"It's not too late, Jewel," her dad teased. "I can send everyone home and keep you here with us."

"Everyone except one," she said. "You can't send him away."

"And I doubt he would leave," he said, taking a step back and looking her over. "Nope, I'm not getting rid of him. Good God Almighty, when did you grow up, Jewel?"

"The last nineteen years, Daddy."

"Eighteen and three-quarters," he corrected her. "I must really trust that boy if I'm handing you over this soon."

"I know you do."

Her dad looked over at her mom for confirmation. "Do I? Do we? Are we really doing this?"

"Just like my daddy did with you," she said, stepping over to snuggle into his side and give him a kiss. "Now it's our turn to give them our blessing and let them be happy together."

They kissed again, and Amber smiled, feeling anxious to be kissed by her groom. What her mom said about feeling better once she had been next to her dad during their wedding made her more anxious to get downstairs and get on with things.

"Are you ready, Jewel?" her dad asked, checking his watch. "I think it's about that time."

She took a deep breath and sighed. "I think so. Am I, Mom? Are we forgetting anything?"

"I don't think so. I'll go down and tell Aunt Beth to get everyone in their places, and I'll see you in a few minutes." She gave her a kiss on the cheek and a sweet smile and stepped from the room, leaving Amber with her dad.

She stepped into his arms once again and let him hold her for a minute. "I love you, Daddy."

"I love you, Jewel. And I know a certain young man does too. Don't ever doubt that about him, okay? Marriage isn't just about loving the other person, it's about allowing yourself to be loved; and I know it's hard for you to imagine right now, but sometimes life gets in the way of even the best marriages, and you have to let that love carry you through those difficult moments."

Her dad's words stayed with her as they went down the stairs, through the main part of the house, and onto the back deck that led to a small courtyard area. Her dad's workshop and her mom's painting studio were off to the left, and a hedge of lilac trees were to the right, blocking her view of the backyard for now. She could hear the music playing and saw her bridesmaids ahead of her on the path, waiting to

298

round the bend leading to the rows of chairs set up facing a gazebo her dad had built just for today.

Mandy came over to give her a hug, and she clung to her quiet strength. She suddenly didn't seem as nervous about being in front of a bunch of people but more about seeing Seth. The enormity of what they were doing hit her like a cresting wave, and she didn't think she could stand to wait another second to see him.

"Have you seen Seth?" she asked her cousin.

"Yes. I was talking to him five minutes ago. He's very anxious to see you."

"Good anxious?"

Mandy laughed. "Yes, Amber. Good anxious. Relax. It's Seth."

She took a deep breath and tried to remember what she had been thinking upstairs about Seth smiling when he saw her. He had the best smile. Not just in a photogenic sense, but in a way that always made her feel like he was happy to see her and be with her, whether he was laughing at something she said, or if he was looking at her and couldn't seem to hold a joyful expression inside.

Mandy took her hand and walked beside her toward the wooden gate under the big maple tree. From there the enclosed area opened up into a wide field overlooking the barn and creek canyon at the back of their property, but there was a wide lawn area off to the right where Seth would be standing. Mandy handed a bouquet of white roses to her and stepped ahead of her to walk into the backyard at Aunt Beth's cue. Amber had chosen Mandy to be her maid of honor but considered all four of her closest friends to be special to her in different ways.

Colleen, Stacey, and Hope had already gone ahead of them in their simple white dresses that were a similar style to hers on the top but had straight skirts that hung just past the knees. Her grandmother, Aunt Beth, and her mom had helped so much with all of the details. It was turning out the way she had envisioned in her mind and had tried to convey to them, mostly with the use of pictures she had collected, and she felt grateful for all of their help. This was so not her thing.

When her turn to step through the arbor came and she saw all of the people turning back to look at her, along with the elegant transformation of her country-home backyard, she felt out of her element. One of the things she thought often was, 'Why all the fuss for one day? What difference does it make if I have flowers or a special dress or a gazebo to stand in when I get married? If we went to the courthouse or had a simple ceremony in my living room with only family there, we'd still be married. Does the way we do it really make any difference?'

And she felt that way as the music changed and she began walking down the grassy aisle with her dad at her side. She felt ridiculous, like she wasn't being herself and she and Seth weren't being who they were. She felt conspicuous wearing a fancy dress and having flowers in her hair and making her guests and wedding party get dressed up for a ceremony that wasn't going to be longer than thirty minutes. All the planning and money and excitement she'd had over little details seemed insane. How had she talked herself into doing things this way?

She was on the verge of tears over it, feeling like an idiot and more nervous than she had ever felt in her life. But then she came close enough to Seth to see his eyes and the look of love they held for her.

He smiled, and everything else faded away. She'd had visions of tripping on her way up the aisle and falling flat on her face or some other klutzy thing, but nothing horrific happened, her dad gave her away like they had rehearsed it yesterday, and Seth stepped toward her and took her arm into his.

They stepped into the gazebo from there, standing under the wide front entrance laced with flowers and small white lights, and Seth looked down at her before Pastor Cooke began to speak. She met his gaze, and he whispered something that made her smile.

"Let's enjoy this, sweetheart. It's all for us."

The pastor began to speak, and she was half-listening to what he said, but her mind went back to the question of 'Why all the fuss?', and in that moment she knew the answer. This was a sacred day that was going to affect the course of their lives, and they didn't need the fancy clothes and flowers and romantic setting to make it happen. But it was a moment that deserved all of that and more.

The joining of their lives was worth all the hours of planning. It was worth standing before all of these people and sharing it with their families and close friends. It was worth stepping out of her element to wear a fancy dress and have flowers in her hair.

Having Seth in her life, becoming his wife, and him becoming her husband was a priceless thing, but having a setting that had taken time and money to put together was a small attempt to show the value of what they were doing.  An expression of the beauty of their love and the time and energy they were willing to give, not only for their wedding day, but for their marriage that lay before them.

*** 

Seth had been feeling calm all morning, but the moment he saw Amber walking down the aisle toward him, she entranced him into another universe.  He'd seen her last night, looking like the Amber he had spent the last three years dating and sharing his world with, but today she looked different to him; And not because she was wearing a beautiful dress and had her hair in a style he'd never seen before.

It was more than that.  Good God Almighty, when had she gone from being the beautiful girl he enjoyed talking to and kissing and having fun with to becoming this young woman who made him feel like he was going to pass out?  It was her, but it wasn't.  She was a vision of beauty and purity and heart-stopping loveliness that transported him into another reality.  A reality where she was going to belong to him, but he had no idea why.

How could she be looking at him that way?  How could she be standing before him appearing so fearless about what they were about to do?  How was he ever going to become her husband tonight in every way?

He knew he probably appeared more confident than he felt.  He was the same way with acting on stage or talking in front of a group of people.  Inside he would be a jumble of nerves and random thoughts, but on the outside he came across as being fearless and in-the-zone. But today he wasn't acting or saying things that most would forget by tomorrow. He was making very serious promises to Amber that entitled him to be her husband.

The reality of that hit him in full force as he stood before Pastor Cooke with Amber at his side. He couldn't remember walking up the steps or the confident words he'd just whispered to Amber. They had probably been something ridiculous that sounded great in his head but came out sounding cheesy and left Amber thinking, 'What am I doing marrying this loser?'

What had their parents been thinking in allowing him to do this? He hadn't planned on dating until another three years from now. This wasn't something a rational, smart, wise young man did. This was the behavior of a crazy and irrational person. Of a fool. Of a guy who thought he knew everything at the grand age of nineteen.

*Please, someone stop this! Amber, wake up to the huge mistake you're about to make with me. Mom, Dad, Mr. and Mrs. Wilson, Pastor Cooke? You know this is crazy. Stop pretending to have faith in me. You thought I would have come to my senses by now and told Amber we should put this off for another five years, but I haven't, so step in and tell me I'm not ready for this. I'll listen now, I promise.*

"Amber and Seth," Pastor Cooke said, interrupting his thoughts. He had been speaking for a few minutes now, but Seth had missed most of it.

'*Are you sure you want to do this?*' Seth imagined him asking, but he said something else.

"I want you to know that I perform some wedding ceremonies I'm reluctant to perform. Maybe because I think the couple is too young, or they don't know each other very well, or because they have different values and religious beliefs, or because they have obvious problems I don't see marriage making any better for them."

*He's going to say it. He's going to express the absurdity of my reckless ways. Go for it, Pastor. Let everyone know how you really feel, and I'll be the first one to say, Amen! Amber, listen to the man. Run for your life!*

"But I stand here today before you, in the presence of these witnesses, to say I know you're going to make it. And not just make it, barely hanging on to your marriage by a thread; but you're going to flourish.

"You two are the epitome of what God intended when He made us in His image. He created us to love each other in the same way He loves us. To trust each other in the same way we can trust Him. To love passionately, even recklessly at times. To put everything else aside and say, 'This is it. This is what we live for. It's all about love. If we have that, we have everything, and if we don't, we have nothing.'"

## Chapter Thirty-One

Seth took a deep breath and allowed the truth to seep into his fearful soul. On the surface, what he and Amber were doing today might seem crazy, especially to someone who didn't know them well. But in his heart, he knew it was right. He knew this is what he wanted, what Amber wanted, and what God wanted for them.

*I call as my heart grows faint, Jesus. Lead me to the rock that is higher than I. I want to enjoy this moment, not be plagued by doubt. I want to live in the reality of my love for Amber, Amber's love for me, and Your love for us. Take me there, Jesus. Remind me that You are my God and I can trust you. That You have led me here. That Amber is the love of my life, and a very special gift, and someone I want to make serious promises to right now, feeling confident I can keep them because your grace is always enough for us. When I trust You, that's always enough.*

Turning to face Amber when the pastor instructed him to do so, Seth took her hands and looked into her eyes and felt his smile form easily. His heart filled with love for her that was so familiar. He'd always loved her. From the first moment he saw her sitting in the Taco Bell dining area, having her splatter Pepsi all over his legs, and getting to know her during their week at camp. He used to be a practical guy who never would have believed in love at first sight; until it happened to him.

But their love had grown a lot since then. Mostly by showing it day after day, and week after week. Somehow they had fallen into something that felt easy and right, and they had taken steps of obedience and faith to keep anything from destroying that. They had fallen in love with God together, and he didn't feel like he had a relationship with God and a relationship with Amber that were separate things. They were tied together with the same cords. To walk away from Amber, He would have to walk away from God. This was His plan for them. To truly love God, he had to love Amber too. There wasn't any way around that.

"I love you, Amber," he said, speaking vows from his own heart. They were rehearsed so he would say all he wanted to say, but they were truthful and filled with promise. The promise in his heart to do his best to fulfill in every way for however many years he had with her.

"Today I promise you forever. And that's not a difficult thing for me to do because you're so amazing and fit my heart so perfectly. I never imagined you until I met you, and now I can't imagine life without you. I used to think life was about succeeding at things, and what I did, and pursuing goals and dreams, but with you I have learned it's about this. It's about love.

"God loving us, and us loving God, and you loving me, and me loving you, and letting everything else flow out of that. Goals and achievements and ministry and other noble things may be a part of our life together, but without the love, they're all meaningless. I can survive without those things, but I can't survive without love—both giving and receiving it.

"And so today I promise to love you for the rest of my life, Amber, no matter what our circumstances may be, and I ask that you will never stop letting me. I'll take care of you, Amber. I will be faithful to you as a man of integrity and holiness. I take responsibility for your holiness by doing everything I can to uphold you in prayer and encourage you in your faith and walk with God. And my consideration for you will always be at the forefront of every decision I make, every path that lies before us, and every moment that you are my wife. Which I hope and beg God is a really long time, because the more time I have with you, the more I want, and it's never as much as I wish it was."

***

Jessica smiled and brushed away tears from her eyes as she listened to Seth speaking his vows to Amber. Today's event was no surprise to her, nor were Seth's words. They sounded just like him, not words spoken for one day, and they sounded like words that Chad would say to her.

As Seth took the ring from Matt and gave it to Amber, Jessica's eyes shifted to Chad standing at the base of the gazebo as one of Seth's groomsmen, and she had this thought: *He loves me like that. He could be speaking those words to me today and giving me a ring, and I would accept them.*

She knew Chad felt like he wasn't in a position to take care of her yet in a financial sense, and she wouldn't want him to bear that burden right now, so she wasn't pestering him about getting married. In fact, she had never mentioned it, and she was content to wait until Chad felt ready. But there wasn't a doubt in her mind Chad would take care of her in every way, even financially right now if he had to.

He would work as hard and as much as necessary. He would let go of his own goals and dreams if it meant making her happy. But she wasn't asking that of him or even wanting it. His happiness was just as important to her, and she knew it would probably be a few more years before they were doing what Seth and Amber were doing today, but she was okay with that because she knew once they did, it would last for the rest of their lives.

She never would have imagined feeling this way about someone she had been dating less than a year, but she did, and as Amber began to speak her own vows to Seth, that reality was only confirmed, because she could be speaking the same words to Chad right now, and in her heart she knew that someday she would.

*\*\**

Amber was still letting Seth's words sink into her heart as he took the ring from Matt and placed it on her finger. One of the thoughts she often had was, 'What is this guy doing in my life, and why does he see me the way he does?' That had never made sense to her, and she felt that way more so now than ever. He wasn't saying anything she hadn't heard before, but he wasn't telling her privately when it was just the two of them together, he was saying it for all to hear!

She didn't fully understand his love for her, but she believed it, and she accepted it. And once Seth had slid her ring into place and said a few words about how it was a symbol of the promises he was making to her today, she knew it was her turn to speak, and the words flowed easily. She had written them several months ago and rehearsed them to death, but they were just as true now as when she first thought of what she most wanted to say to Seth today.

For the moment she forgot about all the people who were here, looked into the eyes of her best friend and the man she loved very much, and she told him exactly how she felt. Not just today, but every day since they had gotten engaged last summer. Her reasons for saying yes then were the same as her reasons for marrying him now.

"Being loved by you, Seth, has become a reality that defines who I am. I am loved. I don't understand why most of the time, but I accept it. I accept your love for me, and I live in that reality every day. That's what today is about for me.

"When I first met you, the thing that stood out to me the most was the way you made me feel. You made me feel accepted, worth your time, worth that sweet smile, and someone who mattered to you, even if we had just met. And two years, nine months, and eighteen days later, you still make me feel the exact same way."

She mirrored his smile and continued, giving his hands a gentle squeeze and feeling him hold hers a little more tightly too. One of the things she had always appreciated about Seth was how he listened to her, and she knew he was hanging on her every word right now, not just waiting for her to finish so they could get this over with.

"Today you are making some promises to me, and there is no doubt in my mind you will keep them. I trust you to take care of me, and I also trust God to carry us through whatever we face in the future. I know you are committed to trusting Him just like I am, and I promise to follow in His ways with you and to go wherever He leads us.

"I can't live any other way. And today I don't just make these promises to you, but I also make them to myself. To not live in the reality of your love for me and not go wherever God takes us wouldn't be living for me. I would only be existing. And I don't want that for you or me. I want us to live."

Taking the ring from Mandy, she slipped the gold band into place on Seth's finger. "I give you this ring as a token of my love for you and the promises I am making today. I love you, Seth. I love you with all of my heart, and I'm never going to stop."

Amber heard the music begin as she finished speaking, and she retook Seth's hands and listened to the familiar words. She had originally chosen another song to be played now that was a very good song about loving each other, but she had changed her mind a few weeks ago. This song wasn't about them and their love for each other, it was a modern worship song about the love of God. Amber let the words penetrate her heart afresh as she had a huge example of God's love right before her eyes, holding her hands with love and security.

As the music played, Seth was able to whisper things to her only she could hear. He placed his hand on her cheek, and she closed her eyes at his touch. She hadn't been thinking about what they would share tonight until now, but her longing for it awakened, and she began to have some clear images about allowing Seth to touch her body and be with her fully.

Opening her eyes, she didn't stay there too long, knowing they had the rest of this ceremony to get through along with the reception and a couple hours of driving. But she was looking forward to it and didn't feel as scared and nervous about it as she thought she might.

The chorus of the song played one more time, and she refocused on the words as they permeated the gazebo and surrounded her with a blanket of truth.

*God's love is true*
*His love is real*
*It's for me*
*And it's for you*

*It lights our way*
*In it we'll stay*
*No matter where*
*We go from here*

Pastor Cooke prayed for them when the music ended, and Amber felt the sacredness of what they were doing. She knew Jesus was right here with them, and she welcomed His presence, even begging for it. *Don't let go of us, Jesus. I know you won't. Help me to always believe that. Keep taking us to the high places of blessing in you.*

Someone else who had been standing in the gazebo with them stepped forward to say a few words after that. Dave West, the director of Camp Laughing Water, was also licensed to marry people, and she and Seth had asked him to be a part of that today since he had been a spiritual mentor to both of them during their summers at camp. He didn't take up a lot of time before getting to the part of the ceremony he had been assigned to do, but he did say a few words about them that Amber found touching.

"As I'm sure most of you sitting here today already know, these are two outstanding young people we all can admire. Like Pastor Cooke said, these two have what it takes for a marriage that will last. Their foundation is love, and the basis for their love is God's love for them.

"And so, Amber and Seth," he said, directing his words to them and flashing a big smile. "It is with great pleasure and confidence in your love for one another that I pronounce you to be husband and wife. And what God has brought together, let no one separate."

Seth smiled and winked at her, and she got teary-eyed. She knew this was real, but she couldn't believe it. She felt anxious to be alone with Seth and have something more tangible than words to let her know she was really his wife now. But she did get a little taste of that reality when Dave gave Seth permission to kiss her, and she felt his sweet lips for the first time today.

It wasn't a quick kiss, but he didn't linger too long either. Almost as if he was breathing in her presence and saying, 'More of that later, my love.' His eyes on her when he pulled away seemed to say that too.

Turning to face the crowd then, Amber took her flowers from Mandy, feeling much different about being in front of everyone than she had earlier, and she listened as Dave introduced them by their married name for the first time. She always had a confident feeling whenever Seth was at her side, and she felt that way now more than ever.

She may have walked down the aisle today as Amber Kristine Wilson, a young single woman who felt scared and ridiculous with everyone watching her, but now she was going to be walking down that same aisle as Mrs. Seth Kirkwood, and that made all the difference. She looked at Seth and smiled, and he kissed her on the cheek.

"You're all mine now," he said. "I love you, babe."

"I love you," she laughed.

## Chapter Thirty-Two

Jessica enjoyed the romantic moment with Chad. Dancing with him in the gazebo was something she had been hoping for ever since they arrived but hadn't had the chance to do until now. Matt and Mandy were dancing beside them, talking softly with one another, but she was content to be silent. One of the things she loved about being with Chad was his quietness.

Once they were all alone, she still felt that way, but Chad became more talkative. First he commented on the wedding itself, the craftsmanship of the gazebo Amber's dad had built, and the beautiful setting they were in. She agreed with everything he was saying and added a few comments of her own. When there was a moment of silence, she didn't mind, but Chad seemed unsettled somehow. Like he had something he wanted to talk about besides all that.

"What are you thinking?" she asked. "Got something to say?"

He didn't answer immediately, but he didn't deny it. "I have something to ask you."

"What?"

"Before I ask, I want you to know it's okay to say no."

"Okay."

"Do you remember how I told you I was trying to save up as much money as I could to pay my own way to Florida?"

"Yes."

"That wasn't exactly true. It was at first. My mom said they hadn't been able to save up as much as they were hoping, and so I offered to pay my own way, and she said that would help, but then after I had saved most of it, she said they were going to be okay after all. I decided to go ahead and save the rest, just in case, but my mom told me yesterday they don't need it."

Jessica waited for him to go on, having an idea of what he might ask but not wanting to guess in case she was wrong. She would love to go to Florida too, but she didn't want to invite herself. She only wanted to go if Chad wanted her to.

"So, anyway," Chad said. "I actually planned to ask you this before, but then when I thought I was going to have to pay my own way, I knew I couldn't afford to pay for both of us."

She smiled, knowing she was likely right about her guess at that point. But she still waited for Chad to invite her.

"Do you want to go with us? I have the money, and I'd love for you to go, but if you don't want to, it's fine."

"I'd love to."

"You would?"

"Yes," she laughed. "Why does that surprise you?"

"You know why," he said, holding her close and letting out a mild laugh.

She didn't scold him for his insecurity. There were times she felt insecure about the way he felt about her too, even if he did absolutely nothing to make her doubt. That was an ongoing process for both of them. Hopefully by the time they were dancing at their wedding, they would both be more secure in each other's love.

"I want to tell you something too," he said.

"Aren't you Mr. Chatty today," she said, smiling at him.

"Just one more thing, and then I'll be quiet, I promise."

"You can talk all you want. I just wasn't expecting it."

He kissed her before revealing his heart. "I want to marry you someday, Jessica. I'm not asking yet, but I want that. You're the one for me."

She knew there was only one way for her to respond. The truthful way.

"I want to marry you too."

He didn't respond, but she knew he was happy to hear that.

"Say, 'I know,'" she challenged him. "In your heart you already knew that before I said it."

He did the best he could. "I was hoping I knew that."

*** 

Amber gazed at the scene around her. This was the first chance she'd had to take a breath and relax for a moment. The reception was dying down, and many people had left. She thought she had talked to everyone, even those she didn't know, and she was thankful for those who had come. But the constant interaction with others following the ceremony, having pictures taken, cutting the cake, dancing, throwing her bouquet, and giving a million hugs had been draining. She had anticipated the stress of the ceremony, but not this part, and she felt a headache coming on.

Glancing over at the gazebo, she saw Chad and Jessica coming down the steps appearing very sweet on each other today. She thought about going over to say hello, but she didn't have it within her. They appeared happy, so she left them alone and hoped she would have a chance to say good-bye later.

"Do I get a dance with the bride today?" she heard someone say over her shoulder.

Turning around, she smiled at Ben. Of all the people she would want to see right now, he would be the one. Seth had left her side momentarily to have more pictures taken with his photo-neurotic relatives. Seth had more family than she could attempt to keep track of.

Stepping into her brother's arms, she received a long hug from him she hadn't had all day. She had seen him, and he'd been around, but this was the first chance she had alone with him.

"Too tired to dance?" he asked, sensing her weary mood.

"No, not for you."

"You did good, Amber. I know this isn't your thing, but you pulled it off, and it was great."

"I had help," she said.

"Great dress, by the way. I'm surprised Seth hasn't whisked you away from here with you looking so amazingly beautiful."

"I don't think he likes it."

"What?" He laughed. "Why would you say that?"

"He hasn't said anything."

"That's because you made him speechless. There are no words for the way you look today, Amber. Not that you aren't always beautiful, but this dress and that hair and—everything. I promise, Seth loves it."

Since Seth hadn't seen her dress before the ceremony, Amber had expected him to say something about it afterwards, but he hadn't. And it wasn't like they hadn't had any moments when he could have. He'd been right by her side for the last two hours, but he hadn't spoken one word about her dress. She was convinced he didn't like it, no matter what Ben said.

"You two need to get out of here," Ben said as they reached the steps of the empty gazebo. "Where is Seth, anyway?"

"Having pictures taken with his relatives."

Ben stopped her from taking another step. "If I whisper in his ear he needs to get you out of here, will you go change and be ready when he comes knocking on your door?"

"Ben, you don't have to do that. When Seth is—"

"You need to let him know what you need, Amber. He's not a mind-reader."

"He usually is."

"It's a big day for him too. If you need him to say something about your dress, you should ask him. He probably doesn't realize he hasn't. All the words are in his head, I promise."

It seemed like a silly thing to be all bent out of shape over. Seth had promised his undying love and devotion for a lifetime. Why did she need him to say something about her dress?

"Come here," Ben said, taking her hand and leading her back toward the field where Seth was with his family. "I'm going to get you time alone with your husband right now, and I want you to tell him whatever you need to say. About your dress, about when you want to leave, about that headache you're getting, and then—"

"How do you know I have a headache?"

"I've been your brother for awhile now, Amber. I know that look. Did your period start today too?"

"Ben!" she laughed.

"Did it?" he asked. "That's usually when you get headaches."

"No, I had it last week, thankfully," she replied, wondering when Ben had ever noticed anything about her monthly cycle. They were close as brother and sister, but not that close. "Since when have you known that?"

"I don't know. Since I heard you and Mom talking about it, I guess. I did live in the same house with you for sixteen years. You think I didn't notice just because I never said anything? Hmm, why does that sound familiar?"

Ben spotted Seth and told her to wait there. Someone came up to talk to her while she was trying not to look too conspicuous, not the easiest thing to do as a bride on her wedding day. It was friends of the Kirkwood family she had met earlier, but she couldn't remember their names.  They were on their way out and told her good-bye.

"Good-bye," she said graciously.  "Thanks for coming."

"It was a beautiful wedding, dear," the woman said.  "Seth is a very fortunate young man."

"Thank you," she replied.

Once they had wandered away, she looked over to where Ben had gone and could see him talking to Seth.  She felt ridiculous.  He had only been away from her for five minutes, and her brother was already over there saying she needed him?  What was the matter with her?  She couldn't function for five minutes without Seth at her side?  She felt hurt because he hadn't said something about her dress?  That wasn't like her, especially when she was surrounded by family and friends and so much happiness.

She saw Seth glance at her and then turn away to go back to the cluster of relatives.  Feeling frustrated with him for not rushing right over, and more frustrated with herself for having such a thought about her husband on their wedding day, she turned away from her hide-out spot and went to mingle with the dwindling crowd of guests.  Headache or no headache, she was still the bride and didn't need to act like a baby at her own wedding.

*Good grief, Amber.  Pull it together.*

\*\*\*

Seth excused himself from his aunt and uncle who had begun this picture-taking frenzy.  They were always doing that during the last hour of family reunions, weddings, or holidays when everyone was together. He had only planned on indulging them for ten minutes, but if Amber needed him after five, he was more than happy to escape.

Heading back to where she had been standing thirty seconds ago, he didn't see her there anymore, and he hoped she hadn't gone too far. He didn't know what exactly she needed, but he wanted to help and hoped he wasn't too late. He also wanted to find her so he could let her know he was ready to get out of here.

Seeing her standing on the grassy area beside the lilac trees leading to the back veranda, he realized she was talking to Dave and his wife, Robin. Approaching her from behind, he slipped his arms around her waist and held her gently in his arms as she listened to something Robin was saying.

She looked fantastic in this dress, and she felt amazing too. It hugged her shape perfectly and was incredibly sexy in the way it exposed her shoulders and upper back and yet had a modesty about it that was so like Amber.

He had tried not to stare too much, but right now he had a desire to touch every inch of her and kiss that beautiful neck. He was definitely ready to get out of here as soon as possible. He had been patient for two years, nine months, and eighteen days, not to mention the last three hours since seeing her walking down the aisle toward him. And now here she was, legally his wife and looking more sexy and beautiful than he'd ever seen her, and he still had to wait. He was all out of patience.

She smiled at him as he made her aware of his presence, but she kept listening to Robin and then responded to her. They were talking about Megan, the West's daughter, whom he and Amber knew and worked with at camp together. She was getting married next weekend.

"We should probably get going," Robin said, looking to her husband for confirmation.

"It's about that time," he said. "How about you two? I hope you're not hanging around too much longer."

"No," he was quick to answer. "Any advice on how we can escape? We didn't really plan this part."

"Just decide to go, and go," he said. "It's your day, you can do whatever you want. If you offend anyone, they'll get over it."

Dave and Robin gave them both hugs, and Seth thanked Dave for his words during the ceremony and said they would see him next Saturday. Once they turned away, Seth took advantage of the semi-alone moment with his wife, giving her a kiss and asking what she needed.

"I'm just ready to get out of here," she said.

"You all right?" he asked, sensing there was more to it than that.

"I'm getting a headache," she said. "And I'm tired."

"Do you have anything you need to do before we go?"

"Just change out of my dress."

He kissed her cheek right by her ear and whispered, "That sounds fun. Can I help?"

She looked at him like she wasn't sure how to respond. She wasn't used to him talking that way. Even in the last few weeks he had been keeping stuff like that to himself.

He had always believed if he went somewhere verbally, it would be more difficult to not go there physically. He tried not to have the thoughts, but if he did, he kept them to himself. It was an exhilarating feeling to finally say what he was thinking, and he couldn't imagine how amazing it would be to take the step beyond that.

"Or, you could wear your dress all the way to the beach, and I could help you with it there. I kind of want to see you in it for awhile longer."

"Do you?" she asked, sounding strangely skeptical about that.

"Sure, but if it's uncomfortable and you would rather change, that's okay."

"It's actually pretty comfortable, so I'll leave it on. I just need to go upstairs and get my stuff."

"Okay. I'll have Matt tell everyone we're leaving so those who want to see us off will be out there."

"Okay."

"Are you sure?" he asked.

"Yes."

"And what is it you're not telling me?"

"What?"

"I don't know. There's something. Or is it just the headache? Is it bad?"

"No. I can just feel it starting."

"Have you taken anything?"

"Not yet. I will upstairs."

"I love you, Amber.  It's okay to let me take care of you."

"I know," she smiled.  "And I am."

They were interrupted then by Matt and Mandy. Matt wanted to know if he could change now, and he said he was about to do the same thing.  He gave Amber a quick kiss and said he would see her in a few minutes.

"Mandy, make sure she goes directly to her room, doesn't stop to talk to anyone, and takes medicine for her headache when she gets upstairs."

"I will," Mandy said.

# Chapter Thirty-Three

Amber and Mandy saw a few people inside, but no one kept her too long, and getting upstairs and into the quietness of her room made her breathe a heavy sigh and appreciate her cousin's quiet nature more than ever. Even when Mandy spoke, it had a soft quality that was always welcome.

"Do you want me to help you get out of your dress?" she asked.

"No, I'm going to wear it. I just need to finish packing."

"Can I help?"

"Yeah, thanks." She told Mandy the items she needed from the bathroom, and Mandy went to get them while she checked her suitcase and bag to make sure she had everything else. Mandy returned and brought her medicine for her headache too. Once Amber felt like she had everything packed, she closed her bags and set them by the door.

"Do you want a few minutes by yourself?" Mandy asked. "Or do you want me to wait with you?"

Amber felt she could use a minute to be alone and pray, so she told Mandy that. "Thanks for all your help," she added, giving her a hug and hanging on for a few moments.

"I'm so happy for you, Amber. I prayed so many times this would be a perfect day for you, and I'm glad it has been."

"Thanks. Me too. I'll pray your wedding day goes just as well."

"I'll be praying about tonight too," she said. "Are you nervous?"

"Yes, I think I am," she said, realizing that may be what was making her feel a little tired and stressed right now. "It seems unreal to me that Seth is actually my husband."

Mandy released her and smiled. "Keep in mind that he is and he's still Seth. It's not like you married a stranger, Amber. He's your best friend."

"I know. And I also know you may be my quietest friend, but you always say the right thing."

Mandy said she would see her when they got back. Amber closed the door behind her and took a moment to think if she was forgetting anything and then walked over to her bed and sat down, leaned against her pillows, and closed her eyes.

*Calm me down, Jesus. Give me peace. I don't want to feel stressed-out right now. Remind me that Seth is my best friend and I can trust Him. Remind me you are my God and you are faithful in every circumstance.*

God seemed to bring to mind memorable times with Seth, starting with the first time she had met him, the canoe ride they'd taken together at camp, Seth surprising her at her birthday party two weeks later and kissing her for the first time. The way their relationship had felt easy and right from the start and how she kept expecting it to come to a disappointing end one day, but it never had.

She thought about how he had proposed to her last summer and the confidence he seemed to have about wanting to marry her. He had never wavered from that. Sometimes they got caught up in trying to plan their future too much and work out details on their own, but Seth never said, 'Maybe this isn't going to work,' or 'Let's wait another year.' And she never had the impression he felt that way but didn't say it.

Seth's love for her had always been something she felt she had no control over. It was just there, all the time, day after day, and week after week. It wasn't something she had to try and gain or maintain in any way. He just loved her, and she couldn't stop it.

Someone knocked on the door, and she invited them in. It was Seth, and Ben was with him, but Ben had only come up to get her things and take them out to the limo. She got up from the bed to give her brother a hug before he left, and she thanked him without saying specifically what she was thankful for. In her mind she was thinking about what he had done twenty minutes ago with helping to get them out of here, but it was more than that. Years and years of him taking care of her and doing what he could to protect her. She was very blessed to have a brother like him.

"Bye, Jewel," he said. "We'll see you in two weeks, right?"

"Yes. I'll call you and let you know what time we're coming." They had already made plans to spend a day with Ben and Hope before camp started, and she was glad they had, or she knew saying good-bye to her brother right now would be more difficult.

Ben gave Seth a hug too. "You're a good man, Seth," he said. "I left the air in the tires."

Seth laughed. "Thanks, Ben. I appreciate that. It would be difficult to get my bride away from here otherwise."

Ben picked up her bags and spoke to both of them before stepping away. "My best advice for you tonight: relax and enjoy each other. All right?"

"All right," Seth answered. "We'll be down in a few minutes."

Ben left the room, and Seth closed the door. Today had been a day of suddenlys for Amber. Suddenly she had been walking down the aisle after a morning of anticipation. Suddenly they had gone from being two single people to becoming husband and wife. And suddenly she was completely alone with Seth for the first time all day. She could feel the peace of his solo presence instantly.

He seemed to feel it too, taking a deep breath and shutting out everything except her. He took her into his arms and held her gently. His extended hug alone would have been enough to calm her down completely and make her feel as loved as ever, but he had kisses for her too, and she accepted them freely. On her lips. On her cheek. And down her neck.

She stroked his soft hair and breathed in the scent of his fresh clothes mixed with his familiar smell. Yes, he was still the same Seth she had spent so much time getting to know and sharing special moments with, but he was also her husband. It felt new, and it felt right.

She knew from his earlier comment about wanting her to wear her dress that he must like it, but she still wanted to hear him say how he had seen her today, and she was about to ask, but then he said it.

"Thank you for wearing such a special dress for me, Amber." He kissed the bare part of her shoulder and ran his hands over the long satin sleeves. "You sure know how to reward a guy who's waited two years, nine months, and eighteen days."

They both laughed.

"That was great," he said, smiling at her and giving her another kiss on the lips. "I can't believe you said that."

"At least I didn't narrow it down to the exact number of days," she teased him. He'd always had a habit of knowing exactly how many more days they had to go before a significant event they were looking forward to, like how many days before they would see each other again, or be at camp together, or get married. He wouldn't round it off and say, 'four months', he would say, '112 days'. And he was great about remembering all of their little anniversaries for different things too. That's when she had gotten the idea. She had been working on her vows the same day he had taken her to Taco Bell to celebrate their two and a half year anniversary of the day they met.

"I loved what you said to me out there," he said, turning serious again. "I am so incredibly blessed to have you."

He caressed her cheek similar to the way he had during the ceremony, and his loving touch affected her in the same way. She took his hand and kissed the base of his palm, but she kept her eyes open and looked at him in a knowing way. The day they had waited a long time for was over, and the evening awaited them.

"Let's go," he said.

She followed him to the door and stepped out when he opened it for her. When they got to the stairs a few paces away, she let go of his hand to hold her dress up while she went down the steps, but he wasn't taking any chances.

"No, no," he said, lifting her into his arms. "Let's do it this way. I don't want to be taking you to the emergency room instead of our honeymoon suite."

He carried her down carefully, but she wasn't afraid of him dropping her. One of the things that had always amazed her about Seth was his strength. He wasn't a big guy, and yet he could be very strong when he needed to be. The night he had carried her across the camp to the nurse, she hadn't known who it was until they got there, and she had been envisioning someone who looked more like a football player with how effortlessly he had carried her that far.

When she realized it was Seth, she had been in too much pain and too delighted by his presence to think about it much, but since then whenever he carried her, she always remembered that day and silently admired his gentle strength. He was strong, but he never used it against her in a negative way. Only for her protection and care.

As he carried her out the front door and onto the porch, she laughed and said, "Aren't you supposed to do this on our way into the house instead of out?"

"This isn't our house," he said, "and we have more stairs." Carrying her all the way down to the area in front of the steps where family and friends were waiting to say good-bye to them and wish them well before they left, he set her down then, and she turned to hug her mom and dad who were standing there, along with Ben and Hope and her friends. The last person she hugged was her grandmother who seemed pleased to see her still wearing the dress she had made for her.

"Thank you, Grandma," she said. "Thanks for the dress. I think Seth likes it."

"I'm sure he likes you in it, Princess."

People had begun blowing bubbles from the little bottles that had been handed out. Seth took her hand, and they stepped toward the white limo that was waiting for them. It wouldn't be taking them all the way to the beach, just to Seth's house in Portland where they would get Seth's things and take his car from there. She got in first, and he followed her. He closed the door but put down the window so they could wave good-bye to everyone.

Once the limo had pulled away and he put the window back up, they both sighed and looked at each other, and that feeling of being alone together returned. Seth kissed her seriously for a few moments in the privacy of the luxury car, and Amber recalled the times Seth had told her how much he desired her even if he couldn't show her yet. She wasn't certain she believed him until now, but she was definitely going to be experiencing a new side of their relationship tonight.

She had felt nervous about it earlier when she was waiting for Seth to come upstairs and she hadn't been alone with him all day, but now she felt like she always did with Seth. She felt safe and loved, and she knew she could trust Seth to make this a very special time for both of them.

"I meant every word I said to you today, Amber."

"Will you say it again? When I'm not standing in front of two hundred people?"

He did, and she repeated her vows back to him also. They both laughed when she got to the part about them being together for 'two years, nine months, and eighteen days', and the remainder of her words were delayed as Seth tickled her gently and gave her playful kisses on her neck.

"Hey, I'm trying to say my vows to you," she laughed. "This is serious."

"You are not being serious," he accused her. "You just wanted to have a chance to say that again."

They attempted to get serious then, but she couldn't do it. She would start to say her next sentence and end up laughing instead. She finally made it through the first, but then laughed during the second.

"You are hopeless," he said.

"I know," she laughed. "Maybe I'll try again later." She leaned her head against the back of the seat and wiped tears from the corners of her eyes. "It feels good to laugh. I was too uptight today."

"You were perfect," he said seriously, laying his hand on her cheek and smiling at her. "I know this kind of thing is stressful for you, but you did beautifully. Everyone was mesmerized with you. I could see it on their faces."

"And you? How did you see me?"

"Like I always see you. Beautiful, amazing, irresistible, and mine."

She smiled and enjoyed a tender kiss. "Do you know how I saw myself today?"

"How?"

"As someone doing something really scary, but with total peace. I woke up this morning telling myself I could trust God in this and I could trust you. And even though I had some frazzled emotions occasionally, that was my mindset. When I trust God, everything always turns out okay, even if there are bumps along the way. And when I trust you, I never go wrong. I love you for a lot of reasons, but that is the biggest one. You are trustworthy, Seth. Two years, nine months, and eighteen days have taught me that about you."

He kissed her sweetly, then more intimately, and he spoke intimately as well. "So, when I tell you tonight you have an amazing body and you are my beautiful bride, you'll believe me?"

"Yes," she whispered.

"I don't expect tonight to go perfectly, Amber. I'm sure it's going to take us awhile to figure out what we like and what works best for us. But I liked Ben's advice. My dad said that too."

"So did my mom," she said.

They both smiled.

He turned his body so he was leaning against the back of the seat, and he pulled her against him. She laid her head on his chest, and they rode in silence. Her headache had gone away, and she relaxed in Seth's arms.

She fell asleep, and when she woke up they were getting close to his house. She didn't feel the need to apologize, especially when Seth smiled at her and made a little joke.

"You can't relax that much tonight."

By the time they reached the house, she felt refreshed from her nap, and after her bags had been transferred from the limo to the car and Seth had gotten his things from the house, she decided to ask him if it would be all right if she changed out of her dress now. It wasn't as comfortable to sit in as it had been with her standing most of the day, it was warmer here than in the mountains, and Seth had suggested them getting something to eat before they headed for the beach, and she didn't want to go into Taco Bell looking like this or spill something on the dress.

He said that was fine and asked her the same question as he had earlier about if he could help, but she didn't feel ready for that yet, and she told him. But she did tell him something he liked.

"This isn't the only pretty thing I have to wear for you today, Seth David Kirkwood."

"Oh, is that right, Mrs. Kirkwood?"

"That's right."

"Are you going to wear that to the beach?"

She laughed. "No. Then I would be too cold."

She wasn't used to talking that way with Seth, but it was fun and gave her a little taste of how different things were going to be between them from now on. She hadn't thought about it before, but as she went inside and changed out of her dress in his room, she wondered how many times Seth had held back on saying something he was thinking but knew wasn't appropriate at the time.

After she returned to the car, she asked him about it, and he admitted he had often held his tongue when he had an intimate type of thought he could have spoken.

"How did you know that was the better thing to do?"

"Just didn't feel right," he said. "There's more to intimacy than sex, sweetheart, and I wanted to save as much of that as possible until now."

"Thank you," she said. "Thanks for being who you are, Seth. I appreciate it now more than ever."

They did stop at Taco Bell for dinner, and after she had refilled her cup with Pepsi at the self-serve dispenser, she asked Seth if he wanted her to drop it on the floor for old times' sake.

"I think we can go on to making a lifetime of new memories," he said.

"How am I going to top that? How much more embarrassing do you want me to be?"

"You don't need to embarrass yourself to be unforgettable, sweetheart."

"And you don't need to be sixteen and desperate for a girlfriend to throw out sappy stuff like that."

"That's not sappiness. That's the truth."

They walked out to the car and still had a bit of a drive ahead of them. When they reached the narrow highway that wove its way through the mountain passes and forested setting, she had moments of feeling nervous about being with Seth tonight, but mostly she felt relaxed and ready to enter this new phase of their relationship.

Seth's family's beach house was in the same town where they were staying, but they had decided to make reservations at an oceanfront inn. They both felt the house was too big and familiar to them. They wanted something more cozy and intimate and a place they could return to in the future for a weekend getaway that would have special meaning for just them.

Seth's family had been at the beach house together for a few days during Winter Break, and the two of them had snuck away one afternoon to check out the various places to stay in the heart of Cannon Beach, and the place they had chosen had been their favorite. Amber couldn't remember exactly what the rooms looked like until they entered theirs, but as soon as she saw it, she remembered why she had liked it so much.

It wasn't super fancy, but the room was larger than an average-size motel room, and it had a magnificent view of the beach. The bed and other furniture and decorations on the walls had a very romantic feel to them. A beautiful room she felt was deserving of such a special time. She had felt that way in December and even more so now.

She had been alone with Seth since leaving her house three hours ago, but she felt the level of privacy take on a new dimension of reality here. How many times had she imagined this night? And now it was real. They were here. They were married. And Seth, her incredibly handsome and special husband wanted to be with her.

They decided to go for a walk on the beach because the sun was about to set. They watched the sun disappear behind the clouds along the horizon in silence. Amber didn't know what Seth was thinking, but she felt like it had all already been said. There wasn't anything she could tell him about herself or how she felt about him that he didn't already know.

They returned to the room, and they were almost completely silent on the way there and after they entered it. She took off her coat, and he did the same, and then he reached for her and pulled her close to him.

He still didn't say anything, and she smiled.

"You're being quiet," she said. She was too, but it was more unusual for him to be this way, especially on such a momentous occasion.

He kissed her tenderly. "We don't need words tonight, baby. Just you and me. That's enough."

*I'd love to hear how God has used
this story to touch your heart.*

*Write me at:*

living_loved@yahoo.com

Made in the USA
Middletown, DE
03 June 2020